THE
ROGUE
WORLD

THE DARK GRAVITY SEQUENCE

———•◆•———

— BOOK THREE —
in the
DARK GRAVITY SEQUENCE

THE
ROGUE
WORLD

Matthew J. Kirby

BALZER + BRAY
An Imprint of HarperCollinsPublishers

Balzer + Bray is an imprint of HarperCollins Publishers.

www.harpercollinschildrens.com

ISBN 978-0-06-222493-4

Typography by Carla Weise
17 18 19 20 21   CG/LSCH   10 9 8 7 6 5 4 3 2 1

First Edition

—◄•►—

To my students, many of
whom feel different and alone.
You are my heroes.

THE
ROGUE
WORLD

CHAPTER

1

ELEANOR HAD MADE THE CHOICE. THEY HAD JUST USED the chaos of the Cairo mob to escape from Watkins and the Global Energy Trust. Luke now taxied *Consuelo* toward the runway for takeoff, but they were leaving Eleanor's mother behind. And that was Eleanor's decision. Not even Uncle Jack's presence, large and comforting beside her, could make her feel better about what she was doing.

"The Himalayas?" Luke asked from the cockpit. "Is that where you said we're going?"

"Yes," Eleanor replied. That was the location of the Master Concentrator, perhaps the key to understanding and stopping all the alien devices.

Everyone else in the plane's small cabin sat in silence. Uncle Jack sat beside Eleanor, while Betty sat next to Dr. Von Albrecht. Finn was by himself, staring out the window. He had left his brother and father behind, too.

"The, uh, Himalayas are pretty big, you know." Luke twisted around in his pilot's chair, and through the cockpit door Eleanor could see his eyes and his beard. "Can you narrow it down?"

"Just get us in the air and fly east," Dr. Von Albrecht said. "I'll direct you when we're safely away from this place."

Eleanor agreed. The most important thing now was to get away. Her Egyptian friends had used the city's protesters as a distraction to help Eleanor and her friends escape from the G.E.T., but that wouldn't keep their enemies occupied forever. Watkins and his chief henchman, Hobbes, might even be coming for them right now. Eleanor gave Luke a firm nod in agreement with Dr. Von Albrecht.

Luke turned back around to face the runway. "Roger that."

The plane lurched forward, a motion that had become familiar to Eleanor, like someone's morning stretch and yawn. But then she felt something else, something uncomfortable, and not familiar at all.

2

It started as a hum at the back of her head, but the hum quickly surged and crashed against the backs of her eyes like a wave. It hurt. Bad. Worse than any headache she'd ever had, and her vision went blurry. Then a shriek filled her ears, a howling storm that came from inside her skull, and she leaned forward, clutching her head.

Her words tumbled out with a grunt and a wince. "Something's wrong."

"I feel it, too," Uncle Jack said beside her.

She squinted at him and found him grimacing, his head pressed back hard against his seat, his eyes closed.

"Are you okay?" Finn asked.

"No." The seams of Eleanor's skull felt like they might be splitting apart.

"Stop the plane," Betty called.

"What?" Luke said. "Why—"

But the shriek drowned him out, growing louder, swelling with pressure behind her ears. She thought she might be screaming, too, adding her voice to the hurricane, but she wasn't sure. She knew only that something had reached into her mind. Something powerful. Something that couldn't fit inside. Something she couldn't banish or fight.

Then it simply went silent and withdrew. The storm

abruptly ceased, leaving Eleanor feeling stretched, scattered, sagging, and dizzy.

She turned to Uncle Jack, who was breathing hard. He heaved his head forward from his seat, opened his eyes, and coughed.

"What was that?" Finn asked.

Eleanor turned toward him. He, Betty, and Dr. Von Albrecht were out of their seats, crowding over them, Luke at Finn's side.

"I . . . don't know," Eleanor said. But the fact that she and Uncle Jack were the only ones to have experienced it meant it must have had something to do with the Concentrators, and the rogue world that had invaded the earth's solar system. The ability to sense the alien presence was hereditary, and Eleanor and Uncle Jack were the only two people on the plane who had it. "It was something new," Eleanor said.

"I don't like the sound of that," Luke said. "What kind of something?"

"Uh . . ." Uncle Jack pinched his eyes between his thick thumb and index finger. "What's worse than a migraine but not quite a baseball bat to the head?"

That described it well enough for Eleanor.

"Hey," Luke said. He looked at Eleanor in a way that carried the weight of everything they'd been through together. "What was it?"

He was worried. And so was she. "I don't know."

"That's not good enough," he said. "I won't let you—"

"Shh," Eleanor said.

She felt something else now. A very different sensation. A tingling across her skin, as if the wind were changing direction around her, only she sat in a stuffy airplane, and there was no wind. She turned to Uncle Jack.

"I feel it," he said. "It's like . . . some kind of static."

"It's energy," Eleanor said. "Telluric energy."

"The earth's energy?" Uncle Jack asked.

Eleanor nodded, holding still, paying attention to the way the currents raised the hair on her arms and the back of her neck. She didn't fully understand this power she had, and yet she was beginning to understand how to use it, to listen to the earth. "It's changed direction. It's all flowing the same way now."

"What is?" Finn asked.

Eleanor held her arms and hands out flat, as if she could see what she felt. "All the telluric energy."

"Which way?" Dr. Von Albrecht asked.

Eleanor used the subtle tingling as a guide and pointed across the cabin, halfway between the cockpit

5

and the first row of seats. "That way."

Luke glanced in that direction. "Just a little north of east."

"The Himalayas," Dr. Von Albrecht said.

"But are you okay?" Betty asked.

Eleanor still felt the tingling, but it had already faded slightly, and the pain in her head was gone. "I think so."

In the seat next to her, Uncle Jack looked down at his own hands, rubbing his thumbs against his fingertips. "I'm already getting used to it."

"Do you think it's okay to fly?" Betty asked, but seemed to be directing the question to the others.

"I'm not sure we have a choice," Dr. Von Albrecht said. "If we stay here much longer, the G.E.T. will eventually catch up to us, riot or not."

"I'm not taking us up in the air until I know they're okay." Luke looked at Eleanor, and she could see the worry in his eyes.

"I'm fine." She tried to put some strength into her voice. "Really. Let's get out of here."

Luke stood a moment longer, and then slowly turned back toward the cockpit. "Buckle in. And tell me the moment you feel anything else that's *new*."

Finn, Betty, and Dr. Von Albrecht returned to their seats. Next to Eleanor, Uncle Jack reached over and took her hand in his, her little fist like a ball inside a warm baseball mitt. A few moments later, they were airborne, and as they rose higher, putting distance between her and the ground, the tingling faded until she almost couldn't detect it anymore. Her ability to hold thoughts together returned as well, and she turned her mind to the question of what had just happened.

So, it seemed, did everyone else in the cabin. "What do you think that was?" Dr. Von Albrecht asked, his voice pitched with curiosity. He had been studying the Concentrators for longer than Eleanor had even known about them.

She tried to find the words to answer him. "First there was . . . something in my mind. It felt similar to the power I feel when I'm near a Concentrator—"

"Hold on," Uncle Jack said. "Can we just— Can we back up for a minute?"

He hadn't been with them from the beginning, in the Arctic and Peru. Watkins and the G.E.T. had brought him to Egypt only as leverage to get Eleanor to do as they wanted, and he was understandably a bit lost.

"Explain this to me again," he said. "What are the Concentrators?"

"Alien devices," Eleanor said. "They look like . . .

big black trees. They were planted here tens of thousands of years ago."

"By aliens," he said.

Eleanor nodded.

"And the Concentrators do something with the earth's telluric energy?" Uncle Jack asked.

"They gather it up," Dr. Von Albrecht said. "They concentrate it and convert it to dark energy, which they send into space, to the rogue world."

"Rogue world?" Uncle Jack said.

Eleanor looked up at the ceiling of the plane. "There's a whole planet up there. An alien planet, which came into our solar system. Its gravity is pulling us out of orbit, away from the sun. That's what caused the Freeze. And now it's draining the earth's energy. For what, we don't quite know."

"And until just a few minutes ago," Uncle Jack said, "that energy flowed everywhere on earth, correct?"

"Right," Dr. Von Albrecht said. "The ley lines crisscrossed the globe. Concentrators can be found at points of confluence where many currents come together. But now, Eleanor, you're feeling the currents all flowing toward the same place. In the Himalayas?"

"Yes," Eleanor said. Everything had changed right after that shrieking presence in her mind, almost like it had caused it, and she suddenly realized what that might mean. "I think it was a command," she said.

"What was a command?" Finn asked, his voice sounding heavy.

"That pressure in my head," Eleanor said. "I think it was some kind of command, ordering the Concentrators to reroute the energy."

"A command from whom?" Betty asked.

"I'm guessing the aliens," Finn said before Eleanor could respond. "Maybe they're pissed off."

"Now there's a pleasant thought," Betty said.

But Eleanor didn't think that was the case. Each time she had connected with a Concentrator, she had felt the artificial intelligence wriggling within its machinery, primal and utterly foreign. Even though the Concentrators had each possessed their own individual intelligences, with their own "personalities," they had shared one trait: loneliness. The Concentrators felt very, very isolated. She assumed that was because they were stuck on earth, separated from their creators for thousands and thousands of years. But the shrieking in her mind had felt the same, just much more powerful. It seemed just as angry and lonely, even though she assumed it had come from the rogue world. That would mean there weren't any aliens on the rogue planet, either.

"So we're trying to shut the Concentrators down," Uncle Jack said.

Eleanor didn't know the answer to that anymore. That had been their initial goal, and she had succeeded in stopping the Arctic Concentrator, the Peruvian Concentrator, and the Egyptian Concentrator. But then she had learned that Watkins shared her ability, and he had simply switched them back on. She wasn't sure how he had done that, because she had destroyed the artificial intelligences within them. But, somehow, he had.

"Wait a minute," Finn said. "Watkins said that when you do . . . whatever it is you do with the Concentrators, it has an effect on you. Like, it might actually kill you or something."

Eleanor frowned. "That's what he said."

He had also revealed that there were many people around the world who shared the ability to connect with the alien technology. That mattered, because every time Eleanor had shut down a Concentrator, it had temporarily weakened her and everyone else like her, including Uncle Jack. And it was getting worse. After stopping the most recent Concentrator in the Valley of the Kings, she could barely move. Eleanor didn't know what would happen to her and the others if she stopped the Concentrators altogether, but Watkins had claimed the result might be fatal.

The reason her mother had joined Watkins and turned against Eleanor's plan wasn't just because of the futility of it. It was because she didn't want Eleanor connecting with the Concentrators anymore. She didn't accept who Eleanor was. But Eleanor had known from the beginning her mission was a very dangerous one. She still wasn't ready to give up, even if her mom was, and that was just one of the many differences between them.

"So if you turn off the Himalayan Concentrator," Finn said, "what will happen to you guys?"

"Good question," Uncle Jack said.

"We need to figure that out before we do anything else." Eleanor didn't want anything to happen to Uncle Jack or herself, but she was ready to do whatever was necessary to save the earth. She looked at Dr. Von Albrecht. "You've seen the Himalayan Concentrator. You know more about it than almost anyone else."

"As far as your connection to them," Dr. Von Albrecht said, "anything I might say would be pure speculation." He pulled his glasses off and rubbed their lenses with a white handkerchief from his pocket. "If Watkins found the answer through his own connection to the alien power, he kept it to himself. We would need access to his files."

"Yeah, that's not gonna happen," Finn said.

He was right, and the cabin fell silent for a moment.

"So, where does that leave us?" Betty asked.

Dr. Von Albrecht cleared his throat. "I know someone in Mumbai who might be able to help us."

"Who?" Eleanor asked.

Dr. Von Albrecht carefully put his glasses back on and adjusted their position on the bridge of his nose, holding the frames between his index fingers and thumbs. "Well, that is an interesting question. I suppose I should clarify that I don't actually know this person. Not personally, at any rate. But I have had contact with them, online. They reached out to me several times after Watkins fired me."

"Who is it?" Eleanor asked again.

"Grendel," Dr. Von Albrecht said. "They go by the name Grendel. That's all anyone knows about them. Their name. And what they've done, of course."

"Okay," Finn said. "So what have they done?"

"It is widely believed that Grendel is responsible for some of the most sophisticated hacks ever perpetrated against the G.E.T. and the UN."

"Wait, they've hacked the UN?" Eleanor said.

"That can't be easy," Finn added.

"No," Dr. Von Albrecht said. "No, it most certainly isn't."

"And that makes you think Grendel could help us?" Uncle Jack said.

"Yes. Grendel hosts several servers on the darknet."

"What's the darknet?" Uncle Jack asked.

"An underground internet," the professor said. "Grendel's little patch of it is devoted to the conspiracy theories surrounding the G.E.T. and the Freeze. They have continued to post classified information there that no one is supposed to have, which means they still have access to some G.E.T. data."

"Can we trust this Grendel person?" Uncle Jack asked.

"The enemy of my enemy is my friend," Dr. Von Albrecht said.

Eleanor wasn't sure that saying always held true. "But will they even help us?" she asked.

Dr. Von Albrecht shrugged. "I would like to think so. But I can't promise anything."

"Mumbai isn't that much of a detour from the Himalayas," Betty said. "And it seems to be our only option."

Eleanor agreed with her. "I'll go tell Luke we're headed to India."

She unbuckled from her seat and moved up through the cabin into the plane's cockpit, and took a seat in the empty pilot's chair on the right. Over the past few weeks, this place had become both familiar and comfortable. One of her favorite places, actually, with the smell of old vinyl, the wide panel of instruments, and the endless blue of the sky before her, with Luke at her side.

She pulled her feet up to sit cross-legged in the chair. "Dr. Von Albrecht thinks we should go to Mumbai."

Luke frowned. "Does he?"

Eleanor nodded. "I do, too."

"And what's in Mumbai? Another Concentrator?"

"No. A Grendel."

"What's a Grendel?"

"Someone the professor thinks might be able to help us find out what Watkins knows."

Luke gave Eleanor a long, sideways glance, without expression. "That sounds good."

"What is it?"

"What is what?"

"What are you looking at me like that for?"

He returned his gaze to the sky ahead. "Like what?"

Eleanor almost took a swipe at his arm. "You know what I'm talking about. So just say it."

He nodded. "Okay, then. I'm wondering if your mom was right."

Eleanor leaned away from him and her voice came out sharp. "What?"

"At least partly," Luke added. "She may not have been right to sign on with Watkins, but she was right to worry about you. I'm worried about you, too. I had to carry you out of that tomb, if you remember."

Eleanor glowered. "I remember."

"Look, I'm not trying to be like your mom, here."

"You're nothing like my mom, Luke. You accept me the way I am."

"Of course I do. But I know your mom loves you. That's why she worries. That's why I worry."

"You don't need to worry."

"I don't?"

"No. I'm way ahead of you, and that's why we need Grendel. I need to figure out this connection before I do anything else."

Luke nodded. "Sounds like we're on the same page, then."

"Same page," Eleanor said.

"Okay." Luke turned to *Consuelo*'s controls. "So the professor trusts this Grendel person?"

Eleanor rose to leave the cockpit. "I don't think so, no."

Luke twisted to look at her with a raised eyebrow,

15

but said nothing, and Eleanor left.

Back in the cabin, she flopped into the seat next to Finn and let out a sigh. "Have you ever been to Mumbai?"

He opened his eyes and swung his head slowly toward her. "My dad went there for research after the earthquake. But he didn't take us with him."

Eleanor tried to read his expression and the tone of his voice, to see if he had any regrets about leaving his dad and brother behind. "Are you okay?" she finally asked.

He looked up at the ceiling of the cabin. "That is a weird question."

"Sorry, I just—"

"No, it's fine. It's not you. I was about to say that yes, I'm okay. But then I stopped to think about the Freeze, and the Concentrators, and my dad and Julian, and I realized how screwed up everything is. So . . . no, I'm not okay. Are you?"

"No," Eleanor said. "Not when you put it like that."

"We can put it another way if you want."

"What way?"

"Things could be worse."

"How?"

"Pissed-off aliens."

Eleanor laughed. "You're right. That would be worse."

But she stopped laughing when she remembered the shriek in her mind, the power of the command that had ordered all the Concentrators in-line. She still had no idea where it had come from, or what it was, and she dreaded facing it again.

— CHAPTER —
2

Eleanor remembered a little bit about the Panvel Earthquake from her science class. As the Freeze had turned much of the earth's water into glaciers, the sea level had fallen, and the water table around Mumbai had fallen with it. The area was already prone to earthquakes, but the loss of groundwater destabilized the fault lines even further.

Eleanor had seen images of the aftermath on the news. Several of Mumbai's skyscrapers had simply toppled. Over three hundred thousand people had died, and even though Mumbai was a city of almost twenty million, it still hadn't recovered from the devastation. It was fortunate that Asia didn't have the same refugee crisis facing South America and Africa, or the loss of life might have been even greater.

"What about the G.E.T. presence in the city?" Betty asked. "Will it be hard to avoid them?"

"The G.E.T. has less influence in Mumbai than in other parts of the world," Dr. Von Albrecht said. "Even after the earthquake, when the G.E.T. offered to help with the reconstruction efforts, the people of Mumbai resisted. Mumbaikars take care of each other. I think that's one reason Grendel lives there."

"That's one good thing, at least," Uncle Jack said.

"I wouldn't count on good things," Finn said.

Eleanor appreciated Uncle Jack's optimism, but agreed with Finn. Going forward, they couldn't take anything for granted or make any assumptions about the G.E.T. They had done that in Peru, which had led to the death of their guide, Amaru. Eleanor's memories of him brought pangs of sadness and guilt, and renewed the promise she had made to him: to make the world safe for his wife and son.

A few hours later, Luke called back from the cockpit that they would be landing soon. Everyone settled in, and Eleanor watched out the window as the plane descended through a thick cloud of smog that reminded her of the one that covered Mexico City. The plane flew over a long stretch of beach that reached into the distance on both sides. Even from hundreds of feet in the air, Eleanor could see the crowds of swimmers and sunbathers, little flecks of color against the sand, which meant it was still warm enough here to enjoy the water.

She almost couldn't imagine that. And she still found it jarring to remember once again that most people on the earth were unaware of the Concentrators and the rogue world. There were people out there who could actually enjoy swimming.

A few moments later, Luke touched *Consuelo* down and then taxied the plane to a private part of the airfield, where they disembarked. From there, they made their way to the main terminal and sat outside near the taxis, where Dr. Von Albrecht used the airport Wi-Fi to attempt contact with Grendel.

"They have always replied quickly," the professor said quietly, staring at his laptop.

"When was the last time you heard from him?" Luke asked.

"Who says it's a him?" Betty asked.

"Four months ago," Dr. Von Albrecht said.

Travelers hurried in and out of the terminal. The air around Eleanor felt humid and warm, the sunlight somehow heavy. She noticed businesspeople in suits, families traveling with children and grandparents, everyone moving about as if making their flight on time was the only thing they had to worry about.

"Where are they all going?" she asked.

"Other parts of India," Dr. Von Albrecht said. "Countries in Africa or Asia. This part of the world has seen less disruption from the Freeze than you're probably accustomed to."

"Unless you count earthquakes," Finn said.

The professor's laptop pinged. "Ah, Grendel replied."

Eleanor leaned toward him. "And?"

"Good news." Dr. Von Albrecht scanned the screen. "There are no promises, but we have a meeting scheduled. Two hours from now, in the middle of a place called the Five Gardens in the Parsi Colony."

"Parsi Colony?" Uncle Jack asked.

Dr. Von Albrecht closed his laptop. "Yes. But I don't know where that is."

So, Eleanor thought, *we are about to venture into a completely unknown city to meet with a stranger who goes by a code name.* The image of the gunshot wound in Amaru's stomach suddenly forced its way into her mind. "Maybe this isn't a good idea," she said.

"What do you mean?" Uncle Jack asked.

"I mean, we don't know who this Grendel is," Eleanor said. "What if this is some kind of trap?"

"That is highly unlikely," Dr. Von Albrecht said.

"But not impossible." Eleanor turned to Luke. He had been there when Amaru died. He had been the one to pull the trigger. "We thought we could trust Amaru, too."

Luke bowed his head a moment, and his voice softened. "I hear you. I do. But I think this is different—"

"How?"

He sighed. "Grendel is already a known enemy of the G.E.T. So we at least know he—or she—isn't working for Watkins."

"That makes sense to me," Finn said. "And can you think of any other way to find out what you need to know?"

Eleanor wiped at the sweat that had risen on her brow in the warm Indian air. She had no answer for Finn. She didn't like it, but if she didn't gain a better understanding of who and what she was, she wouldn't be able to do what she needed to do. And if they couldn't stop the Concentrators, they were all dead anyway.

"Fine," she said. "But I don't like this."

"How are we going to get there?" Betty asked. "Last time I checked, we're low on funds."

"I have some money," Uncle Jack said. "I pulled it out before the G.E.T. brought me to Egypt."

"Hopefully it's enough," Luke said. "I've got enough credit to take care of fuel for *Consuelo*, but we'll need cash for everything else."

They hailed a couple of black-and-yellow taxis, and after agreeing on a price in dollars, they left the airport and set off through the city of Mumbai. Eleanor ended up in a cab with Uncle Jack and Finn, while Betty and Luke went with the professor in the second car.

At first, Eleanor saw no signs of the earthquake, but then she realized she was looking at the city in the wrong way. She was looking for rubble, or vacant spaces where buildings had once stood. But instead, everywhere she looked, she saw new construction. New buildings, new offices, new apartments, rising high and narrow, a honeycomb of concrete and glass. And none of it, to Eleanor's relief, with a G.E.T. logo. Their taxis took a busy highway that seemed to cut through the middle of the city, but from that thoroughfare Eleanor could see side streets thick with pedestrians and hawkers selling their goods from carts along the sidewalks. Their cab shared the road with more cars than it seemed the highway could fit, and they moved at a crawl.

Some distance on, over the tops of some low buildings to the right, Eleanor could see a development of high-rise skyscrapers going up, clad in scaffolding, crawling with construction workers.

"What's that?" she asked their driver, a young man who appeared to be in his twenties.

"That used to be Dharavi," he said. "Very poor. Very crowded. You would call it a slum."

"What happened to it?" Eleanor asked.

"The earthquake." He paused. "The buildings in there were no good. Everything was destroyed. Two hundred thousand died, just in Dharavi."

"And now?" Uncle Jack asked.

"No longer a slum," he said, his tone flat. "Rich Americans and Europeans are buying apartments instead."

Eleanor looked again at the high-rises, built on the terrible misfortune of others. That didn't seem right to her. And yet some would probably say that Mumbai was recovering, finding a way to turn the tragedy around, to keep growing. None of that would matter if they didn't stop the rogue world.

"The Parsi Colony is much better," their driver said. "They never constructed tall buildings there. The earthquake wasn't as bad for them, and they took in many people from the city."

"Who are the Parsis?" Finn asked.

"They were Persians," their driver said. "They came to India, oh, a thousand years ago. Now they are

Indian, but they are also still Parsis."

The buildings to either side of the street suddenly fell away, and they drove onto an elevated road over a wide, circular park, with palm trees and playgrounds. Eleanor smelled coffee in the air, and not long after that, they left the busy highway and turned to the left, into a part of the city that felt very different from what Eleanor had seen so far.

There were more trees, and more space, and no hawkers selling from carts on the sidewalks. The streets lay in shade, and the buildings, though tidy, appeared older, but Eleanor preferred their charm and character to the sleek and soulless new construction they had passed. She saw balconies and colonnades, gardens and arches, and noticed some of the buildings bore a motif she hadn't seen before, that of a bearded man standing between two feathered wings.

"This is Parsi Colony," their driver said, and he ambled them through the neighborhood until they reached a large area of green. They drove in a wide circle around open spaces of grass, numerous trees, and playground equipment, with people out strolling, jogging, and just sitting in the shade. "And this is the Five Gardens."

He turned the car inward, and eventually they reached the hub of the parks, a green space in the middle of the others with a large fountain. Uncle Jack paid both drivers, and after the cabs had pulled away Eleanor looked around for someone who seemed like they might be Grendel. But how would they know?

"What do we do now?" Luke asked.

Dr. Von Albrecht marched toward the fountain. "We wait here. Grendel will come to us."

They followed him to the center of the park and they sat down. The muggy air smelled of vegetation and flowers, spices, and something rotten. After a few moments had passed listening to the fountain bubble behind her, Eleanor grew warm, warmer than she had felt outdoors in a long time. While she enjoyed not worrying about layers of clothing, she wasn't used to the tropical heat raising sweat from her skin.

She watched a young couple walk by with an infant girl in a stroller. They looked at Eleanor and her companions with open curiosity, but their stares did not feel rude. The other people around them in the park wore a wide range of clothing, including robes, jeans, turbans, and other head coverings. A small cow even wandered by, unconcerned with anything going on around it, and Dr. Von Albrecht pointed out that cows were sacred to Hindus, and thus the animals were allowed to go where they pleased in the city.

"No sign of the G.E.T.," Betty whispered. "At least

we have that going for us."

"Let's hope that lasts," Luke said.

"I still don't quite understand what exactly the G.E.T. wants," Uncle Jack said.

Eleanor noticed a woman sitting on a bench nearby, wearing a long turquoise blouse with embroidery around the neck and hem, loose white pants, and sandals.

"What the G.E.T. wants is the end of the world," Finn said.

"No, it doesn't," Eleanor said. "Watkins thinks the only way to beat the Freeze is to conserve all the energy we can, so that a small number of people can survive. He wants to save the planet. A piece of it, anyway. He's just willing to sacrifice most of us to do it."

"Are you sure that's what he wants?"

The question had come from the woman in the turquoise blouse seated nearby.

Eleanor looked at her again, more closely this time. A thick braid held her graying black hair over her shoulder, and she appeared to be approaching middle age.

"Grendel?" the professor asked.

The woman smiled. "Partly."

"Partly?" Eleanor asked.

The woman rose to her feet. "Grendel isn't a single

person. Grendel is the thief in the night, and Grendel could be anyone. We're a collective. Follow me." She turned away from them and set off on foot through the park.

Uncle Jack looked at Eleanor, and she gave him a reluctant nod. If they didn't plan on trusting Grendel, they shouldn't have come. So they all followed after her, in and out of the shade of the trees, a light breeze through the fronds and branches.

Several blocks away, down wide and pleasant streets, they reached a building in one of the older styles they had seen. It seemed made of stone, or concrete, with wooden balconies and columns, rising three stories above the road. Flowers and plants grew from planters hanging outside its windows.

Partly-Grendel led them to a locked front door of iron bars, which she opened for them, and they entered through a small, tiled foyer into a courtyard at the center of the building. Large rosebushes grew in a few raised beds, softening the air with their perfume. Overhead, each floor opened onto the courtyard from a columned walkway, with dark wooden staircases climbing between them. Silken curtains billowed from doorways, and sunlight angled down upon them. Eleanor would have believed they had somehow stepped back in time, were it not for the satellite dishes and antennae she then noticed jutting out from the roof.

"In here," the woman said, and led them into a small apartment on the ground floor that smelled of cinnamon and cloves.

Simple but elegant furniture filled the living room, and ornate woven rugs covered an old and creaking wooden floor. Eleanor took a seat in a soft, upholstered sofa, nudging aside a few decorative silk pillows. Uncle Jack sat next to her, with Finn. Betty, Luke, and Dr. Von Albrecht took armchairs nearby. The woman sat on a wooden stool against the wall, a hallway next to her down which Eleanor glimpsed the kitchen.

"Your message surprised me," the woman said to the professor.

"We appreciate you meeting with us," Dr. Von Albrecht said. "But I am even less sure of who you are now than I was before."

"It is a necessary precaution," the woman said. "But you may call me Badri if you wish."

Eleanor wondered if that was her real name, or simply something she had chosen in that moment.

"Who are your companions?" Badri asked.

Dr. Von Albrecht introduced them all, giving their real names. Badri nodded toward each of them in turn, her expression placid and unreadable. An overhead ceiling fan stirred the air, cooling Eleanor down a bit, even as it dried out her eyes.

"It is hard not to notice," Badri said, leaning forward, "that your party bears a certain resemblance to a band of terrorists the G.E.T. wants apprehended. There's even a substantial reward involved."

Eleanor couldn't tell if that was a threat. Her fear of betrayal clamped her mouth shut and chilled the middle of her back. Badri looked at her with a fraction of a smile.

"Your face is so morose you could advertise flu medication," she said.

Eleanor said nothing.

"If you're thinking of turning us in," Dr. Von Albrecht said, "I would remind you that the G.E.T. wants you apprehended as well."

"Me?" Badri laughed. "Who am I but an old Parsi woman? No, Watkins wants Grendel, and we've already established that Grendel is no one. But not to worry. I have no plans of turning you in."

"Thank you for that," Uncle Jack said, with a subtle sarcasm that Eleanor heard clearly.

"But you did take a risk in coming to me," Badri said. "Why?"

Luke folded his arms. "It was our only option."

"Option for what?" the woman asked.

"How deeply have you hacked into the G.E.T.'s

files?" Dr. Von Albrecht asked.

Badri shook her head. "You first. What does the G.E.T. want with you? And why have you come to me?"

They had nothing to lose, and it didn't seem to Eleanor that they had a reason to keep anything from her. "Do you know about the Concentrators?" she asked.

Badri nodded. "The Trees of Life."

Eleanor nodded back. "That's what Watkins calls them. Do you know what they do?"

"They gather telluric energy," Badri said. "From the earth."

"And they convert it into dark energy. Do you know what Concentrators do with that dark energy?"

"They send it to the shadow." Badri flicked a glance toward the ceiling. "Up there."

"That's right." Badri already knew more than most everyone on the planet, and for some reason, this comforted Eleanor and gave her confidence. "I've been shutting the Concentrators down. That's why Watkins wants to capture us."

Badri leaned toward Eleanor. "You shut them down?"

Eleanor looked into her brown eyes. "Yes."

"How did you do this?"

"She connects with them," Finn said. "Like . . . telepathy."

Badri's lips parted, as if she had just sucked in a silent breath. "Is this true?"

"Yes. I can talk to them, even control them. So can my uncle Jack, though he hasn't tried yet."

Badri looked at Uncle Jack for a moment, and then turned back to Eleanor. "How many of them have you shut down?"

Eleanor sighed. "None. I thought I had shut down three of them, but Watkins has the ability to turn them back on, apparently."

Badri closed her mouth and was silent for a few moments. Then she turned to Dr. Von Albrecht. "What do you need?"

The professor explained the rest of the situation to Badri, after which Eleanor described the recent changes to the Concentrators and the telluric currents that she and Uncle Jack had felt before leaving Egypt.

"So," Badri said when they'd finished, "you need Grendel to comb the G.E.T.'s files and find out what Watkins knows about your connection to the Concentrators. That way you can shut them down permanently."

"That's the hope," Eleanor said.

"There is too little hope in the world these days," Badri said.

Luke chuckled. "Tell that to the fools building sky-scrapers out there."

Badri waved away his comment. "That is not hope. That is denial and pride."

"So will you help us?" Eleanor asked.

Badri sat back on her stool, touched her fingertips to her lips, and narrowed her eyes. She remained this way for a long moment.

"Why must the Concentrators be shut down?" she finally asked. "Why not simply take control of them yourself?"

Eleanor felt the question to be a kind of test. "Because we can't control them. Not really. That's what Watkins has been trying to do, but that hasn't stopped the Freeze. As long as the Concentrators are running, the earth is in danger."

Badri nodded. "The Preservation Protocol is an evil trying to convince the world it is a necessary one."

"So will you help us?" Uncle Jack asked.

"It's not a question of whether we will help you," Badri said. "It's a question of whether we can."

"What do you mean?" Dr. Von Albrecht asked.

"We've already hacked into the G.E.T.'s servers, but have never seen anything like what you're talking about. The information you need must be in Watkins's confidential files, on a separate server. To get a look at them, we would need direct access."

Finn raised his hand. "And by direct access, you mean . . ."

"A terminal connected directly to that server."

"Is that possible?" Eleanor asked.

"Possible?" Badri rose from her stool and paced around the room. "I wouldn't say that it is impossible. But such a thing would be very difficult and dangerous."

"And just what would such a thing entail?" Luke asked.

"We would have to physically break into the G.E.T. facility in the former Kingdom of Mustang. In the Himalayas. That's where Watkins has established his primary research station."

"Near the Concentrator?" Dr. Von Albrecht said.

Badri nodded. "I hear Watkins calls it Yggdrasil. The World Tree of Norse mythology."

A fitting name for the Master Concentrator, where all the earth's currents had just been directed.

"You're right," Betty said. "That sounds pretty dangerous."

"But that's what we were going to do anyway, right?" Finn tugged at the collar of his shirt as if it was too tight, or he was too hot. "I mean, assuming we figure out how to shut down this Iggy Tree safely, that's where we were going to end up eventually."

"That's true," Eleanor said. "So maybe we can do both at the same time."

"We've been watching the Yggdrasil Facility for some time," Badri said. "Until this moment, we didn't have a good enough reason to justify the risk of breaking in."

"If we can find out what Watkins knows," said Dr. Von Albrecht, "we can shut down all the Concentrators and sever our connection to the rogue planet for good."

Badri smiled. "Now Grendel comes. Like a thief in the night."

— CHAPTER —
3

THAT EVENING, AS THE REST OF THE GRENDEL COLLECTIVE prepared for the operation, Badri brought Eleanor and the others to a dining room. The wooden table where they sat appeared to be an antique, with deep grain and a dark, smooth surface. Then Badri and a few others brought in plates bearing steaming bundles of green leaf, as well as platters with potatoes in a curry sauce, and a sharp cucumber and onion salad.

If Eleanor's mom had been there, she would have politely declined to eat any of it. She was way too picky about food. But Eleanor could see the glee in her uncle Jack's eyes, an enthusiasm Eleanor shared with him.

"What do you call this dish?" he asked, exploring

the green leaf bundle on his plate with his fork and fingers. "Is this banana leaf?"

"Yes," Badri said. "This is patra ni macchi."

Eleanor unwrapped her own bundle, releasing the aromas of coconut, mint, coriander, and fish. Inside the banana leaf she found a delicate, flaky fillet enrobed in spicy chutney. She couldn't remember the last time she had tasted half of these flavors. She took a bite, and closed her eyes at how juicy and delicious it was. Everyone else at the table did the same.

Uncle Jack sighed. "This is incredible."

"Yes, it is." Badri wiped her mouth with her napkin. "Now, the one piece of the puzzle left to figure out is how to get from here to Nepal. I must ask, how did you get to Mumbai from Cairo?"

"We have a plane," Finn said.

"*My* plane," Luke said.

Badri leaned back in her chair. "Well, that simplifies things."

"Maybe," Eleanor said. "But the G.E.T. knows exactly what our plane looks like, and they might be expecting us. If we fly too close to their facility, they'll know it."

"I see," Badri said.

After Eleanor and the others had stuffed themselves with fish and potatoes, Badri showed them to a couple of adjoining rooms with beds, cots, and couches. Rugs softened the parquet wooden floor beneath her feet.

"We'll leave tomorrow at first light for Kathmandu." Badri looked at Luke. "May I assume you can fly us at least that far?"

"Sure," Luke asked. "Then what?"

"We take a chartered plane to Jomsom in Nepal," Badri said. "From there it's a thirty-five-mile trek to the Yggdrasil Facility in the Upper Mustang."

"Thirty-five miles?" Finn said.

"Yes." Badri smiled. "Unless we freeze to death before we reach it."

"We can't afford a chartered plane," Betty said.

"But Grendel can," Badri said, on her way out the door. "Get some rest."

When she was gone, Eleanor looked at the others, and no one said anything for a few moments. Badri seemed trustworthy, but Eleanor still felt hesitant. There was simply too much at stake, and the bitter memory of Amaru's betrayal lingered.

"I think we all could use some rest," Uncle Jack said.

The moment he said it, Eleanor realized she was exhausted. She'd been up the entire previous night, delving deep into a hidden tomb in the Valley of the Kings. That felt like days or weeks ago, and now she was in Mumbai. Tomorrow she would be in Kathmandu. Her journey had taken her from Phoenix to the other side of the world, and she could only wonder where it would take her next. Hopefully back home, so long as they succeeded.

Then she could begin to make things right with her mom.

Eleanor woke up the next morning to the sound and smell of rain. Badri served them a breakfast of eggs scrambled with herbs and shredded potatoes, and they left the Grendel home and quiet streets of the Parsi Colony in two vans. Eleanor and her friends rode with Badri in one vehicle, while the other carried five members of Badri's team. The squeaking windshield wipers worked hard, and Eleanor watched the city passing by them through runnels and blurry sheets of water over her window.

"India used to have a monsoon season," Badri said, "with rain much worse than this."

"Used to?" Eleanor said. "Has the Freeze changed that?"

Badri nodded. "It's complicated, but the glaciers that now cover the Tibetan Plateau reflect sunlight back into space, instead of the earth absorbing heat the way it used to before the ice. That means we don't get what they call a thermal low, so no monsoon season like we used to have."

Eleanor didn't quite follow that, but she didn't doubt the effects of the Freeze.

Eventually, they reached the airport and boarded Luke's plane from the wet tarmac. Badri's crew carried on several duffel bags and suitcases and filled every extra seat in the main cabin. As the unrelenting rain pelted *Consuelo*, they took off and climbed above the rough and heavy clouds into the sun.

Badri sat next to Eleanor, and as the plane leveled off, she leaned in close. "How do you do it?"

"Do what?" Eleanor asked.

"How do you connect with the Concentrators? This ability you have . . ."

"I don't really know. It just kind of happens. The real trick is to stay in control of it."

"Interesting," Badri said.

"I think you are very brave."

Eleanor snorted. "My mom calls it recklessness. Or she used to say I was devilishly clever, but now I'm not sure that was ever really a compliment."

"I call it bravery." If this stranger thought Eleanor was brave, why didn't her own mother? Eleanor folded her hands in her lap. "I think you're brave. You know the risk you're taking by helping us, don't you."

Badri nodded. "I do."

"So why are you doing it?"

The woman cocked her head to the side a bit. "Good thoughts. Good words. Good deeds. That is the Parsi way. To be among those who renew the world. The G.E.T. has stretched their control across the globe, and is now engaged in draining the world of life and vitality. They must be stopped."

She said it as if the answer should have been obvious, and the integrity of Badri's motive surprised Eleanor. She wanted very much to believe that the older woman spoke honestly. It gave Eleanor hope that there were still people out there who wanted to do the right thing simply because it was the right thing to do.

The flight across India to Nepal was supposed to take two and a half hours, but after three hours, they still hadn't arrived. Eleanor left her seat and climbed into her chair by Luke in the cockpit.

"What's taking so long?" she asked.

Luke scanned the console of instruments and gauges before him. "With all the back-to-back flying we've been doing, we're putting a lot of strain on *Consuelo,* and she's showing it. I'm going easy on her."

"She's earned it," Eleanor said.

Luke nodded. "That she has."

Eleanor decided to stay with Luke in the cockpit

for the remainder of the flight. Since Uncle Jack had joined them, she hadn't spent as much time with him. As they talked, she watched the ground below rising and falling with valleys and mountains, and off in the distance, she saw the Himalayas, a towering icy rim against the sky that climbed higher and more impressive with each passing minute.

Soon, Luke began their descent into a valley bowl surrounded by snowy hills, and Eleanor studied the city of Kathmandu. From above, its sprawl was not unlike Mumbai, with some areas densely packed, and others more spacious and green, dotted with parks and open squares. Ornate towers and pagodas rose up periodically in the skyline, marking what Eleanor assumed to be temples and palaces.

But she didn't see any more of the city than that. Once they'd landed, Badri led them across the tarmac to the private jet she'd chartered. A cold wind swept down from the mountains carrying a threat that Eleanor recognized. She felt the chill of it and remembered the menacing whisper of ice, its patience and its teeth. She had left the Arctic and traveled around the world, but the glaciers were still waiting for her.

The private plane was cramped inside, not the glamorous kind of aircraft Eleanor had imagined. She sat between Luke and Uncle Jack. Luke fidgeted with his seat belt and shifted in his chair, looking up toward the cockpit.

"You wish you were driving?" she asked him.

"Maybe," he said.

Eleanor elbowed him. "No backseat flying."

He chuckled, and soon they were in the air. From Eleanor's window, she could see the Himalayas above them, and even when they'd reached cruising altitude for their short flight, the peaks rose higher than their plane. Their white lines looked sharp and raw against the sky, as if newly carved.

"Did you know the top of Mount Everest is made of marine limestone?" Uncle Jack asked.

"Marine?" Eleanor asked. "As in . . ."

"As in, it was once underwater," Uncle Jack said.

Luke shook his head. "From one of the lowest spots on earth to the highest. Now that's power."

It awed Eleanor, too, that the earth's plates could lift each other up in that way, turning everything upside down with their conflict. She studied the folds, crags, crevices, and summits as they flew between two large mountains and into a valley.

Before long, the ground below them became a field of untouched white. It was snow, and the memory of a shiver wrapped its cold fingers around Eleanor's neck. She tried to shake it off, but it stayed until they landed on a tiny airstrip next to a tiny village. Before leaving the plane, they all suited up in cold-weather gear that Badri and her Grendel team had brought: coats, boots, gloves, and goggles. It wasn't quite so cold that they needed the breathing masks they had worn in the Arctic.

"Here we go again," Finn said. "I wonder if we'll find any Paleolithic warriors resurrected here."

Eleanor thought back to Amarok and his people, wondering where they had gone, and whether they had found a new home. She hoped they had. But then she thought about the dusty mummies deep in the Egyptian tombs. It wasn't always a good thing that the Concentrators' energy could bring things back to life.

"I'm hoping that anything dead has stayed that way," she said to Finn.

The largest clothing they had was still a bit tight on Uncle Jack, but he wore it without complaint. As they opened the plane's hatch and descended to the tarmac, a sharp wind shoved glittering ice into Eleanor's eyes. She blinked and pulled her goggles on, then looked up at the towering mountains, higher than anything she had seen before, higher even than the clouds that clung to them.

"We should cover as much ground as we can today,"

Badri said. "It will take at least two days to reach the facility."

Eleanor didn't like the idea of another overland trek through snow, but they set off, leaving the small town behind, following the contours and course of the valley. At times the gorge narrowed, and in other places it opened wide, its cliffs both violent and beautiful, one of the most dramatic landscapes Eleanor had ever seen. It seemed that the wind, the water, and the ice had each taken their turn in shaping it. A frigid river wound down the middle of it, runoff from the Tibetan ice sheet high above them.

Their party made a steady and even march northward, and Eleanor's muscles warmed up with exertion, driving away some of the cold. They followed a narrow road to the east of the river as it traveled along the base of the valley, occasionally climbing partway up the side, granting them impressive views of the mountains jutting endlessly all around them.

"Tourists used to come here seeking enlightenment," Badri said.

"I wonder if any of them thought they found it," Luke asked.

"I suspect that had everything to do with them,

and little to do with this place."

Eleanor had come here seeking enlightenment, too. She wanted to know what made her different, and how she could use that to save her world. And perhaps like the tourists who'd preceded her, she couldn't find her answers anywhere else. She knew she was traveling in the right direction, because she could feel the gentle static of the earth's telluric currents rushing beneath her. The energy still flowed powerfully in one direction, a rising tide gathered to this single Concentrator, in the same way the moon pulled at the earth's oceans.

"Do we have a plan once we reach the facility?" Uncle Jack asked Badri.

"There were maps of its layout in the files we've recovered," the woman said. "We have an idea which entry points will give us easiest access to a computer terminal. But we won't know for certain until we are there."

"So let's just get there," Luke said, huffing a little.

Eleanor soon found the exertion getting to her as well. The elevation here made her feel a bit lightheaded, and after a few hours, her muscles ached. Their party stopped periodically to rest and eat. Badri gave them all squares of a chewy bar made from dried fruit, nuts, and honey. Clouds came and went. The miles passed slowly, a winding course up and down narrow side

46

canyons, and the sun moved steadily across their path. They periodically passed freestanding miniature towers that Badri said were Buddhist chortens, places of meditation. Toward the late afternoon, the far side of the valley lay in shadow, and Eleanor watched that shadow swelling, drawing closer to them, but before it reached them, they climbed up an incline and out onto a promontory, where they arrived at another village.

The cluster of buildings overlooked the valley and river below, and unlike the town where they had landed, this place seemed to have been abandoned years ago. The stone, brick, and cement remained behind, snowdrifts piled up in the doorways, a Himalayan ghost town. Eleanor imagined eyes watching her from the shadows and haunted windows, felt the prickle of them against her scalp.

"We'll sleep here tonight," Badri said.

Eleanor looked at Finn, who seemed equally unsettled. "This place?" he asked.

"Yes," Badri said. "The forecast calls for snow tonight. I'd rather be indoors than in a tent."

Eleanor didn't know how to argue with that. She didn't like the idea of sleeping in a tent during a snowstorm, either. But she also didn't like the unease she felt here. At the edge of town, she saw what looked like the ruins of an ancient fortress, with square towers and thick walls the color of sand.

"What was this place called?" she asked.

"Tangbe," Badri said. "The Tangbotens were once a proud people with their own language. They were salt traders many centuries ago, and then they became farmers. But the G.E.T. drove them out when they discovered the World Tree."

"And no one stopped them?" Finn asked.

"It's not the first time a group of people has been forcibly relocated from their land. You have much experience with that in the United States, I believe."

Finn went quiet at that. They all did. With the backing of the UN, Watkins could probably get just about anything he wanted.

One of the other Grendel team members, a man named James, pointed at a nearby building that was wide, whitewashed, and newer in appearance than some of the others. "That one looks large enough, and it's still in good shape."

Badri nodded. "Yes, good."

The team moved toward the building, and when they found the narrow front door locked, they used a crowbar to force it open.

Once inside, Eleanor discovered the interior was entirely empty, no furniture or fixtures of any kind, with bare white walls and a bare cement floor.

Someone had boarded up the windows from the inside, but James had been right. The space in here would be plenty big enough for all of them to sleep that night, and this was only the main room. A few members of Badri's team went deeper into the building, exploring the rest of it, but returned a few minutes later to report that they hadn't found anything—no supplies, and certainly no people.

After that they all settled in and made their beds with the pads and blankets they had brought with them. Then they had a meal of a kind of flatbread and salty cheese, with more of the chewy honey bars for dessert. It tasted wonderful, and Eleanor went to sit by Badri as she ate.

"Thank you for this," she said.

"You're welcome," the woman said.

"No, really. I don't know what we would have done without your help."

"I don't know what we would do without your gift," Badri said.

Eleanor snorted. "It doesn't exactly feel like a gift."

"It is a burden?"

Eleanor tipped her head a little to the side. "I guess, yeah, it's a weight. A responsibility. I feel like I'm the only one who can do something."

"I wonder what the difference is between a

responsibility to help and the privilege of helping."

"I don't know," Eleanor said. She wasn't sure it mattered, really. This was just who she was.

Badri nodded. "I can say that I would feel it a privilege to have your responsibility. But it isn't mine. It's yours. It is my privilege—and responsibility—to help you."

"I appreciate that," Eleanor said.

"Soon we will reach the Yggdrasil Facility, and we will hopefully find out more about this privilege and burden that you carry."

Eleanor made herself smile, but a feeling of nervous dread weakened it from the inside. This was truly their last hope. If this plan failed, she had no idea what they would or could do next.

Soon they all bedded down for the night, but Eleanor lay awake, looking up at the wooden slats of the ceiling. She found eyes and faces in the whorls of wood grain, and it reminded her of lying in bed with her mom, finding shapes in the texture of the ceiling over her bedroom back home. She wondered where her mom was, in that moment. Still back in Egypt? Or had Watkins sent her somewhere else, another research station, or some kind of compound for those who were part of the Preservation Protocol? Or was she on her way here? Eleanor's breath caught in her throat. Watkins almost certainly was headed to the same place they were, and it hurt to think of her mother with him, helping him.

Before long, everyone around her seemed to have fallen asleep, and sometime after that, a howling wind picked up outside. It was the snowstorm Badri had mentioned. Eleanor lay awake listening to it, feeling warm and protected.

But then she heard a different noise, and she sat up, holding still, listening.

Something moved outside. Something heavy. Something big. It thudded against the walls of the building, and it dragged what sounded like thick fingers across the boards that covered the windows.

The sounds of it eventually roused some of the others. Finn shot up, wide-eyed.

"What the hell is that?" Luke whispered.

Badri whispered, "I don't know."

── CHAPTER ──
4

WHATEVER IT WAS, IT SEEMED TO BE CIRCLING THE building, and the walls shuddered with its periodic thuds. Some of Badri's team produced pistols, which helped Eleanor feel a bit more secure, knowing they weren't defenseless against whatever was out there. But she hoped there wouldn't be a need for them to use their guns.

They kept quiet, speaking in whispers, and eventually the sounds faded away, and once again Eleanor heard only the storm.

"I think it's gone," Badri said.

"What could it be?" Betty asked.

"There are animals in the mountains," Badri said.

"Goats. Perhaps even bears or snow leopards."

A bear seemed the most likely of those, considering how big it sounded.

"We have a long day tomorrow," Badri said. "We should try to get some more rest, but I think we need to establish watches."

"I'll stay awake," Uncle Jack said. He got up and lumbered over to the door, where he sat down with his back against the wall. "You all get some sleep."

"Wake me in two hours," Luke said. "I'll take the next watch."

Uncle Jack nodded.

Eleanor didn't know if she'd be able to get to sleep after that, but knowing Uncle Jack was awake helped. She lay back down and closed her eyes, imagining the storm outside, the hazy bulk of a bear emerging from the darkness, pacing around the building, sniffing and huffing and shouldering the walls before disappearing into the snow and the night.

When Eleanor awoke early the next morning, they all ate a quick breakfast and emerged from the building into the abandoned village. The snowstorm had moved on, but had left six inches of new snow, powdery as dust, on the ground. They scouted around, but saw no tracks or footprints from the night before, the wind having erased them. It would have been easy for Eleanor to imagine their visitor had been a dream, were it not for the fact that everyone had heard it.

"Stay sharp," Badri said. "Bears and snow leopards are shy, but they are less so if they're hungry."

They set off and soon left the ghost village of Tangbe behind. The landscape of valley and ravine through which they traveled remained as dramatic as the day before. The Himalayas towered over them, jagged sentinels observing the world at a scale of time and distance no human could grasp.

Later that morning, their party passed through another abandoned village, but this time they didn't stop. A few miles past the village, they marched under some high cliffs honeycombed with dozens of caves. The entrances were of different sizes, some small enough that Eleanor needed to crouch to enter them, some large enough that she and Finn could enter shoulder to shoulder. They appeared to be man-made.

"What are those?" Betty asked, pointing upward.

"They are called the Sky Caves," Badri said. "They are found throughout this valley."

"They are an archaeological mystery," Dr. Von Albrecht said. "No one knows exactly who built them. Or why. But they number in the tens of thousands."

To reach most of the caves would require a perilous

climb, if it were possible to reach them at all. Eleanor studied them as they passed by overhead, and the sensation of being watched again crept over her. As if the caves were the mountains' black eyes.

The caves continued to watch them periodically as they proceeded along the valley, which narrowed and twisted in upon them. They passed through two more ghost towns, until eventually the road they followed veered to the left, across a bridge to the other side of the river, where it climbed up into slopes and foothills. But Badri led them onward, off the road, directly into a narrow ravine. The imposing rock walls to either side rose hundreds of feet above them, almost vertically, and their party now walked through near-permanent shade and icy wind along a severe and tortuous path.

"This is Kali Gandaki Gorge," Badri said. "According to some, the deepest gorge in the world. We are nearing the heart of the ancient Kingdom of Mustang."

They followed this gorge for a few miles. The previous night's snow made the march more difficult than it had been the day before. Eleanor's thighs burned, but she kept her complaints to herself, eventually falling in beside Finn.

She was about to ask him how he was doing, but that question had become a bit ridiculous. "Do you miss your dad and Julian?" she finally asked.

He nodded. "I guess so."

"What do you mean you guess so?"

"It's not like I wish I was with them." He looked up at the cliffs. "I wish they had made a different choice. I guess that's what it is."

"I get that."

"I mean, they're with the bad guys. Does that . . . does that mean they kind of *are* the bad guys?"

"No, it doesn't," Eleanor said. "Just because the G.E.T. is wrong and we're trying to stop Watkins, doesn't mean they're bad guys. In their way, they're trying to save the world, just like we are."

Finn shook his head. "If you say so. Your mom is with them, too, you know."

Eleanor looked down and placed her next step carefully. "I know that."

"Do you miss her?"

She did miss her mom. But she didn't miss the way her mom tried to stop her from being who she was. "I'm like you. I wish she was here. But only if she was on our side."

"At least you have your uncle."

Eleanor looked up ahead of them at Uncle Jack's broad shoulders. "Yeah."

"He seems like a good guy."

"He's the best guy. I didn't have a dad growing up,

but I had him. Whenever my mom went away on her research trips, which was all the time, he stayed with me. You should taste his cooking."

"Maybe one day I will," he said.

Soon, they left the gorge behind, and the valley reopened, though not as wide as it had been. When they climbed up onto a ridge, and Eleanor could see some distance in all directions, the surrounding mountains and valleys formed an enormous and seemingly endless maze. It was hard to grasp the scale of this place, the weight of the mountains and distances between their high peaks. Eleanor felt very small in the same way she did when staring up into the night sky. Without Badri, she wasn't even sure she could find her way back to the airstrip where they'd landed the day before.

"What's that over there?" Finn pointed at a distant, broken slope of snow. The face of the mountain appeared to have been gouged with an ice cream scoop.

"Avalanche," Badri said.

"Avalanche?" Finn looked around. "Are we safe?"

"At the moment," Badri said, with a bit of a grin.

They kept moving, and as evening fell, the older woman suggested they stop and make camp.

"The Yggdrasil Facility is still a few miles away," she said. "We don't know what kind of security measures they've put in place, so I would rather not approach it in the dark. We'll camp here and go in at first light."

"What about that thing from last night?" Betty asked.

"The animals up here are shy," Badri said. "Curious, but shy. Whatever it was, I think it will keep its distance."

So they broke out four tents and everyone helped set them up. Eleanor knelt in the snow, feeling her knees turn cold and a little wet as she fit tension rods together and threaded them through canvas. It wasn't quite dark by the time they'd finished raising their encampment, but the sun had gone down, and the white snow around them had deepened to blue.

The tents each held three people, and after a quick meal they divided themselves up. Eleanor took a tent with Uncle Jack and Betty. Luke, Finn, and Dr. Von Albrecht ended up in another, with the rest of the team filling the other two.

"Let's keep the lights out," Badri called to everyone. "We don't want to be seen. We need to set up watches, too."

After that was all decided, Eleanor lay in the darkness between Uncle Jack and Betty, staring at the low, domed ceiling growing dimmer and dimmer, until the tent became a dark cave. In the quiet of the night, she felt the subtle pull of the earth's telluric currents flowing beneath her, but more than that, she could sense the hum of the Concentrator. She hadn't felt one from so far away before, but she thought perhaps that was because this one was larger than the rest. She could almost hear the artificial intelligence within it, a very distant howling of rage.

"I've been thinking," Betty whispered. "I know we keep saying that we'll deal with this later, but what if the rogue world doesn't move on? What if it stays in our solar system, even if we shut down all the Concentrators?"

Neither Eleanor nor Uncle Jack answered her. Eleanor wondered if Betty was having doubts about their plan.

"Then I guess we have to find a way to survive the Freeze," Eleanor finally said.

"Right." Betty was silent a moment. "Which is exactly what Watkins is doing, isn't he?"

Eleanor frowned in the darkness. What was Betty trying to say?

"Do you think Watkins is right?" Uncle Jack asked her.

"No," Betty said. "I don't accept any solution where we just write off most of the people on this planet. But I am starting to think beyond this goal we've had. I'm asking what if—and I don't think it's a question we should keep putting off."

But it was still a question for which Eleanor didn't have the answer. "If that happens," she whispered, "then we've lost. And Watkins wins. But that won't mean we were wrong to try, and I still have hope."

"So do I," Uncle Jack said.

"I'll try," Betty said. "Maybe I've worked in the Arctic for too many years. I've seen too much to trust in hope alone."

Their tent went quiet after that, but the conversation echoed into the night, keeping Eleanor half awake. She wasn't sure how long she lay there, drifting, but sometime later she jolted. Her eyes snapped open, and her breathing stopped. Something was out there.

Whatever that thing was, it was back.

She couldn't hear it, she couldn't see it, but she knew it was there. Whoever had the watch in that moment might not even be aware of it. For a moment, Eleanor thought about Finn's mention of pissed-off aliens, but she dismissed that. She felt certain she would know if it was an alien. But it was something, and it was holding still, watching them all in their tents.

Eleanor wanted to wake Uncle Jack, but she was afraid to make any kind of sound. She didn't want to draw any attention to their tent. Whatever it was, it was leaving them alone, and eventually, Eleanor heard heavy footsteps moving away from them, and its presence faded from her mind, leaving a wake of tingles along her neck and shoulders.

After that, it was near dawn before she fell asleep.

The next morning, as everyone stretched out of their tents into the sunlight and snow, Eleanor wondered if anyone else had felt the presence of their night visitor. She waited to see if any of them would bring it up as they ate breakfast, and when they didn't, she decided to keep it to herself. She figured everyone thought she was weird enough, alien enough, without adding to it. Perhaps she had simply imagined it.

Badri led the way ahead, up and over hills, down and out of ravines, along valley floors. The few miles she had said were left between them and the Yggdrasil Facility proved arduous, and Eleanor's lack of sleep the night before slowed her down.

"How does the G.E.T. get all the way out here?" she asked, her mouth dry from panting, her legs sore.

"They take the road," Dr. Von Albrecht said.

"Wait." Finn stopped walking. "You're telling me there's a road?"

"Yes," Badri said. "You are free to use it if you would like to get caught. The rest of us will come in behind the facility, avoiding G.E.T. surveillance."

Finn closed his mouth and resumed his trudge along with the others. A few miles later, around midday, they approached the crest of a rise and Badri stretched out her arm, motioning for everyone to duck down. Eleanor crept forward with the rest of them, slowly, until she could peek over the top of the hill at their target.

The complex below them sprawled at the base of a mountain with the industrial appearance of a power plant or a refinery. Miles of tangled pipes, cables, and wires connected a network of towers and transformers, while tall chimneys vented white, billowing steam. A massive structure sat in the middle of it all, with satellite dishes arrayed across its roof. Eleanor sensed the Concentrator nearby, tugging at the telluric currents.

"The Yggdrasil Facility," Badri whispered.

Luke whistled. "This is sure a different situation from the others."

"They have expanded since I was last here." Dr. Von Albrecht squinted. "Much is different."

"How are we going to get in there?" Finn asked.

Badri pointed at a smaller building at the edge of the complex near them. "If the schematics we have are still accurate, that outbuilding will have a computer terminal. That's as far in as we need to go."

"I assume the Concentrator is inside that big building in the middle?" Betty said.

Before Eleanor could answer, Uncle Jack said, "No."

She turned to look at him.

"I can feel it," he said. "I think I've felt it for a while."

The others turned now. Eleanor recognized the discomfort on their faces, but for the first time, that scrutiny wasn't directed at her, and unlike her, Uncle Jack didn't seem to notice or care.

"I think it's inside the mountain," he said.

Eleanor nodded. "I think so, too."

"So how do we do this?" Luke asked.

"First we disable their security cameras," Badri said. "Then we break through their perimeter without setting off any alarms."

"Cameras?" Finn said.

"I assume you have a way to accomplish all that," Luke said.

"Of course." Badri motioned toward a couple of members of her team, James and another man named Cyrus, and the two of them set off carefully down the hill. "The G.E.T. uses wireless cameras, as well as some other sensors, for their surveillance. Such devices can be hacked and disrupted, with the right equipment."

James and Cyrus reached a distant point below their party and stopped, the G.E.T. facility still some distance away.

"It seems they've reached the first sensor." Badri brought her gloved hand up as though she meant to chew on her thumbnail, looked down, and then lowered her hand again.

"Are you worried?" Eleanor asked.

"I said their surveillance *can* be hacked. I didn't say it would be easy."

That didn't help Eleanor's confidence. She watched and waited, motionless.

After several moments, during which Badri never looked away from her team members, the two of them finally moved again, creeping forward toward the facility.

"Let's move," Badri said. "The first barrier is cleared."

Eleanor took her first steps down the hill hesitantly, still half expecting alarms to sound as they triggered unseen detectors. But no bells or sirens broke the silence, and all she heard was the sound of the wind through the canyons around her, and the scuff of her boots through the snow.

When they reached the spot where James and Cyrus had been crouching minutes before, Badri halted them all. Ahead of them, the advance team members had stopped again, hacking the next round of surveillance devices. When the two had successfully finished with that task, Badri led the rest of them forward to that next point, and they proceeded in this way toward the facility, in cautious steps and stages.

It used up a portion of the afternoon, but eventually they reached the outer perimeter of the Yggdrasil Facility, where a high chain-link fence barred their way. After deactivating the cameras mounted on the nearest fence posts, Badri pulled out a laser cutter. Its searing arc of white heat burned through the fencing, turning the metal ends briefly red, and when the cut segment fell free into the snow, it sizzled and steamed. Badri gestured past it, toward the opening she'd just made.

She smiled. "Now for the hard part."

CHAPTER
5

THEY CREPT ACROSS THE OPEN YARD TOWARD THE BUILD-
ing Badri had indicated from above. Eleanor
expected to see guards or G.E.T. agents, or at least
workers, but they didn't encounter any.

"Where is everyone?" she whispered.

"This part of the facility isn't in use right now,"
Badri said. "All staff are guarding or working near the
World Tree, and have been for months."

They reached the outbuilding, and after a few
moments, Cyrus managed to pick the lock on the door.
Then they all slipped inside, closing the door behind
them.

They stood in a noisy, empty control room walled

with electrical panels covered in switches and fuses, as well as a maze of pipes, valves, and gauges. An old computer terminal stood in one corner, an industrial machine that bore dark, smudgy fingerprints across its beige shell and a yellowed plastic skin over its keyboard to keep the dirt out.

Finn frowned at it. "You're going to use that to access the confidential files?"

Badri stepped up to the machine. "It doesn't have to look pretty." Then she started typing, and one of her team connected a portable drive to the terminal.

As they worked, Eleanor stepped toward the wall in the direction of the Concentrator. Its pull on her had grown stronger since entering the facility. She peered between the pipes, at the painted cinder blocks, and imagined she could stare right through them, and through the rest of the installation, through the Sky Caves and the mountain, all the way to the Concentrator's twisting branches and quivering roots.

"I still don't really understand any of this."

Eleanor turned. Uncle Jack stood beside her.

She looked back at the wall. "That's why we're here. If I understand it, I can stop it."

"I'll help you . . . you know, connect to it. If I can."

Eleanor glanced up at him. The creases at the edges of his eyes seemed deeper. "You already have."

"No," Badri said. She stood at the terminal, staccato typing, shaking her head. "This isn't working. They've increased security. I can't get in from here."

"No wonder they weren't guarding this place," Luke said.

Dr. Von Albrecht shook his head. "Watkins has grown even more cautious, it seems."

Eleanor crossed the small room to the computer. The strings of numbers and letters on the screen meant nothing to her. "So what now?"

"We have to find a new way in." Badri yanked out the cable and shoved the drive into her pack. "We need another terminal. One closer to the main installation."

"Closer?" Finn said. "You mean where they have G.E.T. agents?"

"Yes," Badri said. "I'll go ahead with Eleanor, her uncle, James, and Cyrus. The rest of you will stay here."

"No way." Luke stepped in front of the door. "I'm not letting you take her out of my sight."

"I'll be with her," Uncle Jack said.

Luke's eye twitched. "But I won't."

"Finn is right." Badri slipped the pack over her shoulder. "Security will be an issue past this point. If we all go, we'll certainly get caught. This way, we have a chance. But if the worst happens and we do get caught, the rest of you can still escape."

"We're not escaping without Eleanor," Finn said.

Eleanor looked at him, but he didn't look at her. He stared at Badri, adopting the same resolute stance that Luke had. Eleanor's cheeks flushed. It hadn't been so long ago when all she could see were her differences, when she felt like a freak. Now her friends were here for her. And that gave her the strength she needed to go on without them.

"It's okay, Finn." She gave him a firm nod. "Badri is right. It doesn't make any sense for us all to go. To risk getting captured."

"None of this makes sense." Luke stepped toward her. "I've come this far. I'm not going to just let you walk off with this person we just met."

"I believe you can trust her," Dr. Von Albrecht said.

"It's not Badri I'm worried about." Luke looked right into Eleanor's eyes. "We're in the heart of enemy territory here."

"No," Eleanor said. "The real enemy territory is somewhere up there. In the sky. That's why we're here. That's the enemy I need to understand."

Luke said nothing to that.

"Wait here, like Badri said. I'll be back, and hopefully then we'll know what we need to do."

Another moment passed. Then Luke nodded, his

head heavy, and stepped aside. Badri marched toward the door, and Eleanor followed her, with Uncle Jack behind her. James and Cyrus came next. At the door, Badri turned.

"Stay in this building, but at the first sign of any trouble, I want you to clear out. If they catch us, they'll search the rest of the facility."

"Be careful." Luke gave Eleanor a nod.

"We will," she said, and smiled at Finn, Betty, and Dr. Von Albrecht.

The five of them stepped out of the buzzing control room and let the door close quietly behind them, plunging them into the silence of the mountain valley. Once again, Eleanor felt the tingling sensation she had experienced the night before in the tent, and she scanned the slopes around them for who or what might be watching them. She saw no one, and nothing but snow.

"I think we should head that way." Badri pointed at a large building adjacent to the main complex. "That's the next most likely place where we might find a terminal with minimal G.E.T. staff."

Between them and that building lay a maze of equipment, pipes as big around as tree trunks, vehicles, and towers.

"Let's do it," Uncle Jack said.

James and Cyrus moved first, and Eleanor waited with Badri and Uncle Jack until they'd reached a forward point of cover. There, they assessed the security situation using their instruments, and then waved the all clear.

Eleanor and Uncle Jack followed Badri toward them, and just as they reached that point Eleanor saw two G.E.T. agents come around a distant corner, dressed in gray snow gear. She didn't see any guns on them, but assumed they would be armed, nevertheless. She and the others ducked down low behind a bank of pipes and watched. The guards were far away, and they didn't seem to have noticed anything, but their presence tightened the muscles at the back of Eleanor's neck.

"Let's watch a few moments," Badri whispered. "To figure out their patrol pattern."

So they stayed where they were for several moments. Eleanor worried that doing so posed its own kind of danger, if they lingered too long. But Badri's caution paid off when a second pair of G.E.T. guards came around another corner, much closer, marching in a different direction than the first two, and even though Eleanor held her body still, fear leaped around inside her like a caged and frantic rodent.

A few moments later, after waiting and watching,

they observed the specific moment and place where they could duck between the patrols, unobserved, into a narrow space between two large and buzzing electrical boxes. They proceeded this way farther into the Yggdrasil complex: racing from one hiding place to the next, pausing and watching, hacking surveillance along the way.

Occasionally Eleanor looked back at the way they had come, but soon lost sight of the building where Luke and the others waited for them, and the deeper they went, the more Eleanor felt cut off from escape. That they were approaching a point of no return.

They were also approaching the point where Eleanor hoped to finally understand what made her who she was. What made her and Uncle Jack and Watkins unique. Eleanor wasn't sure how she felt about that. She certainly wanted to know, but a part of her was also afraid of what she might find out, assuming Watkins had been telling the truth and he actually did have the answers.

A short while later, they reached their target, a building several times larger than the control room in which they had left the others. Cyrus set to work on the electronic lock, while Eleanor, Uncle Jack, Badri, and James stayed close to the wall. Eleanor felt exposed, and kept glancing over her shoulder.

"Almost got it," Cyrus said. "Just a—"

"Stop!" a voice shouted.

Eleanor turned to see a G.E.T. agent standing nearby. She didn't know where he had come from, but he didn't look like a guard. He wore regular polar clothing and did not appear to be armed.

"Who—who are you?" he asked.

Uncle Jack held up his big paddle hands. "Calm down now—"

"Don't tell me to calm down. State your names."

"We are Grendel," Badri said.

In the next moment, Eleanor watched as realization lifted the man's eyebrows. "You—"

Uncle Jack leaped toward him, moving faster than it seemed a man his size could, and soon had the G.E.T. employee in a bear hug from behind, an arm around his neck. Eleanor watched the man's face go red and his eyes roll back, and then he went limp in Uncle Jack's arms.

"Got it." Cyrus, who had apparently kept working during the confrontation, stepped away from the door as it popped open.

"Let's get this guy inside before he comes to," Uncle Jack said. "He'll only be out for a few seconds."

He slung the G.E.T. employee over his shoulder and carried him through the open door, the man's arms and legs twitching. The rest of them followed, and they entered a long, cold corridor lined with doors. Eleanor tried the nearest ones until she found one unlocked. It turned out to be a supply closet, and after setting the G.E.T. employee down inside, they stole his security badge and key card and shut the door just as he seemed to be regaining consciousness. Uncle Jack gave the door handle a solid, heavy kick, bending it.

"That won't open easily," he said.

"Then let's not waste another moment." Badri pulled a small tablet out of her pocket and swiped the screen with her finger. "There's a computer terminal this way."

Eleanor and the others followed her down the hallway, where they took a right turn down another corridor, and then a left through an open door. The building was frigid, and Eleanor shivered as they crept along the linoleum floor. Eventually, they entered a space that seemed used mostly for storage, with stacks of folding chairs, and folding tables, and regiments of filing cabinets. A desk in one corner bore a computer, its screen black and cold.

"This thing work?" Uncle Jack asked.

"Let's hope." Badri jabbed the power button. "It should."

"What is this building used for?" Eleanor asked.

"Nothing," Badri said. "This was the first building the G.E.T. constructed on the site. After they built the larger installation, they mostly vacated this one. That's why they keep the temperature just above freezing."

"You mean that's why I can see my breath," Eleanor said.

The old computer let out a little chirp, and then a whirring sound from its fan, as if yawning after being startled awake.

"Here we go." Badri plugged in the portable drive and went to work, the chatter of her keystrokes echoing throughout the room. "Much better. And that fellow's security clearance will help, too."

Uncle Jack opened up a couple of the folding chairs for him and Eleanor, and they sat and waited. In the moments that followed, Eleanor's anxiety over what was about to happen climbed, and pretty soon she had to get back up and pace around the room. What would the information in Watkins's files say? What would that information mean about who she was? Maybe she didn't want to know after all. At least, not for herself. But she felt trapped, because she *had* to know if she wanted to save the earth.

"Hey," Uncle Jack said.

She turned toward him.

He spread his lips in a broad and gentle smile.

"Whatever that computer says, it doesn't change a thing."

"How do you do that?"

"Do what?"

"Read my mind."

He shrugged. "Just remember. You're my Ell Bell. That computer might tell you something about these things you can do. But it can't tell you who you really are."

His words loosened the muscles in her neck and relaxed her shoulders. She stopped pacing and returned to the chair next to him, where she leaned her head against his arm. They sat that way for a few minutes, until Badri called them over.

"I'm in," she said. "Pulling up Watkins's files now."

Eleanor hurried to the woman's side and watched as she scrolled through folders and documents. Eleanor scanned the names, looking for anything that might be related to the Concentrators and the people connected to them.

Within a few moments, one caught her eye. "That one," she said.

"Which one?" Badri asked.

Eleanor pointed and read the name. "Exogenetics."

Badri opened it and found it contained numerous subfolders, some named, some of them simply numbered. Badri opened a few of them, but nothing hinted at the answers Eleanor wanted, until she saw a file called "Summary Report: Longitudinal Effects and Influences of Proximity." Badri opened that file, and Eleanor began reading the document.

She didn't understand a lot of the technical language, but she gleaned enough to make at least some sense of the report. The writers suggested that at some point in the prehistoric past, the Concentrators had emitted a kind of alien radiation that influenced the DNA of those who lived close to them, creating a kind of affinity between them. It seemed that these ancestors had then passed on the gene that made connection with the alien technology possible. That particular gene was turned off for most people. But not for everyone, obviously.

That meant Eleanor's ancestors had lived near one of the Concentrators thousands and thousands of years ago. She didn't know which one, but she wasn't sure that mattered. The point was that Watkins was right, and there were probably many, many people around the world who were like Eleanor and Uncle Jack.

"We need to show this to the professor," Eleanor said. "He'll be able to make more sense out of it. But let's keep looking and see what else we can find."

Badri scrolled down farther.

"What's that?" Uncle Jack asked. "That 'Zooid Theory' file?"

"Let's see." Badri opened it.

"What's a zooid?" Eleanor asked.

"It's a colonial organism," Badri said.

"Like a hive?" Eleanor asked.

"No. A hive is a colony of separate bees or ants working together, but a hive isn't an animal. Zooids are highly specialized animals that combine to form a larger organism. Like jellyfish."

"A jellyfish is a bunch of separate animals?" Eleanor asked.

"Some species are," Badri said. "And judging by this document, it seems that Watkins suspects that the alien biology works in a similar way. He believes they evolved from a type of zooid organism. Their parts are all connected to each other."

"Would that explain Eleanor's connection to the Concentrators?" Uncle Jack asked.

"Yes," Eleanor whispered. Because it made sense. The Concentrators had given off the same kind of energy that connected the aliens to each other, changing the DNA of the humans nearby in the process. Those humans had then gained some of the alien ability to connect to the larger whole. "I think Watkins is right," she said. "Maybe that's why it feels the way it does when I shut down a Concentrator. It's like I've injured the whole, so all the parts feel it. We feel it."

"But what does that mean for the plan?" Uncle Jack asked. "Is it safe to go ahead?"

"I think it might be." Badri read from the screen. "I just followed that last document to the results of several research experiments. It seems Watkins was very careful, and there's a notation here. He writes, 'Though it is possible that some individual humans have the ability to interface with the alien technology, they are only proximal zooids. They are not fully integrated with the alien organism, and though the human may feel some of the alien system's warning signs, results do not suggest the human to be in the same danger as the alien system.'"

"So it's safe to shut them down," Uncle Jack said.

It did seem that way. But only if Watkins was right, and Eleanor knew Watkins had been wrong about a lot.

"Let's just get all this back to Dr. Von Albrecht and the others," Eleanor said. "Then we can plan our next move."

"Good idea," Uncle Jack said.

"I'm copying the files right now," Badri said. "Only take a moment to—"

A distant alarm sounded.

"Oh no," Eleanor said.

"Damn." Uncle Jack looked over his shoulder. "He must've got the door open."

"We need to get out of here." Badri yanked the cable to the portable drive and handed it to James. "Hurry!"

The five of them raced from the room, back down the hallways, toward the building exit. As they neared the utility closet where they'd left the G.E.T. employee, they found the door open, the room empty.

"Once we're outside, we're just going to have to run for it," Badri said, already breathing hard.

Eleanor readied herself. Uncle Jack shoved the exit open, letting in the wail of the alarm from all around the installation. The five of them bolted through, back out into the snow and the sunlight, and Eleanor ran.

CHAPTER
6

SHE BLINKED IN THE BLINDING WHITE, RUNNING EVEN
though she couldn't yet see well, hoping she
didn't bump into a piece of equipment, or worse, a
G.E.T. agent. A few steps on, shapes resolved themselves against the blank of the snow, buildings, towers,
pipes. She fixed her eyes on the direction where she
thought the others waited for them and plowed ahead,
hoping they had heard the alarm and gotten themselves out of there.

"Ell Bell!"

She turned to her right, where Uncle Jack ran next
to her.

"Stay close to me!"

She nodded, her sweat freezing along her hairline in the cold. With a backward glance, she saw G.E.T. agents chasing them, but so far none had flanked them or managed to get in front of them. It seemed Badri had been right about this part of the Yggdrasil Facility sitting unused.

James and Cyrus led the charge, but Badri lagged behind them. Eleanor saw pain and strain across her face as she struggled to run and keep up.

If they could get through the perimeter fence, back into the hills, they could hide. There were endless ravines and caves, too many for the G.E.T. to thoroughly search.

"The rest of them got out!" James shouted back to them, holding a radio.

That relieved a sliver of Eleanor's fear, knowing that at least Luke, Finn, Betty, and Dr. Von Albrecht would be safe. Now she and the others just had to make it out and find them.

A loud shot cracked and echoed behind them. Eleanor gasped and looked back in time to see something streaking through the air toward Badri, crackling and sparking.

"Look out!" Eleanor shouted.

But the projectile struck the older woman in the

back, and she went down hard in the snow, convulsing.

"Badri!" Eleanor skidded to a halt in the snow.

Uncle Jack stopped, too. "What is it?"

"They shot her with something electrical!" Eleanor said.

Badri lay in a heap. "R—r—run!" she shouted at them through chattering teeth.

"Eleanor." Uncle Jack grabbed her arm. "We have to keep going."

The grimace on Badri's face made Eleanor feel sick. "But—"

"G—g—go!" Badri shouted.

Eleanor just stared, unable to take the first step, but Uncle Jack half carried her forward, one arm around her waist, gripping her arm with his other hand, until she resumed running on her own.

James and Cyrus hadn't even slowed down. They were even farther ahead, as Eleanor and Uncle Jack dodged the pipes and conduit, covering the distance a lot faster now that they didn't have to worry about surveillance. As they approached the first control room they'd entered, where the others had hidden, Eleanor knew they were almost there. Not much farther, and they'd be clear of the perimeter fence.

They rounded the building, but a guard appeared,

stepping into their path, and swung some kind of club that caught Uncle Jack in the chest. He went down on his back with a grunt.

"No!" Eleanor lunged at the G.E.T. agent, pummeling him with her fists. He took a few steps away from her in retreat, but he seemed more surprised than afraid of her. "Get away from him!" she shouted.

The agent recovered his footing and deflected the next few blows. He raised his club, and Eleanor closed her eyes.

But then she heard a roar, and the G.E.T. agent cried out as Uncle Jack lifted him off his feet and ran with him toward the building. A few feet shy of the wall, Uncle Jack stopped and hurled the agent, practically overhand. The man struck the wall with a thud, shaking snow from the roof, and dropped to the ground in a pile.

"Go!" Uncle Jack shouted, and together they raced past the building, toward the fence.

Eleanor saw the gap now. James and Cyrus had just climbed through it. She couldn't see Finn or the others anywhere. Hopefully that meant they were already safely hidden in the hills.

Several loud cracks sounded behind them.

Eleanor grabbed Uncle Jack by the sleeve and tugged him to the side, dodging out of the way as several more of the stun bullets struck the snow, popping and hissing.

"Almost there!" Uncle Jack said. She heard a groan in his voice, and hoped that agent's club hadn't injured him too badly.

Just a few yards left.

Then they ducked through, and up the hill above them, James and Cyrus waved.

"That way," Uncle Jack said, gasping.

"Are you okay?"

"I'll be fine. Just keep going."

They ran up the hill, but as they climbed, Eleanor felt her muscles failing. The cold adrenaline fire that had driven her burned out, leaving her exhausted. Beside her, Uncle Jack didn't seem to be doing much better. Up ahead, James and Cyrus had apparently decided not to wait, and they'd already gone over the top of the hill.

Down below, a few G.E.T. agents had reached the fence, while somewhere beyond them, deeper in the facility, the whine and whump of a helicopter could be heard. Uncle Jack looked sweaty and pale next to her.

"I'm not going to make it," he said. "I think that guy cracked a few of my ribs. You need to go on without me. I'll try to hold them off—"

"I am not leaving you." Eleanor took his hand and

gripped it hard. Then she looked around and noticed that if they crossed the hill sideways, rather than climbing over the top of it, they'd reach a little ravine. "Maybe we can hide in there."

She pulled him, and he winced, but he came with her, and they stumbled and hurried along the hill face. The helicopter was in the air now. She could hear it over her shoulders, but didn't turn to look, keeping her gaze locked on their target. When they finally reached it, Eleanor helped Uncle Jack climb down into the shadows of the jagged crevice. There weren't any opportunities for cover from the rocks, but there were several cave entrances like those they'd passed.

"The Sky Caves," she said. "Hurry."

Uncle Jack nodded, and they scrambled forward, the beating of the helicopter rotors growing louder and louder behind them. Just when Eleanor feared they'd surely be spotted, they entered the shadow of the cave and threw themselves deep inside it, stopping only when it grew almost too dark to see. A shadow flitted through the light shining through the entrance, and the helicopter grew gradually distant.

Eleanor leaned against the side of the cave, her glove sliding against the sandy rock wall. The sounds of their breathing filled the narrow space.

"I don't think they could have seen us," Uncle Jack said.

"Let's hope not."

"Those G.E.T. agents are still on foot, though. They'll probably be here soon."

Eleanor looked into the darkness. "Then we need to hide deeper in."

Uncle Jack nodded. "I have a light." But as he reached into his pocket, he let out another pained grunt.

Eleanor reached toward him. "We need to get you help—"

"I'm okay," he said. "It hurts, but I'm pretty sure it's not serious."

"Pretty sure?"

"I'm sure." He looked down at his side. "But the flashlight is in that second pocket. If you wouldn't mind."

Eleanor reached into the pocket of his coat that he'd indicated, found the light, and pulled it out. "You tell me if you start feeling worse."

"I will."

She switched on the flashlight, sending a beam of cold blue light down the throat of the cave. Then she led the way forward, following the tunnel as it twisted and turned, taking them into the side of the hill, down inclines and back up again. Unlike the carved caverns back in Peru, these tunnels had a flowing, natural quality to them. As if they'd been sculpted by wind. When they reached the first intersection, they paused.

Uncle Jack palmed sweat from his forehead. "We need to remember which way we go so we can find our way back."

"Left?"

"Left."

So they turned, and when they reached the next intersection, they paused again, taking note, rehearsing the way back. Eleanor felt safer the deeper they went. Even if the G.E.T. agents entered the cave, they'd never find them.

"This is a good place to hide," she said.

"We can't stay in here forever, though. My flashlight will die eventually." That was true, and it brought back unsettling memories of the seemingly endless Peruvian tunnels. "At least it's warmer in here."

"You know, I always thought we could beat the Freeze if we went underground, below the frost line." He paused. "But now that we know the Concentrators are bleeding the earth dry from the inside, I'm not sure that would do us any good."

"I can still feel it," Eleanor said. Now that her fear

had mostly retreated, she sensed the earth's currents above and below her, surging toward the Master Concentrator. "Can you?"

"Yes."

She stopped walking, the flashlight beam fixed ahead of them. "Wait a minute."

"What?"

"The World Tree is underground, right?"

"That's what they said."

"What if we can get to it from here? We could follow the currents. Maybe the caves connect."

"Maybe they do. But what then? Do we try to shut it down?"

That was a good question. They still hadn't decided if it was truly safe or not, and the Grendel team had the portable drive with the files. But everything they had read before the alarm went off suggested that it was safe. *Proximal zooids.* That's what Watkins had called Eleanor and the other people like her. According to his theory, humans weren't truly a part of the freaky alien system. Eleanor might feel the alarm bells going off, but she wouldn't die. Hopefully.

"Isn't it strange?" Uncle Jack said.

"What?"

"I'm just thinking about how different the aliens must be from us."

"That's sort of what I was thinking about. . . ."

"We evolved from mammals, right? The aliens evolved from . . . jellyfish or something. A completely different kind of brain. Or brains, I guess, all working together. A completely different kind of life-form."

"I think it's weird how you can read my mind."

He chuckled, and then winced. "But now we know why you and I have always gotten along so well. In fact, maybe now we know why some people just seem to connect. Like you know them from somewhere, and they seem to get you right away. You've had that happen, right?"

"Not really."

"You will. I have, and maybe now I know why."

"I don't know if I like that idea."

"Why?"

"I always thought I got along with you because you're you. If it's just our alien DNA, there isn't anything . . . special about it."

He nodded. "Maybe it's some of both. Maybe it's something else even bigger than both of them."

She smiled. "So what do you think? Do we go try to find the World Tree?"

"What does your gut tell you? Do you think it's safe now?"

Eleanor thought about the way she'd connected

with the alien intelligences inside the Concentrators. They had felt alive, and unique, but not complete. Not whole. Maybe those had been zooids, part of the aliens left behind inside the machines. Maybe the Concentrators were actually part of the alien life-form, broken off and planted in the earth like seeds. She might never really know or understand, but one thing she did know was that she had killed those intelligences. Watkins had started the Concentrators back up, but the intelligences were gone. She didn't think she could have done that if she was truly part of the alien system, and that conclusion supported what Watkins had found in his research.

"I think it's safe," she said. "I think Watkins was lying to control me. He wanted me to be afraid so I would stop messing with his plan."

"You? Afraid? That doesn't sound like the Ell Bell I know."

"I'm afraid," Eleanor said. "But I'm not afraid of doing something. I'm afraid of *not* doing something."

"Then let's do something."

Eleanor nodded. She closed her eyes and paid attention to the telluric currents, sensing their direction, leading away deeper into the earth. She opened her eyes and pointed down the corridor. "That way?"

"Feels right to me."

So they set off. She hoped the others would be able to take care of themselves. They would worry about her and Uncle Jack, but if she succeeded in what she wanted to do, she would be able to explain what happened afterward.

The tunnels grew more complex in their layout, like a honeycomb. Like a hive. It occurred to Eleanor that it was possible they weren't human-made—but also not carved naturally. This thought nearly changed her mind about their plan. She did not belong in these tunnels. She was now convinced they had not been made for her, or for anyone from her world. But that led to a new, even more disturbing thought—

"What if it really was an alien?" she whispered.

"What?"

"That thing outside the other night. Badri said it was an animal, but what if it wasn't? I've felt something watching us. . . ."

"I think we'd know," Uncle Jack said. "Did the thing feel like the Concentrators?"

Eleanor thought about that. "No."

"Then it must be an animal, like she said."

Eleanor decided to believe him. She mostly succeeded.

The twisting tunnels carried them on and on. At each juncture, they would stop, take their bearings, and follow the currents. A few times they chose pathways that stopped in dead ends, but each time they retraced their steps and chose a different tunnel. Eventually, Eleanor's instincts told her they had to be right underneath the main building of the Yggdrasil Facility. She could almost feel its weight bearing down on them from above, and she wondered if Watkins knew about the Sky Caves and tunnels. Probably not, or he would have guarded them, or at least closed them off.

"We're getting close," Uncle Jack said.

Eleanor sensed it, too. The currents had begun to swell, as if multiple streams were converging around them into rivers, and the rivers raged ahead. It still felt to her as if the entire world's telluric energy had been rerouted here, following that experience aboard the plane when something profound had changed. The unknowns surrounding that experience continued to disconcert her.

They took a few more turnings, and then the silence of the tunnels, until now filled only with the echoes of their voices and footsteps, gave way to the grinding of machinery. The thrum of engines. Eleanor smelled them, too, like a slick of oil over the cool, old air in the tunnels. She turned off the flashlight, and they crept forward by way of a distant glow that grew stronger with each step.

When they rounded a final bend, the tunnel narrowed to an opening perhaps two and a half feet wide, and through it Eleanor glimpsed what must have been an enormous room. The walls on the opposite side from them seemed hundreds of feet distant. Harsh light flooded the cavern, and when Eleanor reached the opening, she saw it.

The Master Concentrator stood at the center of the space, twice as tall and wide as the others had been, its branches even more numerous, razor sharp and twisted with the same incomprehensible geometry, the same eye-defying shape and color, as if it could not and should not be there. Elevated coils of cable circled the World Tree, tightly packed, connected to large machines that looked like they belonged in a power plant.

"This is it," she whispered. "Here we go."

— CHAPTER —
7

F INN CROUCHED IN THE SNOW. THE GRENDEL TEAM HAD erected a camouflage snow blind similar to the ones Amarok and his people had used back in Alaska, only instead of being made of fur, these were made of a lightweight, white nylon fabric. The blinds covered them like small, partial dome tents, shielding them from detection but offering little shelter.

The G.E.T. helicopter had circled several times before returning to the Yggdrasil Facility. Now they just had to wait out the agents who still searched the hills. The plan was to hold their position until nightfall, if they could, and then move to a safer distance.

Luke had a pair of binoculars, scanning the surrounding terrain.

"Any sign of Eleanor?" Finn asked.

"No." The pilot's voice sounded heavy. Finn knew how much he cared about her.

"I'm sure they're safe," Betty said.

"I told you," Cyrus said. "They got out." He was one of the two Grendel team members who'd gone with Eleanor and her uncle into the facility. He and the other one, James, had brought back the portable drive with Watkins's files, but no Eleanor. "It was *Badri* who they captured." His voice sounded bitter.

"They may have made it through the fence"—Luke lowered the binoculars—"but *you* didn't wait around to see if they got clear of the helicopter and the agents."

James pointed at the portable drive. "Badri gave me orders."

Luke shook his head. "Lot of good those files will do us without Eleanor."

"Stop it, Fournier," Betty said. "This isn't helpful."

Luke waved her off and raised the binoculars back to his eyes.

Finn's body tightened up again, a wave that started in his calves and worked its way through his knees and thighs, up his back. A restless wave that crashed around inside him, so that he had to fight the urge to get up and pace to shake it off. He had experienced these waves since leaving his father and brother behind in Egypt, but now, with Eleanor gone, they'd gotten worse. There wasn't anything he could do, but he needed to do something.

"What about the files?" He turned to the professor. "Maybe we should take a look at them?"

Dr. Von Albrecht half nodded, half shrugged. "I suppose we should."

James hesitated, but then reluctantly nodded. He handed the portable drive to Dr. Von Albrecht, and the professor connected it to a tablet belonging to one of the other Grendel team members.

"We managed to steal quite a bit of data," he said, scanning the screen. "There are things here I knew nothing about even when I worked for the G.E.T."

Cyrus's face looked stony. "Badri doesn't leave anything behind."

Finn understood the Grendel team's resentment, and he felt bad that Badri had been captured, but he didn't think the G.E.T. would hurt her. They would try to get information out of her, for sure, but after the short time he'd spent with Badri, he didn't think that would be an easy task.

"So what does it say?" Finn asked.

"Give me some time." Dr. Von Albrecht adjusted

his glasses, read and clicked and read for several minutes.

Finn's legs crawled.

"Interesting," Dr. Von Albrecht said. "It seems Watkins had a theory about the nature of the alien life-form that would explain how Eleanor and others like her can connect to the Concentrators."

"Is she in danger when we shut them down?" Luke asked.

"I don't know," Dr. Von Albrecht said. "There is a file here that claims it isn't dangerous. Or at least, that is the conclusion Watkins came to. But there is another document that suggests otherwise."

"So which is it?" Luke sounded angry. Or impatient. Or just worried.

"Perhaps both," Dr. Von Albrecht said. "It seems to depend on the strength of connection to the alien technology. Some people have a stronger affinity than others. Most people would be perfectly safe. . . ."

"But?" Betty said.

Dr. Von Albrecht cleared his throat. "Some people may not be."

Luke swore. "Let's keep a lookout." He nodded toward the Grendel team monitoring the surrounding hills for G.E.T. agents. "As soon as she gets back, we'll get her out of here. Regroup."

Dr. Von Albrecht returned to the files. Betty scooted closer to Luke and put a hand on his back. Finn started to rock, trying to work out some of the tension holding him hostage. Looking at the files hadn't helped. In fact, they had made it worse. If Eleanor couldn't safely connect to the Concentrator, do whatever thing she did to shut them down, where did that leave them?

Would that mean Finn had abandoned his father and Julian for nothing? He knew his dad was wrong. Finn still had nothing in common with his dad, or his brother, especially now that they had signed on with Watkins and the Preservation Protocol. Finn didn't believe anyone had the right to decide who survived and who didn't, who was worth saving and who wasn't. But if the world was going to end no matter what, did any of that really matter? Shouldn't they be together to face it?

"It looks like the G.E.T. agents are retreating," James said, pointing.

Finn watched the distant figures moving away from them, back over the hill toward the Yggdrasil Facility.

"Why?" Luke said. "They know we're out here."

"I don't know," James said. "But we may not get another chance like this to—"

"What if it's a trap?" Luke asked.

"We'll wait another twenty minutes to make sure,"

Cyrus said. "And then we move out."

"And what about Badri?" Luke asked. "What about Eleanor?"

"We're an army," James said. "Armies take casualties—"

Luke dropped the binoculars and lunged toward the man, grabbing James by the collar of his coat. "She's not a casualty, you understand me? She's a kid."

James stared into Luke's eyes. "Stay here, then. Wait for her if you want. But Grendel will live to fight another day. That's what Badri would want."

Luke released the man. James then ordered the rest of his team to pack up. They left one of the snow blinds behind, as well as one of the tents and a few provisions, before marching away without a farewell or a backward glance. Finn watched them grow distant, shrinking to the size of grains of rice, and then they were gone over the crest of a hilltop.

"That's that." Dr. Von Albrecht turned to Luke. "So, what is your plan?"

"You wishing you'd gone with them?" Luke asked.

Dr. Von Albrecht blinked. "Certainly not. And I don't appreciate the question."

"Oh, you don't, do you?" Luke scowled. "Well, Professor Dr. Von Skeptic, I don't appreciate your—"

"Shut it, Fournier." Betty glared at the pilot. "What has gotten into you?"

Luke bit his lip and ran his hands through his hair. "She's out there. Somewhere. Or they have her. And I don't know which. I don't know what to do."

"None of us do," Betty said. "But that doesn't give you cause to turn on us."

"I know." Luke picked up the binoculars. "I'm sorry."

Finn had stayed quiet, letting the adults argue it out. He was used to that. His mom and his dad argued all the time, less often since the divorce, but even when they weren't together in person, they tried to argue with each other through Finn and his brother. So Finn had learned to stay quiet, do his best to stay out of it, and make up his own mind about what he was going to do.

The way he saw the current situation, Eleanor had either hidden somewhere and she was safe, or she'd been captured. If she was safe, she was probably working out a strategy to shut down the Concentrator, and to do that, she'd have to get back into the Yggdrasil Facility. If she'd been captured, she was already in the Yggdrasil Facility. It was also possible his dad was down there with Julian somewhere, but Finn tried not to think about that. It seemed just as likely they were still in Egypt, and he didn't know what the point of finding them would be, anyway, if they were still working with Watkins.

Regardless, Finn needed to get into a position to watch the Yggdrasil Facility from a safe distance. That meant higher ground.

He felt the tension in his body loosening now that it had something to do. "I'm going to make my way over there." He pointed at the top of a distant peak, the one across the valley, directly above the facility.

"Are you now?" Luke said.

Finn nodded.

Dr. Von Albrecht looked at the mountain, squinting, and appeared to be thinking about it. "I agree," he said. "Our best option at this point is to wait and watch."

Luke turned to Betty.

"Sounds good to me," she said.

"Fine." Luke rubbed his beard. "Fine, we'll make our way over there. Carefully."

They packed up the snow blind and the other gear the Grendel team had left behind and crept along the hill, staying out of sight of the G.E.T. installation, climbing down into shallow ravines and back out again. They passed more of the Sky Caves, and

Finn thought the openings would make perfect hiding places, if hiding were necessary. But he couldn't keep an eye on things from the inside of a cave, so he kept moving.

They crossed the wider valley far to the north of the Yggdrasil Facility and climbed the mountains on the opposite side. The sun lay near the horizon by the time they reached their destination. Finn looked back across the valley, at the point where they had started, from a ridge that gave them a view of everything below.

They set up the snow blind and the tent and settled in to wait and watch. It didn't take long for the exertion heat in Finn's muscles to fade, and the cold to set back in as night came on. The lights of the Yggdrasil Facility grew sharper and brighter, piercing the darkness with multiple dagger points.

Finn and the others took turns with the binoculars, monitoring the activity down below. They observed guards marching back and forth. They observed vehicles coming and going, supply trucks and transports like those the G.E.T. used in the Arctic. But they saw no sign of Eleanor and her uncle.

"I still can't figure out why they called off the search," Luke said. "They had us. Or they could have had us."

Finn wondered that, too. He'd expected that the G.E.T. would send the helicopter back up, or send agents into the hills, but they never did.

"Maybe they know something we don't," Betty said.

"They're the G.E.T.," Finn said. "They *always* know something we don't."

Dr. Von Albrecht laughed, darkly. "That is what they want the world to believe. It is often the case, but not always."

"You all should stay warm in the tent," Luke said. "We'll take shifts tonight. I have the first watch."

Finn climbed into the tent with Betty and Dr. Von Albrecht. They ate a few bites of dried fruit and settled into their sleeping bags. Finn had worked out enough of the tension in his body, and exhausted himself enough, that he was able to fall asleep quickly.

Luke nudged him awake a few hours later.

"You okay taking a watch?" the pilot asked. "Not much going on down there."

Finn sat up, wondering where he was for a moment, but soon reoriented. "Yeah—yeah, I can take a watch."

"Good man." Luke handed him the binoculars. "Stay right by the opening of the tent. If you need something, we'll be right here."

"Got it."

Finn traded places with Luke and stepped outside into the night. Overhead, the stars were doing their infinite thing, the Milky Way a loose, silken scarf wrapped around the neck of the world. Finn stared up at them for a few moments before turning his attention to the facility below. He didn't even know what time it was, but nothing seemed to be moving down there. Here in the Himalayas, in the middle of the night, Finn felt like the only person awake in the world, and he was fine with that—

He smelled something on the air. Something animal. It was musky, but also . . . sharp, a smell of old sweat that was almost human. It seemed familiar. Finn lowered the binoculars and looked around, sniffing. He was alone, but the smell grew stronger, more pungent, carried toward him on the wind.

Then he saw movement. Farther along the hill, perhaps two hundred feet away, a towering shape loped down the mountain. Finn raised the binoculars, and when he looked through them, he stopped breathing.

It was tall, at least eight feet. Its long arms seemed to reach to the ground as they swung along with its gait. Finn remembered then how he knew that smell. It was the odor of the gorillas in the Central Florida Zoo. But this animal wasn't an ordinary gorilla. It had white fur, and a face that looked more human than ape.

It was a yeti. A Bigfoot.

Finn wouldn't have believed it, except for the fact that he had already seen a woolly mammoth and Amarok's prehistoric wolves—not to mention Amarok's ancient people. And Eleanor had seen living mummies in Egypt. All resurrected by the energy of the Concentrator. *In fact,* Finn thought, *I probably should have expected something like this.*

This must have been the creature they had heard the other night stalking them. This might have even been the reason the G.E.T. had given up their search, if they knew a creature like this lurked in the hills.

Finn held still, trying not to panic, and realized that if he could smell the yeti, it might mean the yeti could not smell him. Their tent was downwind of it, and with their snow blind providing camouflage, the animal probably couldn't see them in the dark, either.

The yeti descended the mountain a short distance and then crouched, sitting on its haunches, staring down at the Yggdrasil Facility. It looked strong, quick, ready to strike, tilting its head from side to side, taking in all the angles. The animal appeared to be contemplating something. Working something out.

A few moments went by, and then it rose up to its

full height, its posture now menacing. Then it slammed the ground with its fists. Finn could hear the impact from where he sat, and could almost feel it. The yeti did it again. And again.

"What is that?" came Luke's voice from within the tent. "Kid—"

"Shh!" Finn said, partly taking his eyes from the yeti for a moment.

Luke fell silent, but when Finn looked back down the mountain, the creature had vanished.

"It's gone," Finn whispered.

"What's gone?"

"You're not going to believe it," Finn said.

Silence.

"Really?" Luke unzipped the tent and poked his head out. "You think there's something left that I won't believe?"

"You tell me," Finn said, and began to explain what he'd seen.

— CHAPTER —
8

ELEANOR SAT AT THE EDGE OF THE TUNNEL, LOOKING OUT from the cave. Dozens of G.E.T. workers surrounded the Master Concentrator, moving about with a frantic energy. She couldn't make out anything they were saying.

"Maybe we should wait until nightfall to try to get closer," she whispered.

"Good idea," Uncle Jack said. He motioned for her to follow him, and then he crept farther back into the tunnel the way they had come until they were a safe distance from the opening. "I don't want to risk getting spotted," he whispered.

"Also a good idea," Eleanor said.

They settled down opposite each other, their backs against the walls of the tunnel, Eleanor's legs parallel to his. He winced and grunted the whole way down, and Eleanor saw sweat gleaming across his forehead in the dim light.

"You look pale," she said.

"I'm fine. That guy definitely cracked a rib or two. But I'm fine."

Eleanor wasn't so sure, and kept an eye on him as they sat and waited.

"I just hope Badri's okay," Uncle Jack said.

"Me, too."

"She's tough. But I don't know if she's tough enough."

Eleanor smirked at the thought of Watkins trying to get a single word out of her. "I doubt he'll hurt her."

Uncle Jack folded his hands in his lap. "You have a higher opinion of the G.E.T. than I do."

Eleanor understood what he meant, but she had actually come to think highly of Watkins, in a weird way, and only when looking at him from a specific angle. He wasn't evil. He didn't want to hurt anyone. He had simply made up his mind about the best way for humanity to survive the Freeze, and he wasn't going to let anyone else get in the way of that. When viewed that way, he appeared determined, and intelligent, and capable, qualities Eleanor actually hoped she possessed. She would need all that if she was going to stop him.

What she didn't understand was why her mom had agreed with him and turned against her.

"What do you think changed?" Uncle Jack asked.

"Changed?"

"With the telluric currents?"

"I don't know." Eleanor laid a palm against the smooth sandstone wall beside her, feeling for the energy coursing through it. "I think the World Tree took charge. Maybe the—the zooid organism finally realized what was going on. We've been threatening it, so its defenses kicked in."

"But what was that thing we felt on the plane?"

Eleanor remembered the arrival of that . . . presence. "I have no idea."

"Do you think we should figure that out before we do anything?"

He had a point. But Eleanor didn't know what they could do about it. "I'm worried we won't have another chance like this again. We need to take our shot at the Master Concentrator. We can figure everything else out later."

Uncle Jack nodded, and Eleanor could hear his labored breathing.

"Are you sure you're okay?"

He closed his eyes. "Trying to keep the pain at bay. I might just hold still and rest for a few minutes if you can keep an eye on things."

"Of course. I think we're safe here."

He nodded and let out a long sigh.

Eleanor watched him rest for several hours, feeling both love and concern. She also felt a knot of guilt knowing it was her fault he got injured. He was here only because of her, and if anything happened to him she knew it would destroy her. She suspected he was already hurt worse than he was letting on, and he didn't seem to be in any shape to continue.

His breathing had settled into a steady rhythm, and she realized he was sleeping, or nearly sleeping. Had enough time gone by for the facility to clear out a bit? It would be easier if it was just her sneaking around anyway. Maybe she could slip away, shut down the Master Concentrator, and be back before Uncle Jack even knew she'd left.

She decided to risk it, for his sake.

Eleanor eased herself up to her feet, careful not to scrape the wall, and stepped over his legs. He never stirred as she crept away, back down the corridor, toward the World Tree. There did seem to be fewer agents around when she reached the opening and peered out, but not few enough to make her job easy.

Like Badri, she sat and watched for several minutes, trying to decide which of the G.E.T. workers were scientists or other technicians, and which were the guards. She watched the patterns of their movement, and quickly noted that some of the women and men marched a consistent route. They had to be guards.

The other G.E.T. staff worked in a more haphazard manner, their full attention on the Concentrator and the instruments they either stood near or carried in their hands. They might not even notice her if she waited until there weren't any guards around.

After a time, she could begin to predict gaps in the guard patrols that would allow her to get close. The hard part would be climbing around all the conduit circling the Master Concentrator. But the coils stood a few feet off the ground, so she decided it would be best to crawl underneath them, military style.

She waited a few minutes more.

This was it. Her stomach, breathing, and heartbeat got churned up in the same storm. But then her moment came, and she made herself move.

She eased out of the narrow opening onto the floor of the cavern, sprinted a few yards, and dove beneath the conduit coils. She felt partially hidden there, at least, but realized Uncle Jack would never have fit.

Overhead, through the space between the conduits, she glimpsed the black branches of the Master Concentrator twisting, the cave's ceiling high above them. She also sensed confusion in the telluric currents here. They now flowed in opposing directions and whirled in vortices, as if someone had stuck a paddle into the middle of them to disrupt them. Perhaps that was the purpose of the conduit?

Whatever the meaning, it didn't matter. Eleanor rolled onto her belly, inching forward on her elbows and knees, keeping as low to the ground and quiet as she could. Occasional shadows moved across her as she got close to the guards and workers, but none of them spotted her.

She crawled a few yards at a time, pausing to make sure she wouldn't be seen, and drawing nearer to the Master Concentrator. Its presence swelled in her mind the closer she got; even at a distance, she felt the strength of this one, waiting for her.

At last she reached the edge of the conduit coils and faced her next obstacle. The conduit stopped short of the Master Concentrator by twenty feet or more. That left a gap that Eleanor would have to cross without any cover. She spotted the alien control panel around the side of the World Tree to her left and crawled toward it. She wanted to be as close to it as she could before emerging into the open. On her way there, she sneaked past two of the G.E.T. scientists, and she overheard their conversation.

"No difference," a woman said. "It doesn't matter how we charge the array. The currents find a way through."

"Let's try again."

"But—"

"We try again. That was the directive Dr. Watkins gave us."

"I wonder how much longer that arrogant old buzzard will be giving the orders." A moment of silence passed. "What about the ship?"

"No change there either, last I heard. But Hobbes is in charge of that site now."

Ship? What kind of ship? Eleanor remembered Hobbes, the severe henchman who had been working for Watkins in Egypt.

"As soon as Dr. Watkins is done here," the man continued, "he's got some major damage control to take care of."

"Glad I'm not him. I hate politics, and politicians."

"At this point, I don't think politics even matter. We're well past that. Rumor has it Dr. Watkins is finished anyway."

How could Watkins be finished? And what did he

mean by damage control? And by *ship*, did they mean an *alien* ship? That might explain the new presence Eleanor and Uncle Jack had felt back on the plane. But the scientists had just answered another of Eleanor's questions.

Watkins was here. In the Himalayas.

"I'll let my team know we're going to prep for a new configuration," the woman said.

"Let's try the calculations we came up with yesterday afternoon," the man said. "I don't expect a change. But it's better than sitting around doing nothing."

The woman sighed. "Okay, let's do it."

They both moved away, and Eleanor's mind buzzed. Everything was changing. There was some kind of ship somewhere. It seemed the Master Concentrator had stopped working like it had been. And it seemed the UN wasn't happy with Watkins anymore, which Eleanor thought might be connected to the ship, or it might be connected to Watkins losing control of the earth's energy. Of course, it might also simply be that Watkins was Watkins, and the UN was sick of him.

Still, none of that made any difference to her plan in that moment. She still had to shut down the Master Concentrator, which was even more important if it was true that Watkins had lost control of it.

She crawled onward and reached the spot nearest

the control panel. When she couldn't see anyone else around, she scrambled out and raced toward the Master Concentrator. She wouldn't have much time, perhaps only moments, to do the job. But she had now done it three times, and knew what to expect.

She laid her palm on the console, feeling the cold contours of the metal, imagining her hand sinking into it, becoming one with it. She let out a deep breath and took control of her thoughts, bracing herself. But when she reached into the Master Concentrator through her hand, feeling with her mind for the intelligence lurking inside it, she encountered something new.

The intelligence that reached back toward her felt stronger than any of the others. And it was . . . curious. Certainly not vulnerable as the others had been, and definitely not afraid.

The trusses of Eleanor's confidence cracked, but didn't yet cave in. She extended herself toward the intelligence, letting it get close to her, wrapping itself around her mind. She felt its shape and its nature, and she knew instantly that it was something else entirely than the intelligences she had encountered before. It was part stars and part earth, its parts forming a new whole.

But none of that mattered. The moment Eleanor

sensed its guard was down, she exerted her will against it, trying to wrestle it into submission and extinguish it the way she'd done before.

But this Master Concentrator fought back instantly, and, too late, she realized that it was much, much stronger than she was.

It didn't move quickly, but attacked her in the confident way of something that knew it could take its time. As it emerged from within the machinery and the vastness of space, Eleanor glimpsed its full shape and size, and she knew she'd made a terrible mistake. She could do nothing to resist as it reached toward her and pulled her in, wrapping itself around her.

Eleanor now felt something strangling her mind, tightening coils around her mind, her heart, shutting everything down, sending her vision down into an inky pit. She couldn't hold on to her thoughts, and soon lost sight of where she was, or what she was doing there. Then she started to lose sight of herself. She couldn't remember her name or . . .

"Eleanor!"

The voice barely reached her. But it sounded familiar.

"Eleanor!" the voice said again.

That was who she was, though she wouldn't have

remembered on her own. Eleanor tried to find the source of the voice, but she couldn't move. She could hardly think, so she focused every thought she had on herself. Her body, her legs, her arms. One of her hands felt icy and numb, frozen to something. She decided she needed to pull it away, but that seemed impossible.

The dark thing smothering her squeezed her tighter, and she lost hold of the voice calling to her. What had it been saying?

Her hand.

Her hand was on fire. She knew that, and she knew that it would burn up if she didn't pull away. So she poured everything she was into her hand. She focused every scrap of thought on it. She let go of everything, every part of her down to her last hair and her last breath, until she was nothing but her hand.

And she moved.

She pulled away from the cold flame. The burning ceased, and the dark thing broke away from her, after which her mind flooded back in, bringing the rest of her with it. She clutched her head and opened her eyes, gasping, disoriented by a pain in her skull unlike any she'd ever felt.

"Eleanor!"

It was Uncle Jack.

She turned to see him scrambling toward her over the conduit, guards in pursuit.

"Get away from it!" he shouted.

Eleanor looked up at the Concentrator. The massive expanse of black branches whipped and writhed in the air overhead as if by the force of a hurricane. Eleanor staggered backward away from it, remembering what had just happened, remembering the dark thing inside the World Tree, knowing now how the intelligences in the other Concentrators had experienced their deaths. The same thing had almost just happened to her, and now this Master Concentrator knew about her.

She turned away from it and rushed toward Uncle Jack just as one of the guards behind him raised a gun.

"No!" she screamed.

The guard fired. Something crackled through the air and struck Uncle Jack in the back.

He made a noise, "Uh-hn," and tumbled forward over the conduit. The metallic clamor echoed through the chamber as he writhed.

"Uncle Jack!" Eleanor tried to reach him, but the guards were already on top of him, and then she felt someone grab her by the arms from behind.

She kicked and thrashed, broke free for a moment, but the guard snagged her again, and by this time a second one had come to help. They pinned her face-down against the conduit, the metal cold against her cheek.

"Uncle Jack!" she screamed again, but no one listened.

"Has Watkins left yet?" one of the G.E.T. agents asked above her.

"No," came an answer from someone else.

"Go get him," the agent said. "He's gonna want to see this."

— CHAPTER —
9

FINN COULDN'T SLEEP AFTER THE APPEARANCE OF THE
yeti. None of them could, because they totally
believed him, even though a few weeks ago he probably would have called himself crazy for thinking he'd
seen what he saw. But that big white gorilla was real,
and it was somewhere out there, probably watching
them.

The four of them stood outside their tent, scanning
the surrounding hills. The night hadn't really lifted
yet, and the light from the stars did little.

"What was it doing?" Dr. Von Albrecht asked.

"At first it was just sitting there." Finn pointed at
the spot where the yeti had crouched. "It was staring

down at the G.E.T. base. Then it started pounding the ground with its fists. Hard."

"That's what woke me up," Luke said. "Thought it was an avalanche or something."

"It was just hitting the ground?" Betty said. "Why?"

"Could it have been angry? With us?" Luke asked. "Gorillas do that, right? Some kind of territorial display?"

"I don't think it even knew we were here," Finn said. "We were downwind, and as soon as you made a noise, it disappeared."

"Luke just might be on to something." Dr. Von Albrecht stared along the mountain slope. "This may sound far-fetched."

Luke put a hand on Dr. Von Albrecht's shoulder. "Professor, that train left the station a long time ago."

"In that case, do you remember the evidence we saw of avalanches?"

Finn remembered that Badri had pointed it out.

"What about it?" Betty asked.

Dr. Von Albrecht paused, opened his mouth, paused, and finally said. "Perhaps . . . perhaps the yeti was trying to trigger such an avalanche."

No one spoke up to accept or reject that hypothesis. Finn didn't know whether to laugh or be afraid.

"We've had fresh snowfall in the past twenty-four

hours," Dr. Von Albrecht continued. "It's warmer tonight by about five degrees than it was last night, and tomorrow will likely be warmer, as well. We've seen recent avalanche activity. Even without the yeti, the warning signs are there. But look—" He pointed toward the place where the yeti had pummeled the ground. "Do you see that crack in the snowpack?"

Finn squinted, and then he saw it against the blue-white. A faint, grim line spread horizontally along the mountain's face.

"The question," Dr. Von Albrecht said, "is whether the yeti *intended* that to happen."

Another moment of silence passed. Finn no longer felt like laughing.

"Why would it want to do that?" Betty asked.

Dr. Von Albrecht looked downhill. "Finn did say it appeared to be preoccupied with the Yggdrasil Facility. Isn't that right?"

Finn nodded. "It was staring that way for a while."

"You see?" Dr. Von Albrecht continued. "Perhaps the yeti wants to find a way to destroy the facility."

"Never thought I'd have anything in common with a yeti," Luke said. "But if you're right, what do we do about it?"

"If I'm correct," Dr. Von Albrecht said, "we must also remember that Badri is down there, and so, perhaps, are Eleanor and her uncle. They would all be buried."

Finn hadn't thought of that, and he suddenly found it harder to ignore the question of whether his dad and Julian were down there, too. "So we need to find them and get them out."

"That's right," Luke said. "I'll go check it out. Alone."

"Why alone?" Betty asked.

Luke looked at her with his jaw set, but his voice was gentle. "Because whoever goes down there will be in the path of any avalanche, and there's no reason to put all our lives at risk."

"Now wait just a minute," Betty said. "I'm not going to sit here—"

"We have other people here to think about," Luke said, and cast a glance at Finn.

"Hold on," Finn said. "You don't need to treat me a like a kid—"

"You *are* a kid," Luke said. "And I'm going to make sure that when this is all over you'll be back with your parents and your brother in one piece. So you stay here. Got it?"

Finn knew arguing wouldn't do any good. Luke had made up his mind, and it seemed like Betty and Dr. Von Albrecht agreed with him.

If Finn wanted to help Eleanor, he would have to do it on his own without asking for anyone's permission.

"Got it," he said.

"Good man," Luke said. He turned to Betty and Dr. Von Albrecht. "Keep an eye out?"

"Of course," Betty said. "What's your plan?"

Finn smirked. "What if you just knock on the front door and tell them the abominable snowman is trying to bury them alive? That'll work, right?"

Luke squinted at him. "That's not a bad idea."

"I was kidding."

"I know. Either way, I'll be improvising."

"Don't forget about those Arctic transports," Finn said. "Seriously, those things are tanks. If there is an avalanche, try to get inside one of them."

"Now that's a good idea," Luke said. "Thanks, kid."

He gave them all a nod and set off down the hill, carving switchbacks in the snow. The three of them watched him go, eventually settling down on the cliff's edge. Finn used the binoculars to scan the surrounding hills, but never caught sight of any further movement.

"Maybe the yeti is . . . What's the opposite of nocturnal?" he asked.

"Diurnal," Betty said.

"Right. Maybe the yeti is diurnal?"

"Let's hope," Betty said.

"Diurnality is common among higher-order primates," Dr. Von Albrecht said. "But of course, in the twentieth century, the North American Bigfoot was thought of as a nocturnal animal."

Betty leaned back. "You're not making me feel better about being out here."

But apart from the risk of avalanche, Finn wasn't worried. The yeti didn't frighten him. It had most likely been following them for days, and it could have attacked them if it had wanted to. Last night, it ran as soon as it realized they were there. To Finn, its behavior appeared more shy than hostile.

Except for the avalanche. The avalanche was definitely hostile.

"Can I see those?" Betty reached toward the binoculars, and Finn handed them over. She brought them to her eyes, wrinkling her nose and curling her lip as she looked through them. "Luke's made it to the bottom of the hill."

"Good," Finn said. "Now what's he doing?"

"Looks like he's trying to find a way through the fence."

"Do you see any guards?" Dr. Von Albrecht asked.

"Yes," she said. "Quite a few."

"Maybe he can—"

"Damn it, Fournier!" Betty said.

Finn looked down the hill. "What is it?"

"That fool just turned himself in!"

"What?" Dr. Von Albrecht asked.

"He just walked up to the gate with his hands in the air," Betty said.

"Why would he do that?" Finn asked.

"Fastest way in, I suppose." Betty lowered the binoculars and shook her head. "He goes to bust them out, and we have to bust him out. This is starting to feel like the old woman who swallowed a fly."

"Maybe he has a plan," Dr. Von Albrecht said.

Finn looked at the professor. So did Betty.

Dr. Von Albrecht shrugged. "I didn't say it was a good plan."

Betty sighed. "It sure doesn't look good from here."

Finn scanned the rest of the Yggdrasil Facility. Activity elsewhere in the complex hadn't changed much. The whole place seemed fairly quiet, but it was still nighttime. By morning, he figured there would be G.E.T. agents everywhere. Maybe they would even resume searching for them, especially now that Luke had just revealed they were still hanging around.

There wasn't anything they could do about it from up where they were except wait and see. So that's what they did for the next few hours, but the only thing that changed was the light in the sky and the color of the snow.

Finn's thoughts left the Himalayas and returned home, imagining his life before this whole thing started. He thought of his mom, wondering what the G.E.T. had told her about her sons, the terrorists. She would blame his dad, like she always did, and Finn and Julian would be caught in the middle. That was a hard place to be, because the truth was that his mom was partially right. His dad definitely wasn't perfect. But that didn't make him a bad guy.

At least, he hadn't always been a bad guy. Now that he had signed on with Watkins's plan, Finn wasn't sure anymore. Still, sitting on that mountain in the cold, he wished his dad and his brother were there with him, just the same.

"Look," Betty whispered.

Below them, something lumbered. Quiet. Slow. Big.

The yeti had come back.

No one made a sound. Finn couldn't even hear Betty or Dr. Von Albrecht breathing next to him, but he wasn't sure he was breathing, either. The creature made its way slowly to where it had crouched before. This time, the yeti knew they were there, and it knew they knew it was there. Apparently, it had decided it didn't care, and watched them with its dark eyes, sniffing the air with its white nose.

"What do we do?" Betty whispered.

"What can we do?" Dr. Von Albrecht asked.

"We can hope it doesn't decide we're with the G.E.T. and turn on us," Finn said.

The yeti let out a deep huff, releasing a jet of fog from its nostrils and mouth. Then it turned and regarded the Yggdrasil Facility with the same interest it had shown earlier that night. Finn could see the muscles underneath its heavy fur tightening in its arms and shoulders. He could almost feel its anger.

"I don't like this," Betty said.

Dr. Von Albrecht blew into his fist. "It seems—"

The yeti raised both of its fists over its head and brought them down hard, slamming the ground. The deep thud reached into Finn's stomach.

"Oh no," he said.

The yeti pounded again. And again. And again. And this time, it also let out a roar that filled the valley. There was no way the G.E.T. agents hadn't heard it down at their facility. But then a new sound reached Finn: a deep rumble that seemed to emerge from everywhere at once.

"It's happening," Dr. Von Albrecht said. "We need to climb!"

The professor and Betty turned and scrambled up the hill. Finn followed after them while looking back over his shoulder. Before he'd climbed far, he saw a group of people spill out of the main G.E.T. building. They were too far away for Finn to see who they were, or whether his dad or Julian or Eleanor were among them. The yeti must have noticed them, too, because it hit the ground and roared again.

The rumble grew louder, and then it seemed the entire lower half of the mountain shifted and sagged. The crack widened, a deep fissure opening like a scream, while the yeti bounded up and away, disappearing as quickly as it had before. Down below, most of the people seemed to be rushing toward the helicopter, but a few broke away from the others and moved toward the transports resting near a radio tower. Finn hoped that was Luke with the others.

In the next moment, whatever had been holding the snow at bay finally gave out, and the mountain released its immense burden. The smooth surface disintegrated, rushing down and away from Finn in a tumbling, churning landslide that appeared almost liquid, its thunder deafening. He lost sight of the facility below, as well as the people running to escape.

"Finn, move!" Betty shouted from above.

Finn looked down as the snow beneath his feet shifted. The edge of the avalanche had leaped up toward him, ready to pull the ground out from under him. He turned and clambered on all fours, scrambling until he reached higher, stable ground, and watched the place where he'd been fall away.

Betty and Dr. Von Albrecht came to his side, and a few moments later most of the avalanche had settled, save a few places where snow continued to tumble in chunks. The Yggdrasil Facility was almost entirely buried, except for the tops of several towers. The snow had covered the helicopter, along with anyone who had tried to reach it. The transports were covered, too, but Finn knew where they were. He spotted the radio tower jutting out at an angle, bent by the force of the avalanche.

"My God," Betty whispered.

Finn turned and ran toward the tent. "We have to hurry! I saw them heading toward the transports!"

"Who?" Betty asked. "Luke? Did you see Luke?"

"I don't know," Finn said. "I'm not sure who it was. I'm not even sure they made it inside. But I'm sure I saw someone." He hoped it was Luke with Eleanor and the others. And he hoped his dad and Julian were still back in Cairo.

Betty nodded as Finn reached into the tent and pulled out a foldable snow shovel. Then he turned and began the now much more treacherous journey down the mountain.

"Are you coming?" he asked. "Even if they got inside the transport, their oxygen won't last forever."

"Right," Dr. Von Albrecht said.

Betty went to the tent and pulled out their second shovel. Then she and Dr. Von Albrecht joined Finn, and together the three of them picked their way down the mountain. The ground was unsteady now, and their boots sank deep in the freshly tilled snow, but eventually they reached the bent radio tower. Finn looked around, trying to fix their position, and chose the spot he thought most likely.

"I think it's here," he said. "Let's dig."

⟞ CHAPTER ⟝
10

ELEANOR AND UNCLE JACK SAT AT A METAL TABLE IN A small room just off the cave chamber housing the Master Concentrator. Closed blinds covered the upper half of one wall; the other three walls were windowless. But Eleanor could still sense the alien structure, could still feel its artificial intelligence inside her mind, and wished she could get farther away from it. Uncle Jack sagged in his chair. His ribs were cracked, and he'd been electrocuted by the G.E.T. guards. But he opened his eyes and gave her a serious look.

"Are you all right?" His breath came in wheezes. "When I realized you'd left me in that tunnel, Ell Bell—"

"I'm fine." She wasn't sure how much to tell him about the Concentrator. She didn't want him to worry, and she could only imagine how he'd felt when he woke up to find her gone. Back in Cairo, he had trusted her. He'd turned his back on Eleanor's mom to help her, and she didn't know how to tell him they had lost. She knew now she couldn't shut the Concentrator down. Somehow, a new intelligence had combined with the first one, and together they were much too strong for her.

He peered at her more intently. "But—"

"I'm fine," she said. "Really. I—"

The door opened, and Dr. Watkins strode in. He was wearing military-style fatigues instead of his usual suit. His hands were clasped behind his back, his brow set low. This was the man her mother had chosen to follow. This was the man responsible for the death of Amaru. This was the man against whom Eleanor had been fighting, one of the most powerful people on the planet. And yet compared to the alien intelligence she had just escaped, he was nothing but a feeble old man.

"Where is my mom?" she asked. "And Dr. Powers and Julian?"

"They are perfectly safe," he said. "But we don't have much time, so I'll make this brief. We've lost control of all the Concentrators, including this one."

"You've . . . lost control of the Concentrators?" Eleanor tried to thicken each word with as much sarcasm as she could.

Watkins either didn't notice or didn't care. "Yes. I'm sure you sensed it. Every other Concentrator in the world has gone quiet, and this one has become the primary nexus for all the earth's telluric energy." He pointed down at the ground. "And we can't reclaim any of it."

"The Concentrator is sending it into space," Eleanor said.

"Yes," he said.

"So why don't you stop it?" Eleanor asked.

Watkins wiped his brow and looked back up. "I told you we don't have much time. And yet you insist on asking irrelevant questions."

"It's not irrelevant," Eleanor said.

"Clearly I would stop it if I could. Clearly I must have tried. You are a very clever girl, and you must know the answer to your question."

Eleanor said nothing.

"What did you just do out there?" he asked.

"What do you mean?"

Watkins crossed the room to the blinds and pulled them open, revealing the Master Concentrator, its branches still wringing themselves together like fingers, twisting as if alive. "Something you did set the Concentrator off. Those . . . spasms began when you touched it."

"You're saying it's my fault you lost control?"

"I didn't say that. But you achieved something out there."

"What did she achieve?" Uncle Jack asked. Eleanor could hear the menace and anger in his voice, weak as it was.

Watkins unfastened the button at the neck of his fatigues. "For the past few days that machine has ignored me. I haven't been able to make contact of any kind with it. But Eleanor clearly did. It reacted to her. Why?"

"I don't know," Eleanor said.

"Stop it!" Watkins nearly spat. "Stop lying—"

"I'm not!" Eleanor said. "I really don't know! I didn't do anything different than before."

"And it let you in?" Watkins asked.

Eleanor nodded.

"Then what?"

"Then . . . it tried to kill me."

From the corner of her eye, Eleanor saw Uncle Jack jerk up straighter, staring at her. She avoided looking back at him.

"How?" Watkins asked.

"It tried to . . . shut down my mind. The same way I shut down the other Concentrators. Like it was strangling me. It was way stronger than the others."

"It's the Master Concen—"

"No," Eleanor said. "It was more than that. There was something else inside it. Like two intelligences had joined together." For now, she kept the presence of the silent observer to herself. "Like they're zooids."

Watkins lifted an eyebrow at her use of that word. "Have you been reading my work?"

Eleanor nodded.

"Where do you think this new intelligence came from?"

Something in the way he asked the question led Eleanor to suspect he already had a theory of his own. "I don't know, but I felt it arrive when we were taking off back in Cairo."

Watkins smiled. "You are a very clever girl."

"Whatever. Tell us what you're thinking."

"Very well. I felt it arrive at the same time you did. When the alien ship landed."

"The—" Eleanor wasn't sure what she had been expecting, but it certainly wasn't that. "The alien ship?"

"Yes. You may be clever, but you would also be

wise to remember you don't know everything. A ship landed in England, near Stonehenge. And unfortunately, the whole world knows about it. Cell phone footage and satellite images went public before we could contain them."

"Well," Uncle Jack said, "it's about time the world knew what was really going on here."

"Really?" Watkins took an empty chair and joined them at the table. "Since you all ran off, the riots in Cairo have spread well beyond my facility at the pyramids. The Egyptians have started destroying the European settlements and expelling—even killing—the refugees."

"Why?" Eleanor asked. "They have nothing to do with it."

"Why, indeed. Because when the human mind is frightened, it searches for a reason. Something or someone to blame. And the first target it lands on is often something—or someone—unfamiliar. An outsider."

"But that doesn't make sense," Eleanor said.

"Neither does an alien race channeling telluric currents to power its civilization while destroying an entire planet in the process. And yet here we are. The world has now connected this latest ice age to an extraterrestrial threat. They have all the details wrong, of course. But that doesn't matter. Now the UN is coming after me, and I need to give them answers. Immediately. Before the world descends into complete chaos, destroying everything I've worked to achieve."

"You think I'm going to help you with that?" Eleanor said.

"I think you care about this world as much as I do," Watkins said. "And you'll do almost anything to save it."

Eleanor looked into his eyes. They were watery and bloodshot from fatigue. He'd probably been awake since the ship had crashed and he'd lost control of his grand plan.

But he was right. She would do almost anything. And she knew he cared about the world, in his own way.

"Is the alien ship doing anything?" Uncle Jack asked. "Has it attacked?"

"No," Watkins said.

"Have we attacked it?"

"Not yet," Watkins said. "And I would like to keep it that way, which is one more reason I need Eleanor's help."

"I'm not going to help you lie," she said.

"I'm not asking you to. Quite the opposite, in fact. From you, I want nothing but the truth."

"I've told you the truth." Eleanor found the room

getting hot, and wanted to take off her snow gear. "You're the one who has lied."

"I admit that readily," Watkins said. "And I will continue to lie when the truth is too dangerous."

"After everything you just told me, you would still lie?"

"Yes."

Eleanor couldn't believe it. She wanted to scream in frustration. "The whole reason we're sitting here is because you believed your own lie! You could never control the Concentrators! You only convinced yourself and the UN that you could."

Uncle Jack let out a satisfied *humph*. Watkins looked at him, and then looked back at Eleanor, and it seemed that the fight had slipped out of him.

"Perhaps you are right," he said. "Perhaps I believed what I wanted to believe. That is another human weakness, and I suppose it is possible that I am susceptible to it."

"You suppose it is possible?" Eleanor said.

Watkins sighed. "Perhaps even probable."

Eleanor leaned away from him, shaking her head.

"So what now?" Uncle Jack gestured toward the Master Concentrator convulsing on the other side of the glass. "We have this thing, and Eleanor can't stop it. Neither can you. And now there's an alien ship."

Watkins propped his elbows on the table and clasped his hands together before him. "Perhaps Eleanor gave us the solution."

"What do you mean?" she asked.

"You say it felt as if two of the alien zooid intelligences had merged." He looked out the window. "What if we adopt the same strategy?"

"What do you mean?" Uncle Jack asked.

"What if Eleanor and I combine our efforts and face the Master Concentrator together?"

"If they can team up, so can we?" Eleanor said.

"Exactly."

"But humans aren't zooids," Uncle Jack said. "What are you proposing?"

"I don't know," Watkins said. "I've never tried anything like this."

"And you want to try with Eleanor?" Uncle Jack shook his head, but it was heavy, without a lot of strength behind it. "No. Not on my watch. She just said that thing almost killed her—"

"Uncle Jack—" He was starting to sound like her mom.

"I understand your concern," Watkins said. "I do, but please remember, I'll be exposing my own mind to the same risk."

"That's supposed to make me feel better?" Uncle

Jack's eyes narrowed. "Here's the thing, Mr. G.E.T. Man. I know your type, and I'm betting that if things turn south, you'll be the one who makes it out."

"Trust me," Watkins said, "you do not know my *type*." He turned to Eleanor. "While I respect your uncle's concern, the decision is not his. It is yours."

Uncle Jack reached a hand toward her, wincing from the pain. "Ell Bell—"

Eleanor cut them both off with a raised palm. She needed to think. She needed to put everything together, if she could.

She now knew that an alien ship had landed just before the Concentrators had changed the earth's telluric currents. The new presence she'd felt back in Cairo must have been the alien intelligence on board the ship, and she assumed from what Watkins had told her that it had come down from the rogue world to take control. It had merged with the Master Concentrator and become something too powerful for her to stop.

But was Watkins right? Was it possible to join forces with him and stop it together? How far did their genetic connection go? Uncle Jack had it, too, but he didn't seem to be in any shape to help.

"If I do help you," she said, "if we stop it, what then?"

"What do you mean?" Watkins asked.

"What will you do?"

"Well, if we are able to shut down the Master Concentrator, that changes everything. But if you're asking me whether the Preservation Protocol will be voided, that is not my decision to make. Contrary to what you may believe, I am not a tyrant. Recent developments certainly call our plan into question, but any deviation would have to be approved by the UN and the Global Energy Trust board of—"

"That's not good enough," Eleanor said. "I'm not going to help you fix this just so you can go back to writing off most of the human race as an acceptable loss."

"I can promise you this," Watkins said. "I will make certain you have the opportunity to plead your case. Your voice will be heard."

"Yeah, right," Uncle Jack said. "You've called her a terrorist!"

"You have my word," Watkins said.

"Don't trust him, Ell Bell."

Eleanor didn't trust him, but she also didn't think he was lying. If Watkins promised something, Eleanor believed he meant it. But was that enough for her to help him?

She turned and looked out the window at the

thrashing branches. Whatever the Concentrator had been doing before, it appeared to have accelerated its activity after her attempt to stop it. Perhaps, strong as it was, the combined intelligence inside it felt threatened. That's how it appeared, anyway, and if that was true, Eleanor felt a momentary flare of confidence. If it was afraid, that meant it believed it could be beaten.

"Let's try it," Eleanor said.

"No," Uncle Jack whispered. "Please, don't do this."

"I need to," she said.

"But—"

"Thank you." Watkins let out a long sigh before rising. "Thank you, Eleanor."

Uncle Jack labored to his feet. "You bastard. If anything happens to her—"

"If this situation turns against us, I will get Eleanor out safely, even if that means I do not." Watkins showed no emotion as he said this. Eleanor saw no kindness or bravery in his face. He was simply stating fact. "Does that appease you?"

Uncle Jack seemed a bit taken aback, but he nodded. "A little."

"Good." Watkins turned to Eleanor. "Then let's go. We don't have time to waste—"

Someone knocked on the door.

"Yes?" Watkins said.

The door opened, and a G.E.T. agent walked Luke into the room.

"Mr. Fournier?" Watkins said.

"Luke!" Eleanor said.

"Hey, kid." Luke's smile was quick, and then gone. "Listen, Watkins, you need to clear everyone out of here. Now."

"Really?" Watkins said. "And why is that?"

"Because an avalanche is about to bury this place."

Eleanor thought at first this must be some kind of ploy. A plan to help her and Uncle Jack escape. But when Luke looked directly at her, she didn't see any sign of that. No wink or nod. He looked afraid.

"An avalanche?" Watkins frowned. "How do you know this?"

"Dr. Von Albrecht," Luke said. "He's seen the signs up on the mountain. You may not trust my judgment, but I bet you trust his."

Watkins pursed his lips. "Unless you're lying."

"I'm not," Luke said. "And I'm willing to bet your men know about that . . . *thing* up in the hills, too. And the other avalanches in the area."

"What thing?" Eleanor asked. Was he referring to the creature she had heard?

Watkins simply nodded, looking even paler.

"Trust me," Luke said. "We need to get out of here."

"Then we must hurry," Watkins said.

"Right. I'm glad you—"

"Eleanor, this way." Watkins stepped toward the door, motioning for Eleanor to follow him. "We need to get started."

"Wait." Luke looked around the room. "What's going on?"

"If this installation is about to be buried," Watkins said, "we need to act quickly."

"And do what?" Luke asked.

"They're trying to shut down the Concentrator," Uncle Jack said.

"What?" Luke's eyes swelled. "But—"

"Luke, it's okay." Eleanor knew she would be safe from an avalanche, there underground. And even if an avalanche buried the facility, blocking the way out, she knew there were caves through which she could find her way. "But you should take Uncle Jack and go."

"What?" Uncle Jack said, clutching his side. "I'm not leaving y—"

"Where is Badri?" Eleanor asked Watkins.

"You mean Grendel?" Watkins said. "Locked up."

Eleanor folded her arms and planted her feet. "Release her. Now."

Watkins hesitated, as if trying to decide whether this was a battle he wanted to fight in that moment, and in the end, he decided not to. He nodded toward the guard who had brought Luke in. "Go and fetch her."

The guard left, and after he'd gone, Luke stepped into the doorway to block it. "Eleanor, what is this?"

"I know what I'm doing," she said. "But you need to get Uncle Jack and Badri to safety. I'll be okay."

Now Uncle Jack stepped toward her. "Ell Bell—"

"We don't have time for this!" Eleanor said. "If there's an avalanche, I know my way out. But I don't know what's going to happen if we don't shut that thing down. I don't know what will happen to you. You're connected to it, too, remember? I want you to get far away from it. You're already hurt."

"I'm fine."

"You're hurt." She turned to Luke. "Please. Do you trust me?"

Luke's mouth hung open. Whatever plan he'd brought into that room no longer seemed to apply. "Of course I trust you."

"Then get everyone out of here."

Just then the guard returned with Badri. She looked tired but unharmed, and if she felt any surprise at what she found in that room, she didn't show it.

"I need someone to update me," she said.

"According to Luke, this whole place might be

buried in an avalanche at any moment," Eleanor said. "You need to get out of here with him and my uncle. Watkins and I are going to try to shut down the Concentrator. We have another way out."

The guard looked at Watkins, and Watkins nodded. "Give the order. Evacuate."

The guard turned on his heel and left, and Badri seemed to finally look past Eleanor, through the window, toward the dark branches. Her eyes opened wider, and she nodded. "Come on, you two."

That seemed to be what the men needed to hear. Badri moved toward the door, somehow pulling Uncle Jack and Luke with her by force of her will. But both moved with slow and hesitant steps.

"Hurry, please," Eleanor said. "I'll be fine. I promise."

Luke stopped and turned to Uncle Jack as they reached the door. "I could just pick her up and carry her out of here."

"Don't you dare!" Eleanor said. "This is the mission. This is why we came here."

"Ell Bell . . ."

Badri tugged on them by the arms. "Come."

"Go!" Eleanor shouted, angry at them now, angry at them for making her feel that way while saying good-bye. "I'll see you later."

The two men let Badri pull them through the doorway, and Eleanor followed them out with Watkins. But while Uncle Jack and Luke kept going down the corridor, Eleanor and Watkins turned through a doorway and entered the chamber of the Master Concentrator.

"Good-bye," she whispered to herself.

Then she sighed, and that sigh threatened to turn into a sob, but she pinned it down until it subsided. Watkins led the way through the coils of conduit toward the trunk, a much slower route than hers had been crawling under them. As several moments passed, the writhing branches grew larger and nearer, somehow more disturbing for their silence.

"I've never had the opportunity to talk to anyone else about the connection process," Watkins said as they walked. "Do you lay your right or left palm on the control panel?"

She hoped the others were out by now. That they had enough time. "Yes," she said, hoping that maybe Dr. Von Albrecht was wrong about the risk in the first place.

"Eleanor."

"What?"

"If we are to do this, you will need your full concentration."

She nodded. But thought she heard a thud. A few of them. Like something banging against the mountain above them.

"We will fail otherwise," Watkins said.

"Fail?"

"Yes." He stopped walking, and his voice grew angry. "You must concentrate, or we will fail."

"I'm sorry. I'm just worried about them."

"They'll be all right," he said. "They—"

"Do you hear that?"

But just then the banging stopped.

"I hear noth—"

A loud rumble filled the chamber, distant and yet everywhere, and the walls shook. The rock at Eleanor's feet vibrated like *Consuelo* during takeoff. Stray tools and equipment clanged against the floor around her. The avalanche had started.

Had that been enough time for Luke and Badri and Uncle Jack to get out? She feared it hadn't been, and Eleanor wanted to race from the room, down the corridor, to find them. But before she could, Watkins grabbed her by the arm.

"There is nothing you can do," he said. "We are safe in here. I'm sure they made it to safety out there."

"But—"

"This is the mission," Watkins said. "This is why you came here. Remember?"

Eleanor blinked at him. Her body had gone numb, and her voice had failed. But she knew he was right.

CHAPTER
11

I T FELT LIKE SOMEONE HAD TIED FINN'S SHOULDERS INTO knots, and then lit those knots on fire. His back felt the same way, but he kept digging. And digging. And digging.

"You're sure this is where you saw it?" Betty asked.

"Yes," Finn said, for the fifth or sixth time. "It's here somewhere."

"How deep do we need to go?" Betty asked.

Dr. Von Albrecht scanned their surroundings. "Two to three feet. If we haven't found the top of the transport that far down, we should probably try a new spot."

Finn had already dug five such holes. Betty had dug three, and Dr. Von Albrecht two. They'd been at it for at least thirty minutes. Maybe an hour.

"How much oxygen do you think they have?" Betty asked.

"That's impossible to estimate," Dr. Von Albrecht said. "It would depend on how many people got inside."

If people got inside. But Finn left that unsaid, because it wasn't useful, and he didn't like that thought at all.

While Betty and Dr. Von Albrecht took turns with the other shovel, Finn worked without a break. He dug down, then drove the handle of the shovel even deeper into the snow, and when it didn't strike something hard and metallic, he moved a few feet away and tried again. This went on for another thirty minutes or so, and he started wondering if he had been wrong. Somehow he had gotten turned around, or maybe the radio tower had broken from its foundation and moved far away from the transport. There were other towers, too. Maybe he'd gotten them mixed up—

He heard the ring of something metallic.

"Over here!" Dr. Von Albrecht shouted from his hole.

Finn raced over, and together they dug until they could see the roof of the transport.

"That's it," Finn said. He banged his shovel on it, hard, hoping that if someone had made it inside, they could signal them.

A moment later, they heard a faint banging in reply.

"Someone's in there," Betty said. "You were right."

It wasn't the kind of you-were-right Finn took any pride in. He felt only relief.

The next step would be to find the transport's main hatch, so they had to dig away enough from the roof to locate the middle of the vehicle, and after they'd done that, they dug down the side, trying to clean enough snow to open the hatch.

Sometime later—Finn stopped trying to keep track, because no matter how quickly he dug, it felt like too long—he stood in the bottom of a white bowl, its rim over his head, throwing snow away from the door. Betty or Dr. Von Albrecht scooped and threw that snow up and out, one with a shovel, one with gloved hands. The top half of the hatch lay exposed.

"We're almost there," Finn said.

Every once in a while, he stopped and banged on the door, just to make sure, and then waited, holding still, until he heard a bang in reply from within.

The sun was up now. Its light struck one side of the crater, while most of the bowl remained in morning shadow. That shadow slowly shrank, and the light inched toward Finn until it was only a few feet away, and that's when he got to the bottom of the hatch. Dr. Von Albrecht and Betty climbed down to join him, and Finn pulled the lever to open it up.

There was a slight hiss of air-pressure release, and the hatch lifted like a wing. Luke stood inside the doorway, squinting and shielding his eyes with his palm.

"That took you long enough," he said.

Betty shook her head. "We stopped for coffee a few times."

Then she stepped toward him and they hugged each other hard, briefly. Finn felt every muscle in his body clock out at that point, and he dropped the shovel in relief. He had been right about the location of the transport, and right to hope it was Luke. But who else was with him?

"Mind if we come in and sit down?" Betty asked.

Luke stepped aside. "What's ours is yours."

Finn followed Betty inside the transport. The bus-sized interior held rows of seats, and by the soft glow of the emergency track lighting, and the sunlight from outside, Finn saw Eleanor's uncle Jack clutching his side, looking pretty pale, and Badri sitting next to him. But no one else.

"Where's Eleanor?" Finn asked.

Luke shook his head.

"We left her behind," Uncle Jack said, his voice sounding strained. "She's trying to shut down the Concentrator."

"What?" Betty said. "But the avalanche—"

"She's safe in the cave," Jack said. "And there are other ways out."

"You just left her?" Finn said, his mouth dry.

Uncle Jack closed his eyes. "Believe me, it wasn't our decision. It was hers."

"So what do we do?" Betty asked.

"We wait," Luke said. "And hope they do the job and make it out."

"They?" Dr. Von Albrecht asked.

"Eleanor and Watkins," Luke said.

"Eleanor is working with Watkins?" Finn would not have thought that possible. Ever. "How did—"

"I'm still trying to work that out for myself," Luke said.

"Watkins isn't in control anymore, and he knows it. He's agreed to Eleanor's plan to shut the Concentrator down." Jack winced in pain.

"Are you okay?" Finn asked.

"No, he isn't," Badri said. "He cracked a few ribs, and I worry there may be some internal bleeding."

Betty stepped toward Jack's seat. "Let me see. And, Professor, there has to be an emergency medical kit somewhere in this thing, right?"

"I'll look," Dr. Von Albrecht said.

Luke tapped Finn on the shoulder. "I'm going to need your help."

"With what?"

"With Jack injured, we can't exactly walk back to the plane. We need to dig this transport out."

Finn's back twisted up in complaint at the thought. "You think it'll run?"

"I fired it up when the avalanche first trapped us in here. I shut it down to save on power, in case we needed it later, but yeah. It's got enough juice to get us back."

Finn sighed and nodded. "Guess we better start digging, then."

Before they went back outside, they searched the transport for extra equipment, and found a storage compartment with better shovels, pickaxes, and equipment for deicing. The discovery would hopefully make the job a bit easier. Dr. Von Albrecht had also found an emergency medical kit, and they were able to give Jack some painkillers and wrap up his chest.

"He needs a hospital," Betty said.

Badri agreed. "I can take care of him once we're back in Mumbai."

"We're not going anywhere without Eleanor," Uncle Jack said.

"Don't worry." Finn strode toward the hatch. "We won't."

He and Luke went outside with their shovels, closed the hatch behind them, and climbed up and out of the hole. The radio tower now cast a latticed shadow over them, and Luke stopped, looking stunned.

"Good Lord," he said. "That's a lot of snow."

"You got lucky."

"Thanks to you. The G.E.T. agents all ran for the helicopter, but I remembered what you said about the transports. I tried to call for anyone to follow me, but they didn't listen."

"Some of them got buried, but it couldn't have been everyone who worked here."

"Lots of G.E.T. agents are probably still inside the facility."

Finn's question caught in his throat, like it wasn't quite ready to be asked. "Did you—was my father in there?"

"I don't know." Luke paused, frowning. "No, I don't think so."

Finn nodded, trying to believe that.

"Hey." Luke clasped his shoulder. "I'm sure of it. Your father and brother weren't in there, or we would have seen them."

Finn hoped that was true, and let out a sigh before

turning toward the front of the transport. "We better get moving."

"Right." Luke pointed and drew two parallel lines in the air in front of them. "We'll dig out a ramp here. I'm hoping the transport has enough muscle to climb it without taking the time to dig out the sides."

"Sounds like a plan," Finn said.

So they set to work, carving out slices of snow with their shovels. Some patches they dug felt light, the top powder that the avalanche had turned under. In other places they hit chunks of old, compacted snow turned almost to ice. When that happened, Finn and Luke spread out deicing chemicals and hacked at it with the pickaxes until they could clear it out of the way.

Hours went by. Around noon they stopped and found some emergency food and water rations inside the transport, but they also discovered there wasn't enough to last them more than a day or two. When Finn and Luke grew exhausted, Betty, Badri, and Dr. Von Albrecht took shifts. Jack wanted to help also, insisting the painkillers were working, but Badri refused to let him get up, and he wasn't really in a state to argue.

Eventually, they uncovered the nose of the transport, and by later afternoon the ramp stretched down under it to the front treads. Finn looked up and thought the climb might be too steep for the vehicle to make it out, but they would have to try to know for sure.

Betty had the most experience with Arctic vehicles, so she took the driver's seat. Luke closed the hatch, and everyone buckled in. Finn felt the engines rumble, and then Betty woke up all the electrical systems. Lights came on and warm air circulated.

"Here we go!" Betty said from the cockpit.

Finn looked over at Luke, who did not seem comfortable in the backseat while another pilot had the wheel. He gripped the armrests on his seat and leaned into the aisle to get a look ahead.

The transport jounced but didn't move forward, and Finn heard the squeal of metal outside. For several moments, the walls to either side trembled as the vehicle tried to break free of the snow encasing it.

"Gun it!" Luke said.

"I'm trying!" Betty called back. "You want me to blow out the engine and strand us here?"

The transport surged, and surged, and surged, until finally, they lurched forward.

"That's it!" Luke said.

The squeal became a grinding as the transport inched forward.

"That's step one," Betty said. "Now we gotta climb out of here."

She revved the engine, and the nose of the transport

lifted, tipping Finn back in his seat. They crawled up, foot by foot, until their angle made it feel as if Finn was lying on his back, looking up at the sky through the cockpit windows.

The vehicle climbed a little, but Finn could hear the strain it was putting on the motor. Then their whine suddenly downshifted in tone, and at the same moment the transport jolted. The vehicle fell backward, and when Betty tried again, the same thing happened. After the third unsuccessful attempt, she called back over her shoulder.

"The tread is slipping. It's too steep!"

"Damn," Luke said.

Betty let the transport ease backward into its resting place before shutting down the engines. The cabin went quiet, leaving Finn's ears ringing.

"We'll have to do some more digging," Luke said.

"Eleanor's not back yet anyway," Finn said.

So they went outside with the shovels and got back to work extending the ramp by half its length, evening out the angle so the transport wouldn't have such a steep climb. Somehow this phase of the job didn't feel as difficult as the first, even though Finn was more exhausted. By the time they finished, the sun had moved low on the horizon, and Finn felt it getting colder.

But their efforts paid off. This time, the tread did not slip, and they steadily inched up the ramp onto the surface.

"We're ready to roll!" Betty said. "Whenever we decide to."

Finn turned to Jack. "You mentioned there were other ways Eleanor could get out?"

"Caves," Jack said. "The Sky Caves."

"Where?" Luke asked.

Jack tipped his head to the left. "Back on the other side of the valley."

"We could go over there to wait for her," Finn said.

"That's a good idea," Luke said. "It'll also put some distance between us and the G.E.T. when they show up, which could be any moment."

"I'm surprised they're not here already," Badri said.

"I'm not," Jack said. "They're dealing with the alien ship."

Finn looked over at him. So did everyone else.

"Alien ship?" Dr. Von Albrecht asked.

Jack coughed, and then grimaced. "Yeah. Um. Watkins told us an alien ship landed near Stonehenge soon after we left Cairo. The whole world knows about it."

An alien ship.

"Does that mean . . . there are pissed-off aliens on earth?" Finn asked. Up to this point, the Concentrators had just been stealing energy and beaming it up to space. The idea of an alien invasion was something else entirely.

"Watkins didn't say anything about little green men." Jack sounded like he was trying to talk through a stupor, perhaps an effect of the painkillers. "It's just a ship."

"But the world knows about it?" Betty said. "What does that mean?"

"Riots," Jack said. "Fear. The UN is turning against the G.E.T., and Watkins is rattled."

"And we left Eleanor in there with him," Luke said, almost under his breath. He hiked his thumb toward the cockpit. "I say we get moving."

Betty climbed back into the driver's seat, and a few moments later they were on their way, rumbling across the valley. They covered the distance much more quickly than they had on foot, especially since they could take a direct route, driving right over and through the shallow, half-frozen river. When they arrived at the place where the caves surfaced, Betty shut down the engine to save power, and Finn felt the rumbling beneath him cease. That gave him an idea.

Finn turned to Jack. "Eleanor said you can feel the Concentrators, too, right? So can you tell if she and Watkins have shut this one down?"

That question seemed to rouse Jack a bit. "If they did, I would expect to feel a weakening, like I did with the others." He closed his eyes and craned his head slightly, like he was listening for something. Everyone in the transport watched him and waited, and a few moments later, he frowned and opened his eyes. "I just don't know. The currents feel the same. I don't know about the Concentrator. But then, I never felt it the way Eleanor did."

"So it might be shut down," Finn said.

Betty looked out across the snow. "Or it might not."

CHAPTER
12

ELEANOR STARED AT THE FAINT IMPRESSION IN THE CON-centrator's control panel. It was about the size of her palm, but thinking about jellyfish zooid aliens suggested it might be intended for an utterly different and perhaps incomprehensible appendage. Her first attempt at taking control had almost destroyed her mind. Or at least, that's how it had felt. And she was about to attempt it again.

"Are you ready?" Watkins asked.

"No," she said. "How do we do this?"

"I don't know. I've never attempted cooperative contact. It should have occurred to me earlier to study it, but perhaps I felt threatened by the idea of anyone else sharing my ability."

His admission startled her. It didn't sound humble or apologetic. It was simply a statement of fact regarding the cause of his mistake.

"The question," he said, "is whether we should attack the intelligence within the Concentrator from two separate angles, or whether we should attempt to join our minds to confront it as one."

Eleanor did not feel comfortable with the second option, but she asked, "How would we join our minds?"

"I don't know. But when I have connected with previous Concentrators, it feels as if my mind has moved into a new medium, like moving from air to water. I wonder if that medium could provide a place in which our minds could meet."

That seemed possible, based on Eleanor's experience.

"Shall we attempt it?" Watkins asked.

Eleanor looked at him askance.

"I made a promise to your uncle," he said. "If I can prevent any harm to you, I will."

Eleanor nodded. Then she took a deep breath and raised her palm. "Okay, let's try it."

Watkins raised his hand and held it side by side with hers in the air. She noticed its wrinkles and spots, its veins and its bones. It seemed frail, much frailer than Watkins had seemed in Cairo.

"On three," Eleanor said.

He nodded.

She counted.

"One. Two. Three."

She touched the cold metal, but this time, the intelligence within the Concentrator seemed to have been waiting for her.

It yanked her into its domain. Her mind recoiled, but had no defense other than to curl in on itself. She thought of Uncle Jack, and her mom. Her mom who she had left behind in Egypt. She thought of her house in Phoenix, and all she wanted was to be back there, to be in her bed under the covers. She had cried herself to sleep there many times, back when she let other people hurt her with the things they said. Back when it pained her to be a freak. Back when her own mom couldn't make it better, because Eleanor knew she was a disappointment to her.

"Eleanor," came a strong voice. "Eleanor, reach for me."

She pulled the covers tighter over her head and kept her eyes closed.

"I can't reach you," the voice said. "You need to come to me."

But she didn't want to. She wanted to stay right where she was, away from everyone and everything.

"I can't do this . . . alone," the voice said. "This is why we came here, remember?"

"Where?" Eleanor asked.

"The Himalayas."

The Himalay—?

She pulled the blanket away, feeling the static corona of her hair. She opened her eyes. The voice belonged to Watkins. She wasn't in her bed. The alien intelligence was attacking her, and she had retreated to the only place of safety her mind could find. But now she felt Watkins nearby, somehow, and she reached her thoughts toward him.

"I'm here," she said.

The intelligence had wrapped itself around her again, like before, and she felt it squeezing.

"What do we do?" she asked.

"I don't know." She sensed him straining, too. "I'm fighting it as hard as I can."

The darkness tightened. They didn't have much time. She tried to push back against the alien intelligence, but it was still too powerful for her. She and Watkins needed to combine their strength, but she had no idea how. He was completely different from her. He thought differently. He felt differently. He made different choices than she would ever make.

"We should retreat." Now she heard fear in Watkins's mind. "While we still can."

"Wait," Eleanor said. "You're . . . you're afraid."

"Of—of course I am."

"So am I. We're *both* afraid. Maybe we can use that."

"You mean find something we share, and concentrate on it."

"Yes." She found it harder and harder to think. Harder to fight the blackness closing in around her. "Something deep."

Another moment passed, and Eleanor lost sight of where or who she was, could only push back the weight that smothered her.

"I—I'm alone," Watkins said, his voice growing faint. "I'm different. And alone."

"So am I," Eleanor said. "I always have been."

She reached out for him, using the feeling she knew well as a guide. The pain she knew well. The loneliness. Wishing someone understood her, wishing her mom understood her, wishing anyone would simply accept her for who she was, knowing who she was.

And she found that pain, inside herself and outside. His pain and her pain.

She found Watkins hiding in a janitor's closet

in his childhood school. He was sitting on an over-turned bucket, eyes and nose burning from the smell of bleach, waiting there until the recess bell told him it was safe to go into the hallways, back to his class. She opened that closet door, reached her hand in, and pulled him out.

The moment their hands touched, the alien intelligence flinched. Eleanor felt it like a ripple, and she felt a deep connection to Watkins unlike anything she had ever experienced. Eleanor knew him now, and knew herself better. She knew his thoughts. She knew his intentions. Though she sensed keenly the differences between them, the things about him she would never be, she ignored them. She maintained the link.

The Concentrator's intelligence had slackened its grip a bit, perhaps uncertain about the combined strength of two human minds. Eleanor and Watkins seized that moment together, without having to say a word to each other, and pushed back. Now they had the strength, and the alien intelligence pulled away from them.

They grappled with it, and though this one was much more powerful than the others had been, they had begun to take control. Eleanor sensed its shifting, alien consciousness, at first one entity. But then she felt the seam between its two parts: the intelligence that had been left in the Concentrator, alone on earth for thousands of years, and the new intelligence that had recently come down on the ship.

She and Watkins focused their attack on the part of the alien that had been isolated in the Himalayas. It gave way before them, and though the stronger entity tried to help, Eleanor sensed the damage she and Watkins could do. If they could destroy one part of the combined intelligence, she hoped they could kill the whole.

They renewed their attack on the Concentrator, strangling it, crushing the life out of it. The ship intelligence tried to defend it, but so long as Eleanor and Watkins maintained their link, it wasn't strong enough to stop them.

Bit by bit, thought by thought, they smothered the Concentrator's intelligence, until it collapsed, dead and scattered.

At that point, the ship's intelligence thrashed. Eleanor felt its pain and rage as it tore itself free from its dead companion. She and Watkins turned their attack toward it, and Eleanor thrilled at the thought of victory. They were doing it. They were winning.

But as they closed in, Eleanor saw their enemy with greater clarity. She saw into its mind, and there she found the dried and frozen husks of countless worlds. The Concentrators like poisoned tentacles, digging their barbs into planet after planet. She saw endless fleets of ships, black vessels streaking through space like the shadows of crawling spiders, with intelligences of their own. Eleanor quavered at the sight of them, but Watkins bolstered her.

"This one is alone!" he said. "Let's be done with it!"

But it didn't feel alone. Not entirely. It seemed that something else was there, watching them, a presence she hadn't noticed before, keeping its distance. Eleanor regained her footing and readied herself for a charge. But as they threw her minds against the ship's intelligence, the entity vanished.

"Where did it go?" Watkins asked.

"I don't know," Eleanor said, feeling as though her mind echoed inside an empty chamber. "It's just . . . gone." The silent observer had gone with it.

"It fled."

"Where?"

"I can't be sure, but I believe it went back to its ship."

"Why don't I feel weak, like I did the other times?" Eleanor asked.

"The nature of the system has changed now that the ship is in control of it. Our reactions to it will likely be different, too."

Eleanor's thoughts returned to Uncle Jack and Luke. "Let's get out of here." She pulled her mind away from Watkins, letting go of their shared connection, and departed the space inside the Concentrator. Then she opened her eyes, back in the cavern, and pulled her palm away from the alien console. Above her, the branches of the Concentrator had gone still.

Next to her, Watkins let out a sigh, looking up at the trunk of his World Tree. "I should be able to get it running again."

Eleanor spun on him. "What did you just say?"

"The threat hasn't passed," Watkins said. "The rogue world is still up there, the ship is still down here, and we still need the energy this device can collect to survive the Freeze."

"I can't believe what you're saying."

"I am being logical—"

"You're being stupid!" She pointed up at the Concentrator. "You can't control that thing! Haven't you learned that by now?"

"I can't control it *yet*," Watkins said. "But we said the same thing about the energy locked in the atom before we made bombs and reactors."

Eleanor couldn't find any of the empathy she had felt for him but moments before. "You—"

"Calm yourself," he said. "I do not intend to do

anything unless we are unable to find another solution. Right now, I suggest we find our way out and travel to England. I think we need to finish the job we started."

"Destroy the ship's mind."

"Precisely."

Eleanor could agree with that plan. "Then let's go."

Now it was her turn to lead Watkins, across the chamber, toward the entrance to the Sky Caves. The opening proved difficult to find, which explained why the G.E.T. hadn't discovered it, but eventually she located it and crawled through. From there, she had to find their way back out.

Eleanor remembered the last few turns she had taken with Uncle Jack, and reversed those to go back the way they had come. But a few corridors and junctions later, she found herself disoriented and confused.

"It's a labyrinth," Watkins said, swinging the beam of his flashlight. "How did you find your way?"

"I followed the Concentrator," Eleanor said.

"Then how will we find our way out?"

Eleanor didn't know the answer to that, and it was only now occurring to her that she had lost her compass when they'd shut the Concentrator down. And Watkins was right. The caves formed a maze in which they could easily get lost, stranded underground until they . . .

"I'll try to remember the way," she whispered, hoping she didn't sound as panicked as she felt.

Watkins nodded, his mouth set in a grim frown. "Lead the way."

Eleanor took several more steps, but felt no confidence in any of them. She worried she could be leading them astray, taking them irretrievably into the darkness. She searched the walls for signs of her descent hours before, for familiar shapes and contours. At times she thought she saw something she recognized and believed they might be going the right way. But then she would see an unfamiliar passageway and doubt herself.

So they proceeded slowly, and it soon felt as if they had been in the cave system for days. Watkins said nothing as they moved through the honeycomb tunnels, but Eleanor thought she could feel his recrimination of her, and his fear.

They walked, and walked, and walked, in silence.

"Can you imagine it?" Watkins finally asked, startling Eleanor.

"Imagine what?"

"A planet of beings like that. A species of advanced

zooid. Can you imagine their combined strength?"

Eleanor shuddered at the thought.

"Humans would be no match for such a species," Watkins said. "Look at our world right now. Look what the Freeze has done to us. Separate groups, tribal and petty, battling each other for survival. The aliens would have that advantage over us."

"I don't believe that. I've seen people work together. Amarok and his people in the Arctic. Nathifa and her family in Egypt. Badri—"

"Those alliances can be so easily broken."

Eleanor stopped walking. The tunnels around them were like the underwater caverns in Peru. She remembered Amaru's betrayal. The gunshot, the blood. The death of a man she had thought was her friend, who Watkins had manipulated with fear. Eleanor swallowed down the knot of grief rising in her chest.

"Fear, anger, and hate," Watkins said. "We will always be ruled by them."

"We don't have to be."

"It's in our DNA. It is who we are. That is why the Preservation Protocol was necessary, and may still be necessary. Humanity cannot be trusted with its own survival, or our species will perish."

"But think about what just happened. What we just did."

"A few of us might occasionally band together for a common purpose, temporarily. But our entire species? Against another species united in a way we never could be?"

"Maybe our individuality is our strength."

"I've been . . . alone my whole life." She heard a crack in his voice. "You know that now. You know my fear. You felt it. I find no strength in it. Do you?"

Being alone had made Eleanor strong, in a way. But she wondered if she could have been even stronger without that pain. That wasn't a question she would ever be able to answer, but that wasn't what she meant when she thought about individuality. "Each of us can choose what we want to do. We make those choices alone, but we can choose to work together. That is our strength."

Watkins bowed his head. "I admire your optimism."

Eleanor looked at him for another moment, and then turned away, resuming her trek through the Sky Caves, trying her best to find the way out. But there was no way of knowing, and she feared they should have found the exit by now, unless she had led them astray.

Their light flickered, plunging them into darkness for a terrifying second.

"The flashlight is almost out of power," Watkins said. "Are we close?"

"I don't know," Eleanor whispered.

"Do you have another flashlight?"

"Luke had it."

"I see."

Eleanor felt the blackness closing in as if the tunnels were collapsing, and she struggled to breathe. Not only would they be lost down here, but they would be lost in total darkness.

"I'm scared," she said.

Silence. "So am I. Let's just keep moving as far as we can, and then we'll feel our way."

Eleanor nodded and took a step. Then another. The flashlight flickered three more times, over the next few minutes, and then it went out. Eleanor heard Watkins banging it with his palm, and even though the light gave off a dim, last gasp in response, it was gone.

Her eyes tried adjusting to a darkness they would never be able to see through. She saw phantoms and shapes trying to resolve themselves in front of her, emerging and disappearing back into the void. She felt lost in nowhere.

"Can you feel the walls?" Watkins asked.

"No," Eleanor said.

"Have you tried?"

She hadn't. Eleanor reached out her hand to her side, and her fingers touched cold sandstone. That simple sensation pulled her out of the void and anchored her. She reached out with her other hand and touched the wall on the opposite side.

"I feel the walls," she said.

"Good. Keep contact with them, and let's keep moving. The caves are no different than they were before. We simply can't see."

Eleanor nodded, and then she kept going, moving ahead by touch. They took a few turns, communicating as they went, now proceeding mostly by instinct. Over time, Eleanor started to feel the telluric currents of the earth through her fingertips, humming through the cave walls. She and Watkins arrived at another intersection, and she was about to turn right. But then she felt something else reaching out toward her through the stone, along the currents. An intelligence, but not an alien intelligence. Something else. Something familiar.

"Uncle Jack?" she whispered.

She heard Watkins's footsteps halt behind her. "What?"

"I think I feel—my uncle Jack. Like he's . . . searching."

"Fascinating," Watkins said. "Can you—can you feel where he is?"

The sensation had grown faint, but Eleanor remembered where it had come from. "I think so."

"Then let us move in that direction," Watkins said.

Eleanor nodded to herself, and turned to the left.

— CHAPTER —
13

Finn had climbed out of the transport as soon as they'd reached the caves. There were at least a dozen openings in the rock, and he and Luke spent some time climbing around each of them, stepping partway inside, calling Eleanor's name. So far, they had neither seen nor heard any sign of her, and the afternoon had become evening, soon to be night. They had the transport to sleep in, if it came to that, but Jack looked like he would need medical care soon.

And he worried about Eleanor.

"Hello!" Luke called again through cupped hands, into one of the caves. His voice echoed through the sandstone chambers, but Finn heard no reply. "Eleanor!"

"What if she doesn't come out?" Finn asked.

"Let's pretend you didn't just ask me that question, kid." Luke cupped his hands again. "Eleanor!"

But Finn had to ask that question. Eventually, Luke would have to ask it, too. They couldn't stay around here forever. Finn wondered if maybe Jack had made a mistake, and this wasn't the place. Maybe the pain he was dealing with had messed up his memory. What if Eleanor had already climbed out of a cave somewhere else?

There was also the yeti.

It was still out there, and even though it hadn't attacked them the night before, Finn didn't think they should take that for granted. He looked at the setting sun and realized they probably wouldn't be driving away that night, regardless.

"Eleanor!" he shouted.

Still nothing.

He and Luke kept calling for her, until the sky lifted up the first few stars.

"Maybe we should go into the caves," Luke said.

"Jack said it's a maze in there."

"Maybe that's why she can't find her way out. Maybe she's lost."

Finn had already thought about going in a couple

of times. Maybe if they fashioned some kind of trail to find their way back out, like Theseus and the thread that Ariadne gave him to find his way out of the Minotaur's labyrinth. They didn't have mythical thread, but they could carve or draw on the walls.

"Maybe we—"

"Shh!" Luke held up his hand, turning his head.

Finn listened. He heard a distant voice, coming from inside the caves.

"Eleanor?" he shouted.

"Eleanor, this way!" Luke shouted.

"Luke!" they heard her reply. "Finn!"

"We're here!" Luke repeated. He turned to Finn. "Go tell the others we have her."

Finn nodded and ran. When he reached the transport, he opened the hatch and jumped inside.

"She's back," he said, closing it behind him to save heat.

Jack sat up higher in his chair, groaning quietly, and craned his neck. "Where?"

"She's in the cave," Finn said. "But we heard her. She's coming."

"Oh, thank God." Jack lay back down, his whole body sagging, and Finn realized it was the first time he'd seen the big man truly relax. Next to him, Badri smiled, looking relieved at the news. So did Dr. Von

Albrecht. Betty looked past Finn, through the hatch outside.

"Probably too late to move out tonight, though."

Finn looked over his shoulder. "Probably. But do we—" He glanced at Jack. "Can we afford to stay?"

Betty shook her head and shrugged at the same time. "I guess we should deal with that when we're all together."

Finn nodded. "I'm going back to the cave."

Then he left the transport and scurried back to stand by Luke.

"She's getting closer," the pilot said.

Finn peered into the darkness, which was even deeper now that night had fallen over them. "Eleanor!"

"Finn!" Eleanor replied. She did sound closer.

"Are you okay?" he asked.

"We're fine!" she said.

Finn turned to Luke. "We?"

Luke looked at Finn with puzzlement, and then called into the cave, "Who is with you?"

The response took a moment to arrive. "I'll explain when we get there."

"It's gotta be Watkins," Luke said.

Several minutes passed, with calls and answers, until Eleanor was close enough that Finn could hear her footsteps. He expected to see her flashlight at any moment, but instead she simply emerged from the darkness. She seemed fine, unharmed, and Finn sighed. Then Watkins came out, wearing baggy fatigues, like he thought he was some kind of general. Finn still didn't understand what had happened to bring Eleanor and their enemy together, but he was just happy to see her safe and put that question aside.

"Eleanor!" Luke said.

Eleanor pulled the pilot into a hug, closed her eyes, and said nothing as she hung on to him for a moment. Then she gave Finn a hug, too, and he felt her hair brush his cheek.

"Good to have you back," he said.

"Good to be back," she said. "You have no idea."

"It's getting cold," Luke said. "Let's all head to the transport."

"You have one of my transports?" Watkins asked.

"None of your guys seemed to want it," Luke said.

They left the Sky Caves and climbed down to where the vehicle waited. When they opened the hatch and stepped inside, the looks on everyone's faces said they were just as uncomfortable at the sight of Watkins as Finn had been.

"Ell Bell," Uncle Jack said.

Eleanor gasped and rushed to his side. "You told me you were fine!"

"I am fine," he said.

"He's not fine," Betty said. "He needs medical attention."

Eleanor's face paled. "Uncle Jack, you—"

"Did you do it?" Jack asked. "Did you shut it down?"

"Yes. Yes, we shut it down."

"Good. I tried to find out by sensing it, but I couldn't."

Suddenly, Eleanor was crying. "I sensed *you*," she whispered. "We got lost in the caves. Our light went out. But then I felt you, and that's how we made it back. You brought me here."

Uncle Jack nodded. "It's good to see you, Ell Bell."

She leaned over and kissed his forehead. Then she turned to Betty. "We need to get him help."

"We can move out as soon as we decide to," she said. "But it'll be more dangerous at night. What does everyone think?"

"I want to go now," Eleanor said.

"He needs help as soon as possible," Badri said.

Watkins cleared his throat. "I would suggest—"

Luke spun on him. "You don't get a say, you miserable old bastard."

Watkins held up his hands. "I only want to point out—"

"I don't care!" Luke said.

"Luke," Eleanor said. "Just let him finish."

Finn didn't know what to make of Eleanor sticking up for Watkins. Something had clearly happened since the last time he'd seen her, but he couldn't imagine what would prompt this reversal. Maybe it had something to do with the alien ship.

Watkins waited. Luke finally turned away with an exasperated grunt.

"I only wanted to say," Watkins continued, "that there is more danger here than you realize."

"What danger?" Dr. Von Albrecht asked.

"I gather from Mr. Fournier that you are all aware of a certain creature? A large primate in the mountains around us? Possibly a relic *Gigantopithecus*?"

"The yeti?" Finn said. "Yeah, we're aware of it. Why?"

"Well." Watkins pushed his palms together in front of him, and then opened them up. "When we built the Yggdrasil Facility, we, well . . . that is, we inadvertently destroyed its den."

They waited.

"And?" Finn said.

"And," Watkins said, "in doing so, I—we injured one of its young."

"So that's why," Finn said. "That explains everything."

"We didn't mean any harm," Watkins said. "And the animal seemed fine. We treated its injuries and released it."

"You make enemies out of everyone, don't you?" Luke said.

Watkins looked at him with a scoff. "That is often true of those who make the difficult choices."

"Leaving you behind in the snow won't be a difficult choice," Finn said.

"We can't," Eleanor said.

Everyone turned to her.

"I need him," she said. "*We* need him."

"Watkins?" Badri said. "Why?"

"Because there's an alien ship," Eleanor said. "It landed at Stonehenge."

"We heard about it," Finn said.

"It poses a threat," she continued. "If we're going to shut it down, Watkins and I are going to have to work together."

"And you think he's just going to start helping you now?" Luke's face was red with anger. "We're just supposed to trust this walking pile of lies?"

Finn looked at Wakins, whose mild expression hadn't changed at all during the exchange.

"Yes," Eleanor said. "We can trust him. On this."

"On this?" Finn said.

Eleanor nodded. "I don't believe a word that comes out of his mouth, and you shouldn't either, but I know he'll help me shut down the alien ship if I can get us there. And Uncle Jack needs medical care. So I say we go now, before it gets much darker."

"I agree," Watkins said.

"And what about your people?" Luke asked. "Your whole base just got buried."

"I am certain the distress call has been sent," Watkins said. "As soon as I am able, I will get a status update. But for now, there isn't anything I can do for them, is there?"

Watkins was right, and Finn knew it.

"Let's move out," Eleanor said.

A quick glance between them all confirmed that they agreed, reluctantly. But Finn also thought about the fact that the man the yeti apparently blamed for injuring its child was now on board their transport, and he suspected that might make the vehicle the creature's next target. But he still didn't know what it meant that Watkins, the man who had been hunting for them across the globe, the man who was directly

189

or indirectly responsible for every bad thing that had happened to them in the past several weeks, was sitting there comfortably in a seat next to them.

Betty went up front to the cockpit and started the engines as everyone buckled in. The transport heaved forward, and Finn tried to settle for the ride but found it difficult. His anger made the seat incredibly uncomfortable.

"You've ruined our lives," he said to Watkins, before they'd traveled far. "You've torn my family apart."

Watkins's voice turned somber. "I realize why you would blame me, but I blame the Freeze. I blame our common enemy—our *real* enemy—the rogue world."

Finn considered that for about half a second. "No, you don't get out of it that easy. The Freeze doesn't give you an excuse for a single thing you've done. That's on you. All of it."

"I accept responsibility," Watkins said. "But I make no apologies. I did what was necessary in response to a crisis. I did what I was authorized to do."

Finn balled his hands into fists and pressed them into his thighs as fury took him. He knew this old man would never be held accountable. Watkins didn't regret what he'd done, and he would never pay for it, and there wasn't anything Finn or anyone could do about it. That wasn't fair, and Finn almost couldn't handle his rage, because he had nowhere to put it.

He turned to Eleanor. "What about you? You just gonna sit there and forget that he almost got your mom killed in the Arctic?"

Eleanor scowled at him. "I think saving the world is more important than my anger right now."

Finn couldn't keep his jaw from dropping open. "But it's all his fault! All of it!"

"Not all of it," Watkins said.

Finn glared at him. "I think you better just keep your mouth shut."

"But Finn," the old man said, "there is at least one thing that is *your* fault."

"I'd be careful, Watkins," Luke said. "You're poking at a live coal."

Finn liked hearing that. He felt a fire burning in him. "What's my fault?" he asked, like a challenge, or a dare. "Please, Mr. G.E.T., tell me what's my fault."

"You made the choice to leave your father and brother behind. I didn't force you to do that."

Finn clamped his mouth shut. He'd expected Watkins to offer up a huge target, something for Finn to fire rage at, but instead, the old man had disarmed him.

"If your family is ruined," Watkins continued, "it's because of the choice you made."

Finn wanted to fight back, but his anger went out as if Watkins had doused it with ice water. He slumped back in his chair, feeling empty and lost, and no one in the transport spoke for a few minutes.

Then Badri said, "What good is blame? We each have choices to make, and we make them. Blame is often nothing but misplaced regret."

"What do you mean?" Eleanor asked.

"Sometimes we don't like our choices," she said. "Sometimes in the moment, sometimes afterward. In such situations, it's easier to pretend the choice wasn't ours. We blame someone else, and somehow, blame makes us feel better. Or at least, we think it makes us feel better. Blame is an illusion."

She was right. What Finn truly felt was pain at the choice he'd made. Not regret, exactly, because he would do the same thing again. But he had made his choice back in Cairo. Watkins had absolutely created the situation, but he hadn't made Finn's dad choose one way, and he hadn't made Finn choose the other. Finn still thought Watkins was wrong, in almost every way, but he realized now that there actually were things he couldn't blame on Watkins.

"Where is my dad now? And my brother?"

"Madrid," Watkins said. "They flew from Cairo with Eleanor's mother, heading for Madrid."

At least they were free of the riots.

After that, Finn rode in silence. He tried not to think about his dad, or Watkins sitting there only a few seats away. Instead, he imagined the yeti up in the hills. He wondered if it felt better in some way after causing the avalanche. Did it bring the creature peace, in whatever form a yeti could feel it? Or would it still roam the mountains angry at the injury to its child, the loss of its home? Finn couldn't blame the yeti for what it had done.

If only he could stop blaming himself for what he had done.

— CHAPTER —
14

ELEANOR COULDN'T LET HERSELF THINK ABOUT FINN'S anger at Watkins. She felt it just as strongly as he did, but if she gave in to it, she risked breaking the fragile alliance she had established with their former enemy. It seemed that working with the old man would be the only way she could do what she needed to do to save the world, and to work with him, she would need to find that connection they'd found while battling the Concentrator. If she let herself hate him, that might not be possible.

Instead she focused on Uncle Jack, who rested beside her. He had finally fallen asleep, which was probably for the best. Betty had tried to assure Eleanor

194

his injuries weren't immediately life-threatening. But that didn't do much to ease her worry.

"Is there a phone I could use?" Watkins asked. "Most of my transports have sat phones."

"Why?" Luke asked.

"I need to make sure the G.E.T. is sending a rescue team to the site of the avalanche. Or have you already forgotten about the lives of those men and women, Mr. Fournier?"

Eleanor remembered the conversation she had overheard, the mention of damage control, and wondered if he needed to check on more than that.

"In the cockpit," Betty called back. "There's a sat phone up here."

"Excellent." Watkins climbed out of his seat and made his way swaying up toward her, his back straight. Eleanor tried to listen to his call, but found it too difficult over the rumble of the engines, and the chewing of the transport's treads over the snow. A few minutes went by, and Watkins remained in the cockpit.

When Watkins finally returned to his seat, his back appeared hunched and his face pale. He toppled into his seat like a felled tree.

"I can't believe it," he whispered.

"What is it?" Luke asked.

"I've . . . been removed."

"What?" Eleanor asked. "What does that mean?"

"The board held a vote of no confidence. I'm—I'm out."

"Of the G.E.T.?" Eleanor asked.

He nodded.

No one said anything for a long time while the transport bumped and ground along. At any other time, this would have been the best possible news. But right now, Eleanor wondered how it would affect their plan, and who would be put in charge instead of Watkins.

"They fired you?" Luke asked.

Watkins opened his mouth, but nothing came out at first. "Yes. I am to report to the nearest G.E.T. head office for debriefing. After that—"

"What about us?" Finn asked.

Watkins frowned. "They have ordered me to bring you in, after which you will surely be placed under arrest."

Eleanor felt the plan tipping sideways, threatening to capsize. "You promised me they wouldn't do that. You promised—"

"I know what I promised," Watkins said, his words sharp. "But it seems I no longer have the authority to keep that promise."

"Why did they take this action against you?" Dr. Von Albrecht asked.

Watkins rubbed his forehead, spreading its many wrinkles. "They'd already learned about the avalanche. This makes the second G.E.T. installation lost under my direction, thanks to your efforts in the Arctic. And the alien ship . . . it seems they have concluded I should have anticipated its arrival. Or at least prepared for it. They have called my leadership and judgment into question, and found it inadequate."

"Sounds like they got it right," Finn said.

"So what happens now?" Eleanor asked. "Who's in charge—"

"The UN Security Council has assumed temporary leadership," Watkins said, "until the threat of the alien ship can be ascertained."

"Security Council?" Luke said. "So the G.E.T. is now under the control of the military?"

Watkins sighed. "So it would seem. All the Concentrator sites will be locked down, as will the alien ship."

"Then how will we get close to it?" This wasn't a scenario Eleanor had considered. It had not even occurred to her that Watkins could be removed and lose all his authority. "How will we stop it?"

"For now," Watkins said, "we won't. We'll follow my orders—"

"Like hell we will," Luke said. "We're not going down with you. You're welcome to get off this ride here and now."

"It is the UN, Mr. Fournier. There is no use in defying—"

"That's all we've been doing," Eleanor said. "We've defied you from the beginning, and we'll defy anyone who tries to stop us."

"I find your determination admirable," Watkins said. "But—"

"No," Eleanor said. "There is no other option. We keep going. And you are going to help us. You saw what I saw. You know what's up there. You know what the aliens have done before, and what the rogue world will do to us. You saw their ships. You—"

"I know very well what I saw," Watkins said.

"Then how can you just surrender?" Eleanor said. "How? That doesn't seem like you at all."

Watkins leaned back in his seat with his chin between his thumb and forefinger. He stared at Eleanor through narrowed eyes, and seemed to be considering what she'd said. He remained that way for several moments, and Eleanor knew intuitively he could not be rushed in this process. She could not convince him.

He had to convince himself. So she waited, and the others waited, too.

Finally, Watkins lowered his hand and spoke. "You are right."

"About what?" Eleanor asked.

"I now know what is up there. I didn't before. I didn't want to know before. But now that I know, I believe we have to do what we can to stop it."

"So you'll help us?" Eleanor asked.

Watkins nodded. "I will."

"Ladies and gentlemen," Luke said, "the Freeze just reached hell and froze it over."

Eleanor felt the same way. This moment had just played out in a way she couldn't quite believe. If this had been a TV show, she would have rolled her eyes at the writers and changed the channel.

"Why?" Finn asked.

"Why what?" Watkins said.

"Why did you just change your mind?" Finn pointed at him. "All this time, everything you've done, and now we're supposed to believe you're suddenly on our side?"

"I am suspicious as well," Dr. Von Albrecht said. "And having worked for the G.E.T., I think I have good reason to be."

"Of course you do," Watkins said. "All of you have

reason to be suspicious of me. To be honest, you would be foolish to trust me. But I can't do anything to change that. Finn just referred to everything I've done, and it's true that I've done a great deal to thwart you, as you have done a great deal to thwart me. But I am a scientist. I adhere to facts, not ideology or even my own pride. The scientific method sometimes presents us with new information, new data we must assimilate, and sometimes that means changing our entire way of thinking. That isn't always comfortable, but what kind of scientist would I be if I refused to recognize the reality of our situation?"

Eleanor shook her head at the peculiarity of Watkins's mind. Not even her mom, as cold and analytical as she could be, would alter her path so radically, so quickly.

"I respect that answer," Dr. Von Albrecht said.

"You believe that answer?" Luke asked him.

"I do," Dr. Von Albrecht said.

Finn snorted. "I don't."

"Then I suppose," Watkins said, "that you will have to make your own observations of me going forward. You can watch my actions, and decide for yourself whether the data changes your mind about me or not."

Finn turned to Eleanor. "What about you?"

"Do we have a choice?" Eleanor said.

"Yes," Badri said. "You have a choice. And you will have to live with that choice, because it's yours."

"What about Grendel?" Luke asked. "Do you trust him?"

"Grendel counts many former G.E.T. employees among its number," she said. "They are some of our best assets. This wouldn't be the first time one of them joined our cause."

"I will not join Grendel," Watkins said. "That I can promise you. But I will help you stop the alien threat to our planet."

Eleanor looked at him for another moment, and once again, she knew he was telling the truth. He would do what he said he would do, so long as he could.

"Okay," Eleanor said.

"Okay?" Finn said. "Just like that?"

Eleanor nodded. "Now Watkins is a terrorist like us."

"So what's our plan, then?" Luke asked.

"We get back to *Consuelo*," Eleanor said. "And we fly to Stonehenge."

"Hey!" Betty called. "Would someone come up here and update me?"

Dr. Von Albrecht turned and moved up toward the cockpit. Watkins settled into his seat, looking much more comfortable than Finn or Luke appeared to be.

Eleanor knew exactly how they felt, and she still wondered how they had arrived here, with everything turned upside down.

Uncle Jack groaned, and she moved closer to him, laying her hand on his stubbly cheek. She would have some explaining to do when he woke up, but for now, she sat next to him as they plowed through the night and pulled into Jomsom early the next morning. Badri had already used the sat phone to contact Grendel to let them know they would need the plane, and they found it waiting for them on the runway. Not long after that, they were in the air, heading back toward Mumbai. It was only then that Eleanor felt safe enough to sleep.

The medical clinic felt old, like many of the Parsi Colony buildings had, but it was very clean and bright. The doctor Badri had brought Uncle Jack to see had a warm smile and dark eyes, and he pointed at the X-rays and insisted that Uncle Jack would be fine. No internal bleeding. But a deep, horrible-looking bruise.

"I told you," Uncle Jack said, already sounding better with the medication the doctor had given him.

"You should still take it easy, though," Eleanor said.

"I'm just glad I'm cleared to fly," he said. "You're not leaving me behind again."

"You still haven't forgiven me for that, have you?"

"Nope. And don't expect me to anytime soon."

She helped him up from the medical bed, and they left the clinic together, his arm over her shoulder for support, which Eleanor knew was more for her emotional benefit than his physical needs. They climbed into Badri's waiting car and returned to her house, where the others sat around the kitchen table eating their first real cooked meal in days.

"How does it look?" Luke asked as they walked in.

Uncle Jack gave a thumbs-up. "Let's get going."

"I'm glad it wasn't too serious," Watkins said.

"Yeah, well." Uncle Jack looked down at the old man. "Let's not forget it was one of your guys who did it." Eleanor had explained the Watkins situation as best she could, and even though Uncle Jack had listened, he sided slightly more with Finn.

"I haven't forgotten," Watkins said. "It was I who authorized the use of force when you broke into my installation."

"Not your installation anymore," Uncle Jack said. "I haven't forgotten that, either."

"Everyone here?" Luke said. "I've been to the airport, and *Consuelo* is ready for takeoff."

"I'm ready," Eleanor said. "How is it out there in the city?"

"It doesn't seem to be as bad here in Mumbai. But I caught some news. Cairo is still rioting, but now so is Mexico City and several other places. The violence and panic have spread to pretty much any country with a large refugee population."

"Phoenix?" Uncle Jack asked.

Luke shook his head. "I don't know."

Eleanor thought about her friends Jenna and Claire, and hoped they would be safe. She turned to Badri, who had decided not to come with them to England. Her place was here, with her family and her team, especially now, and Eleanor understood that, even though she would miss the older woman.

"Good-bye," Eleanor said. She almost hadn't trusted Badri in the beginning, and she wanted to apologize for that, but couldn't think of how to say it. "I . . . thank you for everything."

"Thank you, Eleanor," Badri said. "You may be the bravest person I have ever met."

"I don't feel brave."

"You are. Now go."

Eleanor hugged her, and they all left the Grendel house behind. Some of Badri's team drove them back through the shady and quiet streets of the Parsi Colony, and then through the chaos of Mumbai. They reached the airport and boarded *Consuelo*. Eleanor took a seat next to Uncle Jack, while Finn, Betty, and Dr. Von Albrecht claimed their own. Luke stalked up to the cockpit, and Watkins stood in the aisle, looking around.

"This looks much as I imagined it," he said, "as I thought about you all flying about, and where you might go next."

"Glad we didn't disappoint you," Betty said, her tone flattened with sarcasm.

Watkins smiled as he took a seat. "I didn't say that."

Eleanor saw Finn shake his head, jaw clenched.

Consuelo woke up with engines that sounded rested and eager to fly. Eleanor lay back against the headrest, comforted by the gentle rocking motion as Luke taxied them to the runway, and then thrilled by the power and pressure as they accelerated and lifted into the sky. Mumbai fell away, crowded and beautiful, and Eleanor leaned her head against Uncle Jack's arm.

"I wonder what your mom thinks about it," Uncle Jack said, his voice low.

"About what?" Eleanor asked.

"The alien ship. Watkins getting ousted."

"I don't know."

"I wonder if it's changed her mind at all."

Eleanor leaned away from him. "Maybe it has. I don't know."

"Don't you want to know?"

Eleanor shrugged.

"Don't you want her back on your side?" he asked.

"She shouldn't have left my side to begin with. But she did."

"Oh. So you're not ready to forgive her."

He didn't say it in a judgmental way, but that's how Eleanor took it. "I don't know."

"But you can forgive Watkins?"

"I haven't forgiven Watkins," Eleanor said. But when she stopped to think about that word, she wasn't even sure what it meant to forgive. Was it something earned? Or something she was supposed to just give? "Have you forgiven Mom?"

"She didn't let me down the way she let you down."

That was true. And Uncle Jack never really got mad at either of them, Eleanor or her mom.

"You'll figure it out," Uncle Jack said. "Once you figure out what you want."

"What I want is for her to trust me and let me make my own decisions."

He nodded. "I get that. But maybe that's not all you want."

Eleanor looked up at the plane's ceiling. She was

done talking about this. Uncle Jack was never one to lecture her. That was her mom's job, and she wanted to keep it that way. "I'm tired."

"Get some sleep," Uncle Jack said. "We've got a long flight ahead of us."

— CHAPTER —
15

"BUT WHY STONEHENGE?"

Eleanor awoke to the sound of Finn's voice. She sat up rubbing her eyes and looked around the plane's cabin, trying to figure out how long she'd been out. Watkins was asleep, and so was Betty. Finn and Dr. Von Albrecht were in the middle of a conversation.

"Stonehenge sits on a nexus of ley lines," Dr. Von Albrecht said. "It is perhaps the most connected site on the planet. It's possible the alien ship has the ability to plug into the entire network from there."

"That must be how it contacted the World Tree," Eleanor said, coming fully alert. The other two looked over at her. "And also how it retreated back to its ship.

It's using the network of ley lines."

"It?" Finn asked.

"An alien intelligence," Eleanor said.

"So there are aliens on the ship?" Finn said.

"I didn't say that. It's not necessarily an alien like from movies. It's more of an artificial intelligence, but I'm not sure how artificial it is." Eleanor shook her head. "It's hard to describe."

Finn looked at Dr. Von Albrecht, and then back at Eleanor. "So that's why we're going to Stonehenge? To stop that intelligence or whatever?"

"Yes," Eleanor said. But ever since glimpsing that alien consciousness, she had begun to wonder what the point would be. If there was a whole alien planet up there, with a fleet of ships, what would be the purpose of stopping this one that had landed? Eleanor couldn't answer that question, but then, throughout this entire ordeal, she had let such questions go unanswered. She would do what she could do to stop it, no matter what came after, and right now, this was something she could do.

"I wonder what the ship looks like," Finn said.

Eleanor had glimpsed that, too, and the memory filled her with horror and dread. "A space tarantula. That's what it looks like. A giant space tarantula."

Finn shivered. "Okay, I get you."

"Not something I'm looking forward to seeing in person," Eleanor said.

"I am," Dr. Von Albrecht said. "Frightening or not, this is something the human race has wondered about for generations. We know we're not alone. We've been visited. And now we have a chance to see their ship."

"You go right ahead with that," Finn said. "I might just stay here with *Consuelo*."

"I would if I could," Eleanor said. Then she climbed out of her seat and moved up to the cockpit to sit with Luke. He smiled as she tucked her legs up under her in the chair next to him. This spot had become one of the places where she felt safe, high above the world. The G.E.T. couldn't reach her here. The ice and snow couldn't reach her here. No alien intelligence invaded her mind. She leaned back with a sigh, at peace, for the moment.

"Your uncle's a tough man," Luke said.

"He's a teddy bear," Eleanor said.

"He's a good man, too."

"Yes, he is." She grinned at him. "And even though you've denied it, so are you."

Luke tipped his head to one side. "You know, I think maybe you've been right about that all along. I mean, if you look at what I've done in the past few weeks, I'm practically the hero of this crazy mission."

"I wouldn't go that far," Eleanor said.

"I would."

"How about we call it a . . . six-way tie."

"If that'll make everyone feel better, sure."

Eleanor folded her arms and looked out the windows. "How much longer?"

"We're coming up on Greece. Only a few more hours."

Eleanor wiggled deeper into the seat, and stayed there as they reached what had once been the Mediterranean. They flew over Greece, and Italy, and then France, before reaching the narrow English Channel. Eleanor had learned in school that it had once been nearly twenty miles wide at its narrowest. But now the waterway had shrunk to less than half that size, and parts of the prehistoric region of Doggerland rose above the water once again.

Before long, Eleanor could see the edge of the glacial ice sheet in the distance, not yet fully covering the British Isles, but closing in, having driven people south into southern Europe and Africa. The ice had apparently not yet reached Stonehenge.

"We're coming up on it," Luke said. "Do you want to stay up here for the landing?"

"If that's okay?"

Luke nodded. "Of course. It might be bumpy,

though. I'm going to have to land in a field."

"I'll be fine."

"Okay then."

Eleanor felt her stomach rising, and the pressure squeezed her ears as they dipped lower in the gray afternoon sky. She scanned the horizon ahead of them, looking for a long brown stretch where Luke could take them down. She couldn't yet see the megaliths of Stonehenge but searched for those, too.

"Oh no," Luke said.

"What?"

"I'm getting radioed."

"By who?"

"Guess," he said. Then, into his headset, he said, "This is *Consuelo*, flight—"

Luke's mouth clamped shut. He seemed to be listening to whatever message came over his radio, and the skin around his eyes tightened up.

"What is it?" Eleanor asked.

"They're not playing around," he whispered.

Just then, two fighter jets flew up on either side of *Consuelo*. They weren't so close Eleanor could see their pilots' faces, but they were close enough that she knew they meant business.

"They want us to land," Luke said. "Or they say they're going to fire on—"

"What?"

"Negative!" Luke shouted into his headset. "We have children on board, over!"

Eleanor scrambled out of her seat and hurried back into the main cabin. "We have trouble!"

Uncle Jack raised his head. "What is it?"

"There are fighter jets out there," she said. "They're threatening to shoot us down."

"Pretty much par for the course," Betty said.

"They can't," Watkins said. "That would violate—"

"I don't think they care," Eleanor said. "They just told Luke to land or else."

"Ell Bell," Uncle Jack said. "Come get buckled."

"They must have declared the crash site a no-fly zone," Watkins said, almost to himself.

"And they definitely know our plane by now," Finn said. He was trying to sound calm, but Eleanor could see the fear in his eyes.

"Eleanor," Uncle Jack said. "Come. Sit down."

Eleanor nodded and went to sit next to him, pulling the straps of her buckle tight.

"Luke will talk sense into them," Betty said. "He just needs to follow their orders and—"

The plane heaved sideways, violently, throwing Dr. Von Albrecht's loose notes into the air, and then the sound of an explosion slammed against Eleanor's skull. The plane convulsed, and something outside screamed, like *Consuelo* was in pain.

"They fired on us!" Luke shouted from the cockpit. "I'm losing an engine! We have to land!"

"Heads down!" Betty shouted. "Keep them down! Luke will get us out of this!"

Eleanor believed that. She had to believe it. She ducked her head.

"I love you, Ell Bell," Uncle Jack said next to her.

She seized his nearest hand and squeezed it with both of hers, hard. "I love you, too."

The plane's rapid descent turned her stomach over, and her ringing ears felt like they were about to implode. Then she smelled smoke, the acrid scent of burning plastic, but when she peeked up at the cabin, she couldn't see any in the air. Across the aisle, she glimpsed the back of Finn's neck and head.

"We're coming in hot!" Luke shouted. "Brace your-selves!"

"Heads down!" Betty said again.

Eleanor ducked her head again, waiting, closing her eyes tightly. Uncle Jack squeezed her hands now, hard enough to hurt, but she didn't care.

"Impact in five!" Luke said. "Four! Three! Two!"

The floor of the plane rammed into Eleanor's legs and feet, and it felt like gravity wanted to pull her right through it. Then they felt airborne again, and Eleanor's body lifted up as far as her seat belt would allow, before slamming back down again. This time, they stayed down, and Eleanor felt the plane shimmy and shake, jostling her so hard she bit her tongue and tasted blood.

"Almost there!" Luke shouted.

The jostling slowly eased up, allowing Eleanor to see straight. She risked looking up again, out the windows, and saw the rough ground flying past them. They seemed to be in a field. There were trees and stone fences in the distance, and Eleanor hoped there weren't any in front of the plane, but eventually *Consuelo* ground to a halt and jerked everyone forward one last time before pulling them back into their seats. Eleanor turned to Uncle Jack in the same moment he turned toward her, and they pulled each other into a hug.

"Everyone okay back there?" Luke asked.

Betty stood up and looked around the cabin. "Everyone seems to be," she said.

Luke emerged from the cockpit, his face a ghostly pale above his beard. "I'm sorry," he said. "They didn't even give me time to comply."

"I did not foresee this," Watkins said.

"It's the alien ship," Eleanor said. "People were already scared from the Freeze. I think the ship has pushed the world over the edge."

"But we're clearly not a threat," Finn said.

"They think we're terrorists," Betty said, looking at Watkins. "That makes us a threat."

"If there were something I could do about that, I would," Watkins said. "But I am likely now considered a wanted man, like the rest of you."

"We can deal with this later," Luke said. "For now, they know where we went down, and they'll be heading this way immediately."

"Then let's move out," Uncle Jack said.

Everyone suited up with what polar gear they had on board and grabbed the few provisions they had left. Then they opened *Consuelo*'s hatch, and Luke pulled the cord on the emergency slide. A yellow, inflatable ramp burst outward, leading down to the ground.

"Everyone out," Luke said. "One at a time."

Betty went first, and then Finn. Dr. Von Albrecht pushed up his glasses, and went down clutching his notes to his chest. Watkins took the chute with stiff legs and arms, and then Eleanor went down, feeling the friction of the plastic against her coat. Then Uncle Jack descended, and lastly, Luke.

"Which way to Stonehenge?" Eleanor asked.

Luke pointed. "That way."

"Isn't that the way they'll be expecting us to go?" Finn said.

"Probably," Eleanor said. "But what other direction is there?"

"Away," Finn said. "Escape."

"Then what?" Eleanor said. "The ship is still—"

"They shot us out of the sky!" Finn said. "My dad doesn't even know where I am! I don't even know where he is! I don't want to die for this, Eleanor!"

Eleanor turned back to the plane. *Consuelo* looked broken, sitting there in the middle of an icy field. The grass, brown and covered in frost, bore the deep furrow of her landing. One wing held the charred remains of an engine. The other had broken off at the tip. It appeared as though a giant had taken a sledgehammer to the plane's body, and even with all her Arctic armor, she looked bruised and battered. Eleanor wondered if she would ever fly again, and that clenched her chest with grief.

"You don't have to come, Finn," Eleanor whispered. "None of you do. You can stay here. If you surrender, I think you'll be okay. The danger is in going forward."

"What about you?" Finn asked.

"I'm going." Eleanor turned to Watkins. "And so are you."

Watkins simply bowed his head in agreement.

"Well, I'm coming, too," Luke said.

"So am I," Uncle Jack said.

"Maybe you shouldn't." Eleanor bit her lip and looked down at the ground. Her body started to shake. "Finn is right. I don't want any of you to die for this. I don't even know if this is going to work."

"Ell Bell." Uncle Jack took a step toward her. "We're going to see this through with you."

Luke nodded. "What he said."

Eleanor smiled at them. "You left me to do what I needed to do back in the Himalayas. I'm asking you to do it again."

"Not this time," Luke said.

Uncle Jack stood up to his full height. "Not even an avalanche would change my mind."

Eleanor thought about what Badri had said about choices. Everyone had their own to make, and Eleanor couldn't make this decision for them, as much as she wanted to. She looked at Betty. "You should stay with Finn. You, too, Dr. Von Albrecht."

Betty hesitated. She glanced toward Luke, and he gave her a wink.

"Better stay with Finn," he said. "I'll see you soon."

"I'm holding you to that, Fournier."

Dr. Von Albrecht pushed up his glasses. "I would

like to see the alien ship."

"Is your curiosity worth dying for?" Watkins asked.

"To me," the professor said, "this opportunity feels like the validation of my life's work. Yes, that is worth the risk."

Eleanor nodded, and then turned toward Finn.

"I'm sorry," he said, staring at the ground. "I just—I left them behind—"

"I know."

"I need to see them again."

"You will," Eleanor said.

She gave Finn a hug, and then she turned in the direction of Stonehenge and marched forward. The frozen grass crunched beneath her boots, and she heard the others fall in behind her. Uncle Jack and Luke. Watkins and Dr. Von Albrecht. When they'd walked some distance on, she turned and looked back at the plane. From this distance the damage appeared somehow worse, *Consuelo* more crumpled and broken, but she saw Betty with her arm around Finn, standing next to the wreck, and she drew some comfort in knowing they were safe.

"How far away is it?" Uncle Jack asked.

"Seventeen miles," Luke said. "Give or take. Because of our emergency landing, that's just a guess."

Uncle Jack sighed. "That's a lot of ground to cover."

Eleanor looked up at him. "Your ribs. I don't know if you—"

"Eleanor," Uncle Jack said, "I've lost track of how many times I've had to say this, but I'm hoping this is the last. I'll be fine. You just lead the way and don't worry about me."

Eleanor would continue to worry about him. There wasn't anything she could do about that, even if she wanted to. But she decided not to ask him about it again, if that was what he wanted.

"Seventeen miles might prove difficult for me, on the other hand." Watkins chuckled. "But I shall do my best."

"We'll take it as slow as we can," Eleanor said.

They crossed the field they had landed in and climbed over a low stone wall. Eleanor thought she could feel the cold of the gray rocks through her gloves. A few of the upper stones tumbled down after them into the next pasture, and they saw the freeze-dried carcass of a sheep, its wool a loose and decaying rug upon the ground.

"Listen," Luke said. "Do you hear that?"

Eleanor cocked her head. And she heard a familiar whumping.

"Helicopters," Watkins said.

"We need to hurry," Uncle Jack said. "They'll figure

out pretty quick we left the plane, and then they'll come looking for us."

Eleanor nodded. "We should stay close to the walls and the trees—they'll give us some cover."

They ducked down and scurried along the stone wall single file, listening to the helicopters drawing closer. The cold air tasted of something earthy, and as Eleanor moved along, she thought for a moment about reaching out to see if she could feel the ship's intelligence from a distance. But she decided that might risk alerting it to their presence, and instead kept her mind as calm and blank as she could.

"If we can stay hidden until nightfall," Luke said, huffing, "I think we might make it."

Eleanor looked up. Nightfall was still hours away, and they had a lot of ground to cover.

— CHAPTER —
16

FINN WATCHED ELEANOR AND THE OTHERS GROWING smaller and smaller until they disappeared over a distant rock wall. Betty didn't say anything. She just stood by him and kept her arm around him. He didn't need that, but he didn't mind it either, so he let it be, even though it didn't do anything to close the pit of guilt opening up inside him.

"That was a brave thing you did," she finally said.

"What was?"

"Choosing to stay behind."

Finn scoffed at that. "I feel like a coward."

"I don't see it that way. You stood up for what's

important to you. Even if that meant you might let someone down."

"It seems like I'm always letting people down."

"I don't see it that way. This isn't about right or wrong anymore. Sometimes, you do what you do knowing what the consequences might be. Accepting those consequences makes you brave."

Betty had already shown that kind of bravery. Back in the Arctic, she had burned up whatever credibility she had with the drillers by sending them after a bogus oil well, and she'd done that knowing her career there would be over, to help Finn and the others escape.

"You're a lot braver than I am," Finn said.

"I don't know about that," she said. "I think you—"

Finn heard helicopters. They both looked up in the same direction. Finn squinted back toward the last place he'd seen Eleanor, hoping they were out of sight from the air, and then told himself not to look in that direction again. He didn't want to give away where Eleanor had gone. In fact—

"We need to buy them some time," he said.

"How?"

"I don't know. We just . . ." But he couldn't think of anything they could do.

They stayed together, watching the horizon, and

eventually two black dragonfly shapes appeared. As the helicopters drew nearer, they got louder, and Finn could see their rotors and their skids. Finn blinked in the storm of their landing as they buffeted the ground and churned up the dirt.

"Hold your hands up," Betty said.

Finn did what she told him, and a moment later several soldiers leaped from inside the helicopters to the ground. They wore green camouflage fatigues and the blue helmet of UN peacekeepers. They carried guns, and they rushed toward Finn sighting down the barrels.

That scared him, but he stayed calm, and when they ordered him to the ground, he complied. So did Betty, and the peacekeepers wrenched Finn's hands behind his back, where they bound his wrists with zip ties. After that, two soldiers hoisted him back to his feet, and another of the peacekeepers approached him, a muscled man with darkly tanned skin and buzzed gray hair. Finn recognized him from the G.E.T. facility in Cairo. He had been Watkins's right-hand man.

"Hobbes, right?" Finn said. "Playing for a different team now?"

"Where are the others?" Hobbes asked, ignoring him.

"What others?" Finn said.

Hobbes grabbed Finn by the collar and yanked him close. "Listen to me, you—"

"Keep your hands off him!" Betty said.

"Where are they?" Hobbes asked again, this time close enough that Finn could smell cloves on his breath.

"Outer space," Finn said.

"You think this is a joke, you little punk? In this moment, you belong to me. The rules don't apply anymore. We have your father."

"My—" Finn kept his eyes locked on the guy's pale blue irises. If that was true, Finn needed to say something that would help Eleanor, but something believable, to protect himself and his dad. "They're hiding on the plane," he blurted out.

"Where on the plane?"

"I don't know," Finn said. "It's a big cargo plane."

Hobbes released him, and then the soldier ordered his men to accompany him onto what remained of *Consuelo*. Finn looked at Betty, and they both kept their faces blank. The helicopters stayed grounded, which was exactly what Finn had hoped for, though their engines and rotors were still running.

Several minutes went by. Finn counted the seconds, imagining that each was another step Eleanor and the others took to safety. He wondered if the UN peacekeepers really had his dad, or if that had just been a ploy to scare him.

When Hobbes returned, he stalked right up to Finn, grabbed him with both hands, and threw him backward. With his hands tied behind his back, Finn couldn't do anything to catch himself. He hit the ground hard on his tailbone, sending an electrical jolt up his spine.

"You think it's smart to lie to me?" Hobbes said.

"I didn't," Finn said, groaning. "They were on the plane."

"Do you know what I can do to you, boy? What I can do to your daddy?"

"You want me to just make something up?" Finn shouted. He gestured in a different direction than Eleanor and the others had gone. "You want me to just tell you they went that way?"

Hobbes narrowed his eyes. Then he turned toward Betty.

She only sneered at him. "I got nothing to say to you."

Hobbes took one more look at *Consuelo*, and then turned toward his men. "Load them up. I'll take them back, but the rest of you keep searching. Take this plane apart, and get back up in the air. They can't have gone far."

"Yes, sir."

A peacekeeper grabbed Finn by the shoulder and dragged him toward one of the helicopters, while another brought Betty. Hobbes marched alongside them and took the seat opposite them after Finn and Betty had been shoved on board. The rotors whined louder, and the helicopter lifted off the ground into the gray, overcast sky.

Finn wondered where Hobbes was taking them, but hoped it might be the same place as his dad. The crash in the airplane had done something. The alien ship had done something, too, and the situation felt very different now. The Freeze had been a very gradual threat. A danger off in the distance, creating the sense that there would be time to figure something out and survive. But there wasn't anything gradual about the alien ship, or getting shot out of the sky. Finn could have died, without seeing his dad and Julian again.

Below them, the English countryside heaved and rolled. Finn saw abandoned farms and villages, windows empty and dark, streets overtaken by weeds. But ahead in the distance, he saw floodlights blaring, like a stadium, and as they flew closer, he saw it was a temporary camp. A military camp.

As the helicopter landed, Finn saw columns of assault vehicles, tanks, and armored trucks with heavy artillery mounted to them. There were numerous tents, with satellite dishes in and around them, and peacekeepers marching in formation. Finn had been intimidated by the G.E.T. facilities, but this was something else. It had only felt like war before, but this actually looked like it. The world had finally woken up.

"Out," Hobbes ordered.

Finn and Betty climbed out of the helicopter, after which the peacekeepers ushered them toward a tent with posted guards. Finn noted the guns in their hands and in the holsters at their sides as they saluted Hobbes, and then pulled the tent flaps open.

"Inside," Hobbes said.

They pushed Betty in first. When Finn entered, he saw the kind of setup he'd expected. Spare walls and a floor of rigid plates, with a metal table and metal chairs at the center. The peacekeepers guided Finn to a chair and handcuffed him to it. They did the same to Betty on the opposite side of the table, and then they took up positions around the edges of the room. Hobbes stood at the head of the table, looking down on them.

"Maybe you've started to size up the situation you're in," he said.

Finn looked at the table. It was made of stainless steel, with thousands of minuscule scratches criss-crossing its surface.

"You fired on a civilian aircraft," Betty said. "With children on board. That's the situation I see, and it doesn't look good for you."

Hobbes ran his fingers through his bristly hair. "That wasn't even my order. It came from the top. The RAF jets flew out of New Brize Norton, where I don't exactly have jurisdiction."

He seemed to be saying the Royal Air Force had authorized their jets to shoot *Consuelo* down. If that was true, then maybe Finn and Betty didn't understand the situation after all. Betty seemed to realize that, too. Finn saw her swallow, but she tried not to show it.

"So what is your jurisdiction?" Finn asked.

"Ground security for the ship site," he said.

"Why you?" Betty said.

"Because I handled security for the G.E.T., and I've spent more time around alien technology than anyone except Watkins."

"Guess you know everything, then," Finn said. "Why do you need us?"

"I only need you for information," Hobbes said. "I need to know where the others are, and what they're planning to do."

"You would be smart to just let them do it," Betty said.

"Actually," Hobbes said, "I'd be pretty stupid, considering the job your little team has done so far. Most people think your activities are what brought the alien ship down in the first place."

"Actually," Finn said, deliberately echoing him, "you don't understand what you're talking about."

"Fine." Hobbes folded his arms. "Enlighten me."

"Sure," Finn said. "I'll just spill our whole plan all over this table, and then you'll change your mind, and then we'll all live happily ever—"

Hobbes slammed the metal table with the palm of his hand, and the bang made Finn jump. "You are trying my patience. This is a world security threat. You think you matter?" Hobbes leaned in close and whispered, "You think I can't do whatever is necessary to get you to talk?"

Finn's adrenaline reached his arms and legs, turning them cold. His heart beat faster with the flood of it, and his scattered breathing stayed shallow.

"I see you're starting to get it." Hobbes moved an inch closer, and Finn held still. "So tell me. What are the others planning to do?"

Finn bit down hard to keep himself from talking. Hard enough he thought his molars would shatter.

Hobbes leaned away, and then snapped at one of the guards. "Bring in Dr. Powers."

Finn's eyes widened.

"You thought I was lying, didn't you?" Hobbes smirked.

Finn had assumed that, yes. But it seemed they had his father, after all. That made sense, now that he considered it. When he had gone with Eleanor, during the riot in Cairo, he had left his dad in the vehicle convoy with Hobbes.

A few moments went by, and then the tent flap opened. Finn tried to stand up, but hit the limits of his handcuffs and fell back in his chair. Then his dad stumbled in, pushed by one of the guards, and the bottom fell out of whatever hope Finn had left.

His dad had a swollen black eye and a bloody lip. He walked with a slight limp, his hair and beard unkempt.

"Finn?" he said, looking through his one open eye.

"Dad!" Finn said.

His dad rushed toward him, but Hobbes stepped in between them, cutting him off.

"Get out of my way," his dad growled. "That's my son."

"I know that," Hobbes said. "And you can go to him when I say you can go to him." Hobbes turned and looked at Finn over his shoulder. "If he's still in one piece."

"You dare to threaten my boy?" his dad said.

"That depends," Hobbes said. "Do you dare to defy me?"

"I will rip you apart. You won't—"

"Dad." Finn didn't want Hobbes or anyone to hurt his father more than they already had. "I'm okay. Don't—I'm fine."

"And he'll stay that way," Hobbes said. "If you both cooperate."

Finn's dad looked like someone had taken the supports out from under him. He sagged and shook his head. "What do you want?"

"That's better." Hobbes led Finn's father over to the table and seated him in one of the chairs. Finn wanted to reach out and hug him, but they were both restrained. Instead they looked at each other, and nodded, and smiled.

"Now," Hobbes said. "I need to know what the others are planning to do with the alien ship."

Finn found it hard to form the words that would betray his friends. But he couldn't let them hurt his father any more. "They—they want to kill it."

"Kill it?" Hobbes said.

"There's an alien artificial intelligence on board the ship. They want to kill it."

"Who is they?"

"Eleanor and Watkins," Finn said. "But the others are helping them."

"And how do they know there's an artificial intelligence on board the ship?" Hobbes asked. "We're not getting any readings from it. We can't even get inside it."

"Because they made contact with it," Finn said. "Eleanor can connect with the Concentrators, and with the ship. That's how she shut the others down."

"Eleanor made contact with the ship?" Hobbes snapped his fingers at one of the guards again. "Bring me the girl's mother."

"Yes, sir."

"That's why you should just let them do it," Betty said. "They're trying to help, and they're the only ones who can."

"That's not the way I see it," Hobbes said. "That's not the way the UN sees it. What if they fail? What if they dismantle the energy network, and we all slowly freeze to death? Or what if they end up bringing a fleet of those ships down on us? This is the entire world we're talking about. It isn't their decision to make."

"Yes, it is," Finn said. "Just like you made the decision to threaten us—"

"Where are they now?" Hobbes asked.

That was a question Finn could answer honestly

without betraying his friends. "I don't know."

"Tell me, or I'll break your dad's—"

"I don't know!" Finn shouted. "I have no idea where they went after they left the plane. In case you hadn't noticed, I'm not with them."

"But they're heading toward the ship," Hobbes said. "Correct?"

Finn imagined himself punching Hobbes in the mouth. He didn't say anything, but he didn't have to.

The flaps of the tent opened again, and this time, Eleanor's mom came in. She didn't appear to be injured in the same way Finn's dad was. But she looked just as haggard. Her hair flew about her head in wisps, and she had dark circles under her eyes.

"Finn?" she said. "Betty? Is Eleanor with you?"

"No," Hobbes said. "That's why I need you."

"For what?" Eleanor's mom asked.

Hobbes walked over so that he was standing right in front of her. "You're going to help me find your daughter. And then she's going to help me get on board that ship."

— CHAPTER —
17

ELEANOR STOOD IN THE SHADOW OF THE COPSE OF LEAF-less trees, listening for the circling helicopter that had them pinned down. The next place where they could find cover, another stand of trees, was too far away to make the run. The helicopter hadn't made a pass for several minutes, but she assumed that meant it would fly overhead at any moment. They'd probably have to wait for nightfall to move any farther.

"Since we're stuck here," Uncle Jack said, "explain to me how this works, Watkins."

"How what works?"

"This ability Eleanor has. I get the DNA part. But how does she . . . connect?"

Watkins gestured toward Dr. Von Albrecht. "We've discussed this actually. My theory is that the alien species, a type of zooid, has developed a way to interface its neurology across its component organisms. Some method of communication between its different minds. Perhaps electromagnetic in nature."

That matched Eleanor's experience, though it didn't match anything she knew about the way nature worked. But life on earth could have evolved very differently than it had on the alien home world. She remembered what Dr. Powers had said about the Concentrator upon Eleanor's first glimpse of it. The way it defied her ability to perceive it, the way it seemed to deflect her eyes. Dr. Powers said they had been created by minds that perceived the universe very differently than the human mind.

Eleanor had caught a glimpse of that kind of mind.

"I don't hear the helicopter," Luke said.

Eleanor strained to listen, and heard nothing.

"Do you think they've given up?" Uncle Jack asked.

"Changed tactics might be a better way to put it," Dr. Watkins said.

"Should we risk running for it?" Luke asked.

Eleanor peered through the trees, down the stone fence, to the next grove. She listened again, and heard nothing but the wind. "Let's give it another five minutes. Then we run."

So they waited.

No helicopter.

She didn't know what new tactic they might employ, but it seemed they'd given up their aerial search. "Let's go, before they come back," she said.

They crept from the trees, and then broke into a trot along the pasture's edge. Watkins moved the slowest, so they kept pace with him. Out in the open, Eleanor tried to find the sun, but the overcast sky kept it hidden. The clouds would bring on an early night, a rare, fortunate turn for them.

A few minutes later, they reached the edge of the pasture and entered the trees. Most of them looked dead, tricked into a permanent winter. But there were a few pines that had clung to their needles, and Eleanor inhaled their weak fragrance.

They rested a few minutes, and then looked ahead.

"That's a village," Uncle Jack said.

"Looks abandoned," Luke said.

Uncle Jack nodded. "Might be a good place to spend the night."

"Might be," Watkins said. "Let's assess that once we get there."

Eleanor led the way, and they crossed another series of pastures, until they got to the edge of town. At that point, Uncle Jack stepped forward and scoped each doorway and window before they passed in front of it. They saw no one, and nothing moved. Hardy weeds had sprouted up between the bricks and cobblestones that lined the street. Roofs had caved in. Doors had fallen from their hinges.

"What do you think?" Luke asked.

"Now that we're here," Watkins said, "using this town for shelter seems preferable to setting up camp out in the open."

They all looked at Eleanor.

The place felt eerie to her, but she did her best to ignore that. It did make more sense to stay here. "Okay," she said. "Let's pick a building."

They crept up and down a few more streets until they stumbled on a place that seemed to have been a tea shop. The furniture had been taken, but a long glass case still stood along one wall, empty of the pastries and scones Eleanor imagined had once tempted people from inside it. A layer of dust covered the black-and-white checkered tile floor, which would be a hard surface to sleep on, but the roof overhead looked sound.

"It will keep us dry at least," Eleanor said.

"Looks good enough to me," Uncle Jack said.

They rolled out the little bedding they had packed with them from the plane and ate the little food they'd brought.

"How many miles do you think we covered today?" Eleanor asked.

"Three," Luke said. "Tops. We'll go a lot faster tomorrow, assuming the helicopter stays away."

"But the closer we get to the ship," Dr. Von Albrecht said, "the more likely it is we'll run into ground security."

"We'll deal with that when we come to it," Eleanor said, getting tired of hearing herself say that.

"I think this was probably a lovely establishment," Watkins said, looking around the shop. "I imagine it smelled wonderful. Full of nice village folk talking and enjoying their Earl Grey. The clink of china cups on saucers. Warm scones with clotted cream."

Eleanor closed her eyes and tried to imagine it, but that world had never really existed for her. She knew the kind of place Watkins described only from TV and movies.

"It sounds rather frivolous, doesn't it?" Watkins said. "With everything we face, who cares about tea anymore?"

Dr. Von Albrecht sniffed. "I think if we let ourselves

stop caring about that, we lose the reason why we're fighting."

"What are you fighting for, Professor?" Uncle Jack asked.

"I suppose . . ." Dr. Von Albrecht took off his glasses and rubbed his eyes. "I suppose I want Christmas again. As a boy, I looked forward to the snow. We went to my grandfather's house in Bavaria, and we ate food and told stories. We huddled around the fire, and we celebrated the turning of the season. I suppose a piece of that celebration was the knowledge that spring would arrive."

Eleanor turned to Uncle Jack. "What about you?"

"I don't know what I want for myself," he said. "But I want the world for you. I want you to be able to do anything you want to do, and be anything you want to be."

"You don't want to be a chef?" Eleanor asked. She turned to the others. "Uncle Jack is the best cook in the world. He can take whatever ingredients you give him and turn them into something delicious."

"Don't make promises I can't keep," Uncle Jack said. "Next thing you know, they'll hand me sardines and chocolate."

"Ew." Eleanor laughed. "But seriously, don't you want to go back to being a chef?"

"Maybe," he said. "I don't think about it that much."

"Well, start thinking about it," Luke said. "I think the professor is right. The harder this gets, the more we need to remember why we do it."

"What about you, Mr. Fournier?" Watkins asked.

Luke rubbed under his nose. "Before today, I would've said I want to fly nothing but private island hops in the Caribbean. But now, I'd settle for having *Consuelo* back."

That brought them back to where they were, in a cold and empty tea shop, in a forgotten town, at the edge of the world.

"I'm sorry," Eleanor said.

Luke nodded. "She was a good plane. We've been through a lot together. Even before I picked you up in Phoenix."

"You didn't pick me up. I stowed away."

"I knew you were there, remember?" Luke shook his head. "I shoulda thrown you off, but kid, I'm glad I didn't."

"Even with everything that's happened?" Eleanor asked.

"Because of everything that's happened," he said.

Eleanor sighed and lay down on the hard floor. The tea shop didn't feel so cold anymore, and the tiles warmed up a bit as she lay on them. Unlike the others, she couldn't say what she wanted back, because the world of the Freeze was all she'd known. For her, the hope of ending it was simply the hope of something better.

If she were to say what she wanted back, right then, in that moment, it would be her mom. She wasn't about to say that out loud, but it was true. When her mom had gone missing in the Arctic, and when Eleanor had found her again, she'd realized how much she needed her. Even though they fought, and even though she never felt like she measured up to the girl her mom wanted her to be, and even though her mom had been gone all the time with her job, and even though she'd sided with Dr. Watkins back in Cairo, and even though she refused to eat anything that wasn't a hamburger or a grilled cheese sandwich . . . Eleanor still wanted her there in that tea shop with her. But that was impossible, for many reasons, one of them far more painful than the rest.

Her mom had chosen this.

Her mom didn't want to be there with her, and Eleanor had never in her life felt so alone.

When Eleanor woke in the morning, she realized nothing had disturbed her during the night. Specifically, no helicopter. No one else had heard anything, either, which reassured them that they might be able to keep moving without being followed.

They had no food left, and doubted they could find anything in town before they had to get moving. So they packed up their bedding and set off.

Eleanor could see the sun today, the sky blue and the clouds white. In that light, the village felt a little less haunted, and Eleanor noticed things that the people who had lived here probably loved about it. An old war memorial at the center of town. A stone bridge with an exaggerated hump. An old church sporting a gargoyle in the likeness of a jester.

When they reached the edge of the village, they found a toppled sign that Watkins called a fingerpost. The elements had long worn away the names that had once been there, and Eleanor wished she had something she could call this place. She hoped the people who had lived there could return.

Though the sun was up, a cold wind blew over the fields and pastures, and Eleanor felt chillier than she had yesterday. They found an old road, and they followed it, staying close to the hedgerow to the side, even though they still hadn't heard any hint of the helicopter.

Before long, they'd traveled a mile, and then another, and then another. Eleanor was soon hungry and thirsty, but there wasn't anything she could do about it, so she kept going. Along their journey, they encountered few living things. A few small rodents that made their nests among the fence stones. Some stubborn grass, lichen, and weeds. A large hawk that circled them, perhaps out of curiosity, before flying away to the south.

Around midday the road they traveled came to a fork, and Dr. Von Albrecht pulled out his maps to figure out which way they should go. After a few moments, he indicated the lane to the right, but before they set off again, Eleanor heard the distant sound of a motor.

"There's someone coming," she said.

Uncle Jack nodded. "I hear it, too."

"That's not a helicopter," Luke said. "Let's get off the road,"

They all scrambled over the hedgerow and ran far out into the pasture, where they lay down as flat as they could and waited. A helicopter overhead could have easily spotted them, but a car on what must have been the road they were walking would not.

The hum of the motor grew louder, and then the car appeared, coming around a bend in the road that Dr. Von Albrecht had just said they should take. The hedgerow blocked much of the vehicle from view, but Eleanor could see the top of it, and it looked like a military jeep. It sped away from them, down the road they had just followed outside the abandoned town. Everyone held still until they couldn't hear its engine anymore.

"At least we know we're going the right way," Watkins said. "That was a UN vehicle."

"It's going to be a lot riskier if those keep coming, though," Uncle Jack said.

"I guess we'd better stay off the road," Luke said. "Keep to the fields like we did yesterday."

So that's what they did, crossing several miles of pastures. They passed a few more villages, too, off in the distance. Eleanor noted their bell towers, and from that far away, she could imagine that people still lived there. They also saw a few more vehicles traveling the roads, all of them government or military. Each time, they dropped down low to the ground and seemed to have gone unnoticed.

By late afternoon, Luke announced that they must be getting close to the site of the alien ship.

"I think it might be time to start thinking about how we're going to get near to it," Watkins said. "There will no doubt be considerable security."

"Maybe we don't have to get that close," Eleanor said. "Maybe we just have to get close enough to connect with the alien intelligence."

"Perhaps," Watkins said.

"If that doesn't work," Luke said, "A few of us could just create an old-school diversion. Eleanor and Watkins can use that to get past security—"

"Shh," Eleanor said. "I hear another car."

They all dropped to the ground once more. Eleanor peered through the turf toward the road, waiting, holding still. But then she had an idea.

"What if we steal one of these vehicles?"

"How would we do that?" Luke asked.

"I'll go down to the road and pretend like I've been hit or something. When the car stops, and the driver gets out, you guys jump him. We leave the driver tied up and we take the car back to the site."

"That sounds pretty risky," Uncle Jack said.

"It's all risky," Eleanor said.

"What if you can't just drive the vehicle through security?" Watkins asked. "I imagine they will likely have a gate."

"If we get close and it doesn't look like it's going to work, we ditch the car and go back to our first plan."

"And I suppose," Luke said, "we might be able to get some equipment from the car. Maybe even a radio to listen in."

"If we are going to do this," Dr. Von Albrecht said, "we should hurry. The vehicle is almost here."

Eleanor listened. He was right.

"Are we doing it?" she asked.

"I guess so," Uncle Jack said.

"Let's go!" Eleanor jumped to her feet and ran toward the road. Then she clambered over the hedgerow and lay down alongside it, facing the rocks, hoping she wasn't about to get run over, which was a risk she hadn't considered until this moment.

The rest of them hunkered down behind the wall, just a few feet away from her.

"Eleanor?" Uncle Jack whispered.

"Yeah?"

"I may have to tell your mom about this."

She smiled. And then she played dead.

The sound of the engine grew louder, and then a vehicle came around the bend, going fast. Eleanor held her breath and heard the slight squeal of brakes, which meant the driver had seen her. The car slowed down, then came to a stop. The door opened, and Eleanor heard the sound of boots hitting the road. Then footsteps drew nearer to her, and when Eleanor sensed the driver was about to reach her, she called out.

"Now!"

Commotion came from the other side of the wall as Uncle Jack and Luke leaped up, but then they both went silent.

"Sam?" Uncle Jack said.

Sam?

Eleanor rolled over and looked up, squinting. At first, she simply couldn't believe it. She had to be imagining it. But in a second that disbelief passed, and then Eleanor gasped.

She was staring up at her mom.

CHAPTER

18

Mom!" Eleanor jumped to her feet and threw her arms around her mother.

"Eleanor!" her mom replied, returning her embrace. "Oh, sweetie, it *is* you."

Then Uncle Jack was there, with his long arms around both of them. "Sam," he said. "How—?"

"I'll explain on the way." Eleanor's mom gave her a kiss on her forehead and pulled away. "We need to hurry."

"On the way?"

"To the ship." Her mom moved back toward the vehicle, a white SUV stenciled with a UN label. "That's why you're here, right? So you can shut down whatever's inside it? Come on, get in."

Eleanor didn't know how many scenarios she would have had to imagine before this one came up: a ploy to steal a vehicle out here in the middle of the English countryside, only to discover the vehicle driven by her mom, taking them to the very place they needed to go. And her mom sounded as though she almost supported what Eleanor planned to do.

She climbed into the front passenger seat. Uncle Jack, Luke, Dr. Von Albrecht, and Watkins climbed into the back two rows. The men had barely shut the doors before Eleanor's mom put her foot on the gas, pulled a tight U-turn on the narrow road, and sped down the lane.

"I can't believe it," Eleanor said. It had really only been a matter of days since she'd last seen her mom in Cairo, but it felt like months. So much had happened.

Her mom took her eyes off the road briefly to smile at her. "I can't believe it either. What on earth were you doing lying in the road?"

"I wasn't *in* the road," Eleanor said, grinning. "I was *beside* it."

"But what were you doing?"

"We were going to steal your car," Watkins said from the back row.

"That's a coincidence," her mother said.

Uncle Jack leaned forward. "What are you doing out here, Sam? Are you working for the UN?"

"I am—I was." She twisted her grip around the steering wheel. "I heard they shot down a civilian plane. I worried it was *Consuelo*. But there was talk of searching for the survivors. So I stole this to come look for you."

"Do you know if they picked up Betty and Finn?" Luke asked.

Eleanor's mom nodded, her lips tight. "They're fine."

"What happened?" Eleanor asked. "How did you get here?"

"After you ran away, back in Egypt, Watkins left for Nepal, and Hobbes brought us to a G.E.T. office in Spain. We were supposed to meet with senior UN advisors about the Preservation Protocols. But that never happened. . . ."

"The ship?" Eleanor said.

"Yes," her mom said. "The ship changed everything."

They whipped down the road, along pastures and fields, fences and hedgerows.

"I saw the first news reports with the rest of the world," she continued. "Someone was out here visiting Stonehenge—wanting to see it before it was covered by a glacier—and they caught the whole thing with their cell phone. The UN had no warning before the images were everywhere, and people started asking questions. It didn't take long for them to connect aliens to the Freeze." She paused. "The rioting broke out almost immediately. Even back home."

"No," Eleanor whispered. She'd been afraid of that.

"It started in the Ice Castles," her mom said. "All the refugees who live there. Mexico has closed its borders. Egypt, Libya, and other parts of northern Africa are in chaos. Now it really does seem like the end of the world."

Jenna and Claire lived in the Ice Castles, and Eleanor hoped once again they were okay. As for the rest of the world, in Barrow, Mexico City, Peru, Cairo, Mumbai . . . she hoped the friends she'd made in each of those places were safe, too.

"How did you end up here?" Uncle Jack asked.

"It was Hobbes. Once the alien ship landed, the UN decided the G.E.T. had—" Eleanor's mom glanced in her rearview mirror.

"Feel free to continue, Dr. Perry," Watkins said.

Her mom nodded. "The UN decided the G.E.T. had failed in its purpose. Dr. Watkins hadn't properly assessed the threat. They recruited Hobbes to lead a UN team to secure the site of the ship. Hobbes brought me with him, along with Simon and Julian."

"Why?" Uncle Jack asked.

"We've been around the alien technology. We understand it better than almost anyone else in the world, even though that's not saying much."

"What have you been doing for Hobbes?" Uncle Jack asked, his tone slightly sharp.

"There isn't much we've been able to do," her mom said. "The UN has a position of noninterference with the ship. That's why they declared this a no-fly zone. Some countries were talking about a nuclear strike right away, but the UN Security Council rejected that proposal. They believe we need to understand the ship and the potential consequences better before we make the decision to destroy it. They don't want to repeat past mistakes."

"My mistakes," Watkins said.

No one argued with him on that.

"You're right, Mom," Eleanor said. "I'm trying to get to the ship. I've connected with its alien intelligence, and I think Watkins and I can stop it. How soon until we get there?"

Eleanor's mom seemed to focus all her attention on the road ahead. A muscle quivered in her neck. "Soon," she said.

Now Eleanor felt a suspicion tickling the back

of her mind. Something she couldn't quite put into words. Everything—her mother finding them, driving them to the ship in a UN vehicle . . . it all seemed too easy. Eleanor wanted to believe they might have luck on their side, after the struggles they'd dealt with to get to this point. But still, she couldn't quite believe it. Maybe Uncle Jack had sensed the same thing.

Eleanor turned toward her mom and scrutinized her more closely. She appeared weaker than Eleanor had ever seen her, with bags under her eyes and a deflated posture. Something was definitely off. Her mom hadn't taken her gaze from the road since Eleanor had mentioned connecting with the ship.

"Are you okay?" Eleanor asked.

"Of course, sweetie," she said. "Now that I have you back, safe and sound."

But Eleanor had abandoned her in a mob to go and do the very thing her mom didn't want her to do. And now her mom was driving her to the ship to do that same thing?

"Are you really okay with me doing this?" Eleanor noticed that everyone else in the car had fallen very silent.

Her mom accelerated the SUV. "Doing what?"

"You know what," Eleanor said.

"Where are we going?" Dr. Von Albrecht asked.

"The ship," her mom said.

"But this is not the way to the ship," Dr. Von Albrecht said.

Eleanor turned around in her seat. The professor had one of his maps out, and Watkins frowned at it next to him. Luke was shaking his head, and Uncle Jack was looking right at Eleanor with sadness in his eyes.

The SUV took a sudden turn, throwing Eleanor sideways in her seat. In the distance ahead she saw a roadblock—multiple vehicles, and a few of them looked like tanks. Dozens of armed soldiers stood waiting next to them.

"Mom," Eleanor whispered. "Turn around."

Her mom said nothing. Did nothing.

"Mom?"

"I'm sorry, sweetie," she whispered. "They gave me no choice."

Eleanor's suspicion broke like a dam, and a torrent of pain and betrayal flooded over her. "Mom," she said. "Turn around, please!"

Her mom blinked rapidly, staring ahead through tears. "I can't," she said.

"Sam." Uncle Jack put a hand on her mom's shoulder. "Don't. Not this."

They were almost to the roadblock, maybe a few

hundred yards away, and her mom completely ignored Uncle Jack.

"Sam!" he said again.

"Dr. Perry," Watkins said. "I would have expected more from Eleanor's mother."

That finally drew something out of her. "I *am* her mother!" she shouted. "I'm doing what I have to do to protect my daughter! I'm not letting her anywhere near that thing!"

Eleanor felt too stunned to do or say anything. But as they drew close enough to the roadblock for her to see the soldiers ahead raising their weapons, her survival instinct took over. They had to get out of there. They couldn't be caught, or it would mean the end of everything. She had connected with the alien intelligence; she knew what it planned to do. And she wouldn't let anyone—even her mom—stop her from ending it.

She reached out with both hands and grabbed the steering wheel.

"Eleanor, don't—"

"Turn around!" she said, and wrenched the wheel sideways.

The SUV swerved, hurling Eleanor against the restraint of her seat belt, choking the air out of her. Her hands flew off the wheel, and her mom lost control. The brakes screeched, and they slammed headlong into the stone hedgerow. There was a loud bang, something hit Eleanor in the face, and for a second everything went black.

Then Eleanor coughed. A fine dust coated her skin and filled the air. She refocused her eyes and saw the airbag had deployed in front of her.

"Sweetie," her mom said, leaning toward her. "Are you okay?"

Eleanor felt something warm on her lip and licked it.

Blood. From her nose. It must have happened when the airbag hit her face. "I'm fine. I think." She turned around and looked in the back rows. "Uncle Jack? Luke?"

"We're fine," Luke said.

"We are, too," Watkins said. "Though I suspect we'll all have sore necks tomorrow—"

"Hands in the air!"

Eleanor looked out the window to her side. Soldiers had rushed up to surround the vehicle, rifles and pistols aimed inside. Eleanor couldn't see any way out of this. She raised her hands in the air and looked over at her mom.

She had her hands in the air, too. "Just do what they ask," she said. "No one will get hurt."

"*They* might," Uncle Jack said, almost growling.

"Don't do anything stupid," Eleanor's mom hissed. It sounded very much like an older sister scolding a younger brother, which is exactly what it was. Eleanor didn't like that at all.

"I said hands up!" shouted one of the soldiers.

Eleanor looked back and saw Uncle Jack slowly raising his arms, hands balled in fists. The others in the backseats had already done so.

A soldier standing by Eleanor's door yanked it open, and then rough hands reached in, unbuckling her and pulling her out. She sniffed at the blood still oozing from her nose as soldiers surrounded her and spun her around. They pulled her hands behind her back and handcuffed her.

"Eleanor!" she heard her mom call from the other side of the vehicle. "Sweetie, it will be okay!"

No. It wouldn't be. Not ever.

"We'll figure this out." They'd pulled Uncle Jack from Eleanor's side of the SUV. He towered over most of the soldiers, but he let them handcuff him, while a few feet away, Luke struggled a bit and got a fist to his stomach for it. Next to him, Dr. Von Albrecht had lost his glasses, either in the crash or from the man-handling of the soldiers. Across the vehicle, through the windows, Watkins looked unconcerned, almost serene.

"Secured?" one of the soldiers called out.

"Secured!" responded another from the other side of the vehicle.

"Load 'em up!"

Firm hands pushed Eleanor away from the SUV, toward the vehicles waiting at the roadblock. The soldiers ushered them through a staggered formation of white military assault vehicles and tanks, all of them marked with the UN logo. The soldiers wore camouflage fatigues and blue helmets. These weren't G.E.T. agents, and Eleanor had no idea what to expect from them.

When they reached a large, covered white truck, the soldiers led them around to the back, where they opened the tailgate and forced them up into the bed. Eleanor stumbled up onto a bench that ran down the side, almost falling, and Uncle Jack managed to sit down next to her. Her mom sat down across from her, and she leaned toward Eleanor, trying to look her in the eye, to get her attention.

But that wasn't something Eleanor was going to give.

Once they were all loaded and a few of the soldiers

had joined them in the back of the truck with their guns, the truck moved out. Eleanor couldn't see where they were going, only what was behind them. The UN blockade, soldiers walking to their vehicles, and beyond that, the crashed SUV.

Her plan to steal it had been risky, but it might have worked. If not for her mother.

If not for her *mother*.

"Where are you taking us?" Luke asked the soldier next to him, a young woman with lots of freckles and blond hair.

She looked back at him, stone-faced, and said nothing.

Eleanor raised her voice. "Hey!"

The soldier looked at her now.

"He asked you a question."

"I heard him," the soldier said. Then she looked away.

"Don't antagonize them," her mother said.

Eleanor locked her eyes on the chipped enamel coating the floor of the truck. It seemed they were heading roughly in the same direction they had been traveling since morning. She didn't think they would be taking them to the alien ship, but Hobbes probably had some kind of base of operations near it, and that's likely where they were going.

Out the back of the truck, Eleanor saw abandoned farmhouses and barns, and they passed through another ghost town, before slowing to a stop. The driver of the truck talked with someone else, and then the vehicle eased forward, and Eleanor saw a security gate close behind them.

They had entered an area fenced with razor-topped chain-link. They passed rows of tents, some of them small enough for sleeping, some of them large enough for meetings or research labs, like the G.E.T. encampment in Cairo near the pyramids. Eventually, the truck stopped again, and this time, the driver shut the engine off.

More soldiers approached the back of the truck and lowered the tailgate. Then the soldiers in the bed of the truck pulled Eleanor and the rest of them to their feet before pushing them out onto the ground, where Eleanor got a better look at where they were.

Tents surrounded them, and the base seemed huge. Their truck had come in by way of a road through the midst of them, and there were other streets leading away. Soldiers walked and hurried around them, some of them armed, like their captors, and others not. Eleanor searched in all directions, but saw no sign of the ship or Stonehenge.

"Welcome," said a male voice.

Eleanor looked for its source, and saw Hobbes marching up to them. This was the second time he had captured her.

"Hobbes," Watkins said. "What is the meaning of this? I demand you—"

"I take my orders from the UN now," Hobbes said. "And even if I still worked for the G.E.T., you wouldn't even have the authority to send me out for coffee." Hobbes looked him up and down. "You've been neutralized, Watkins."

The old man scowled and smacked his lips, apparently unable to put even one word together in response.

"As for the rest of you," Hobbes said. "You'll be taken to holding cells, where you will wait for transfer to a permanent facility."

"What kind of facility?" Luke asked.

"A prison. Where you will await trial." But then Hobbes turned to Eleanor. "Except you. You're coming with me."

Eleanor lifted her chin. "I'd rather go to prison with my friends."

"Sweetie," her mom said. "Please, just listen to him—"

"No!" The ferocity in Eleanor's voice made her mom recoil. "You don't get to say anything to me! After what you did? How could you—I trusted you! And you

262

betrayed me!" Eleanor lowered her voice when she felt it was about to break. "I will never, ever forgive you."

Her mom nodded, biting her lip. "I know that, sweetie," she said. "I know."

— CHAPTER —
19

Eleanor sat at the metal table, looking Hobbes in the eye. He sat across from her, while her mom sat on her left. But Eleanor ignored her. They'd taken her handcuffs off, but there were guards both inside and outside the tent. Eleanor still hadn't figured out where they had taken Uncle Jack, Luke, and the others. She assumed Finn and Betty were here somewhere as well, and probably Finn's dad.

"You got heart, Eleanor," Hobbes said. "Probably more than anyone gives you credit for. I admire it."

Eleanor smirked. "You can't good-cop me when you already bad-copped me. It doesn't work that way."

"I'm not a good cop or a bad cop."

"Then what are you?"

He looked up at a spot somewhere over Eleanor's left shoulder, as if he was thinking about it. "I suppose you could call me a . . . planetary patriot. Like you."

Eleanor bristled. "We are nothing alike."

"I think you'd be surprised how similar we are."

"I doubt that."

"Eleanor," her mom said. "Please, you don't understand. Just—"

"Dr. Perry." Hobbes held up a hand. "I'll do the talking."

"Yes, you will," Eleanor said. "Because I sure won't."

Hobbes lowered his raised hand to the table and drummed the metal with his fingertips. "Fine. I'll do the talking. But you're going to listen."

Eleanor shrugged. "Doesn't look like I'm going anywhere."

"I have a daughter," Hobbes said. "Mariah. She's a little older than you. She likes computers, and she might be as stubborn as me. Come to think of it, you two would probably get along." He leaned back in his chair. "Do you know what you're supposed to do if someone tries to mug you? Has your uncle ever taught you?"

The question caught Eleanor off guard, and she answered, "No."

"For some people," Hobbes said, "like me, your first impulse is to refuse to give them what they want. You fight back. But that's not always the smart thing to do, because you don't know what they're capable of. Maybe they have a gun. In that case, fighting back could get you killed, when you could've just handed over your wallet and walked away. You might be broke, but you're alive."

Eleanor wondered where he was going with this.

"Now, I have never in my life backed away from a fight," he continued. "Someone tries to mug me, chances are good I can take them down whether they're armed or not. That's if I'm alone. But let's say I have Mariah with me. . . ."

He paused.

Eleanor waited.

"That changes things for me," he said. "Now I have to ask myself whether I can risk fighting back. The mugger is an unknown. Unpredictable. In that situation, I'm more likely to ignore my first impulse and hand over my wallet, rather than jeopardize my daughter."

"Okay," Eleanor said.

Now Hobbes leaned in toward her. "That alien world up there? It's a mugger. It stepped out of the shadows, and it's demanding that we hand over our wallet. And no one knows what it's capable of. We don't know if it has a gun." He paused again. "If it were just me we were talking about? I'd be right there with you, fighting this thing until it bugged out back to wherever it came from. But I have Mariah with me. So you know what? I'm going to give it my wallet. That alien world might leave us broke, but we'll be alive."

"Alive?" Eleanor said. "The world is freezing over—"

"Humans have survived ice ages before," Hobbes said.

"Not like this," Eleanor said. "This ice age will never end. Not as long as that planet is pulling our world out of orbit and bleeding it dry."

"Unless," Hobbes said, "the mugger disappears back into the shadows after it gets what it wants. What if the rogue world just moves on?" He tipped his head and gave Eleanor a knowing look. "Face it. You don't know what's going to happen any better than anyone else."

"That's not true," Eleanor said. "I've seen what they do. If we don't stop this, we won't survive. I've seen the dead planets they leave behind. Hundreds of them. Thousands—"

"Even if you're telling the truth, it's a risk we can't take. We can't provoke the alien world until we know more."

"What more could we possibly hope to know?"

"That's where you come in. I need you to open up that ship. We need to find out what's inside it, and see if the mugger is armed."

"Don't you think that's a bit . . . threatening?" Eleanor asked.

"We won't do anything to attack the ship," he said. "If you can do what Watkins can do, then you can convince the ship that we mean it no harm."

"You're putting a lot of faith in my ability."

"I'm aware of that," he said. "But based on what you've managed to accomplish up to this point, I don't think that faith is misplaced."

Eleanor shrugged. "Why not just ask Watkins to do it?"

"Because I lost faith in him a long time ago. He's a scientist with his head stuck up his algorithms. We need to pivot our strategy to something . . . tactical. Diplomatic. That's why the UN assigned me to Watkins in the first place."

"To keep an eye on him?"

Hobbes nodded.

"Where is Watkins now?"

"In a holding cell with the others."

"I'll need his help."

"I can't allow that."

268

"I can't do it without him."

Hobbes let out a sigh of irritation. "Why not?"

"It would be hard for you to understand," Eleanor said. "But I'll try to explain. Did Watkins ever tell you about his zooid hypothesis?"

Hobbes nodded.

"Well, the ship's intelligence is strong. Much stronger than me. Watkins and I need to work together to defeat it. That's the only way."

"How do you know?"

"We already faced it together in the Himalayas."

Eleanor's mother let out a little gasp.

"What happened?" Hobbes asked after a moment.

"The ship took control of the Master Concentrator, but we were able to fight it off and shut the Concentrator down. The ship's intelligence escaped and came back here."

"I see," Hobbes said.

He rose to his feet and paced around the tent, arms folded. Eleanor watched him, trying to figure out how much leverage she had. He needed her, so that put her in the position to bargain. But she wasn't sure how far she could push him. He was like the unpredictable mugger he had described.

On the other hand, Hobbes was giving Eleanor the opportunity to get close to the ship. Once she was connected to it, he would probably have no way of knowing what she was doing. Perhaps she could pretend to cooperate with him while sticking to the original plan. For that to work, she would still need Watkins.

Hobbes returned to the table. "Here is my problem," he said. "I can control you, but I can't control him."

"You think you can control me?" Eleanor said.

"I know I can. But Watkins, on the other hand, is an unknown." He turned to the guards. "Take them to the holding cell until I figure this out."

"I'm not doing anything unless we do this my way," Eleanor said, even as soldiers lifted her out of the chair and forced her toward the exit of the tent. "And there's nothing you can do about that."

"You'll find out soon enough," he said, and just as the soldiers prodded Eleanor outside and the door was closing, he added, "Why don't you ask your mom?"

The encampment surrounded her with commotion. She thought her mom wanted to say something to her, but before she could, the soldiers pushed them both along, down the rows of tents, until they came to one of the larger ones. Inside it, Eleanor saw Uncle Jack, Luke, Finn, Betty, everyone. Even Dr. Powers and Julian. And they were in a cell.

The guards marched Eleanor and her mom to a door in the cage, which one of the soldiers unlocked and opened, while the others held their weapons drawn. Eleanor's mom went in first, and then Eleanor followed her. The door closed behind them with a loud clang.

"Well, looks like the whole band is back together," Luke said.

Eleanor glanced at everyone in the cell with her, feeling something different for each of them, from anger to relief. "At least no one is hurt," she said.

"I wouldn't say that." Finn looked at his dad, and Eleanor noticed the purple bruising of a black eye against his brown skin.

"What happened?" Eleanor asked.

"I picked a fight I couldn't win," Dr. Powers said, glancing at the guards. "But I'd do it again."

"I'll be there to help next time," Julian said.

"A fight over what?" Eleanor asked. "With who?"

"With Hobbes. Over the shooting down of a civilian plane with my son on board." Dr. Powers's jaw muscles rippled with anger. "I thought I was doing the right thing, signing on with you, Watkins. I didn't realize . . ."

"Neither did I," Watkins said.

The cell was the size of a large room, with a row

271

of cots and sleeping bags, a sink, and a thick canvas floor. Outside the cell, in a corner of the tent, stood a blue portable toilet. Eleanor didn't like the thought of using it.

"So what did Hobbes want with you?" Uncle Jack asked.

"He wants her to help him appease these . . . aliens," Eleanor's mom said. "And I think we should do what he says."

Eleanor snapped at her. "You have no idea what you're talking about."

"Sweetie—"

"Don't call me that. I'm not your sweetie anymore." Eleanor turned to Uncle Jack. "Hobbes says he can make me do whatever he wants. But he's nothing more than a bully, and I've dealt with bullies before."

"What does he want you to do?" Watkins asked.

"He wants me to convince the ship and the rogue world that we mean them no harm. He wants me to open up the ship."

"Why?" Finn asked. "Does he *want* to meet some pissed-off aliens?"

"Maybe," Eleanor said. "He thinks if we give these aliens what they want, they'll just go back to where they came from. And he wants me to trick the ship into trusting us or something."

"He wants you to be his spy," Watkins said.

"Actually, he wants you, too," Eleanor said. "But he's afraid of what you might do if he lets you near the ship."

Watkins chuckled. "That is very astute of him."

"Eleanor, listen to me." Her mom stepped closer to her and tried to reach out a hand toward her hair. "You—"

"Don't touch me," Eleanor said.

Her mom withdrew her hand and frowned. "Look, I don't expect you to understand right now, but one day you'll—"

"What day would that be?" Eleanor said. "Because if it's after the earth freezes over and dies, I don't think it will matter much to either of us."

"Eleanor," Finn said. "Could we talk—over there?" He nodded toward a cot in one corner of the cage.

Eleanor didn't know what he would want to talk to about in that moment, but she nodded, and they stepped aside. The others moved away to give them what privacy they could in the small space and started up their own conversations. Watkins, Dr. Von Albrecht, Dr. Powers, and Julian seemed to be conferring about the alien ship, while Uncle Jack tried to speak with Eleanor's mom. Betty and Luke said nothing, watching the others.

"There's something you need to know," Finn whispered to her. "About your mom."

"I think I know everything I need to know. She lied to me. She tricked me into getting into her car, and then she turned me over to Hobbes." Eleanor shook her head. "You know, it was hard for me to trust Badri, after what happened with Amaru in Peru. But I did. And it turns out, I should have been worried about trusting my own mom."

"It's funny you should mention Badri. She would say your mom did the brave thing."

Eleanor leaned away from him. "Brave thing? What are you even talking about?"

"She made her choice knowing what the consequences would be. She knew you'd probably hate her."

"And yet she did it anyway."

"Exactly. But you don't know why."

"Do you?"

He nodded. Then he leaned in closer, and whispered even more quietly. "I overheard your mom talking with my dad. And the thing is . . . Hobbes said he would kill your uncle if your mom didn't help bring you in."

"He—" The cage seemed to collapse around Eleanor, shrinking until she couldn't breathe. "Hobbes said that?"

"More or less. He told her that was the only way he would guarantee your uncle Jack's safety."

Eleanor looked across the cell. Uncle Jack stood there, his arm around her mom's shoulder, trying to comfort her. Eleanor realized he was a pillar holding the world up, and she would do anything to keep him safe. And so, it seems, would her mom.

"I didn't know," Eleanor whispered.

"You're not supposed to," Finn said. "I'm not supposed to."

"Why?"

"Because your mom doesn't want your uncle to know he's being used that way. She's afraid he'll do something stupid and get himself killed."

Finn was probably right. Uncle Jack would never allow himself to be a pawn that way, especially if it meant that Eleanor couldn't or wouldn't go through with the mission. When they'd climbed into the SUV, her mom certainly couldn't say anything about it with Uncle Jack right there. Eleanor didn't want to think about what might have happened with all those armed soldiers around.

"Thank you for telling me," she said.

"I just didn't want you to say something you would regret later."

Eleanor didn't regret anything she'd said. "Look, if

she only betrayed us to save Uncle Jack, I could accept that. But that's not what happened. She *chose* Watkins. She's the one who put Uncle Jack in danger in the first place."

"I guess that's true."

"What about you?" Eleanor asked. "How are things with your dad and Julian?"

"Better," he said. "We talked."

"About Cairo?"

"Only a little. We put that behind us."

That sounded a lot simpler than it probably was. Eleanor knew Finn and Julian both struggled with their feelings for their father. He hadn't been around for them and their mother. That's not something you just get over.

"So what are we gonna do?" Finn asked. "Do you have a plan?"

"Not yet. I think Hobbes has to make his next move." She looked around. "I guess we're stuck in here for the time being."

"I guess so."

Eleanor thought about Hobbes, and wondered if he would really follow through on a threat like that. Would he hurt Uncle Jack? Or had that just been something to get Eleanor's mom—and Eleanor—to cooperate?

That whole speech he'd given about Mariah had

seemed sincere. He loved his daughter. Eleanor knew what she was willing to do to protect Uncle Jack. What was Hobbes willing to do to protect his daughter?

She had a feeling that, very soon, she was going to find out.

CHAPTER
20

ELEANOR HEARD NOTHING FROM HOBBES FOR THE REST OF that day, and spent the time telling Dr. Powers about everything that had happened in the Himalayas. Toward evening, soldiers brought them all food in the form of ready-to-eat field rations, probably the same stuff the peacekeepers were themselves eating. Eleanor sat on her cot, chewing and swallowing, watching Uncle Jack inspect each bite as if he wasn't convinced it was actually food.

"I wish we had some of that fish Badri gave us," Finn said. "That was good. Tender and spicy."

"It sounds delicious," Eleanor's mom said.

Eleanor snorted. "Oh, please. You would have

turned your nose up at it like you do to anything that's a little different." It came out sounding like the dig she'd meant it to be.

Her mom went quiet, along with everyone else, but Eleanor refused to feel bad about the tension she'd brought into the tent. She hadn't said anything that wasn't true.After they'd finished their rations, they each took one of the cots. Eleanor ended up between her mom and Julian.

"I wonder what Hobbes has planned for us," Watkins said. "Nothing in the middle of the night, I hope."

Eleanor didn't think they could rule anything out with Hobbes. She climbed into her sleeping bag, her head resting on a very flat pillow, and thought about how she could get them all out of this cell and go after the alien ship.

"So Finn really saw a yeti?" Julian asked next to her, keeping his voice low.

"Yup."

"That is crazy."

"Yup."

"My dad was pretty pissed at him for a while. Now I think he's proud of him."

"He should be," Eleanor said.

Julian paused. "Hey, if there's something I can do to help with the plan, let me know?"

Eleanor rolled her head to the side and looked at him. "How do you know there's a plan?"

"It's you," he said, smirking. "You always have a plan. And I'm glad we're all on the same side again."

"I am, too," Eleanor said. "But I wish it didn't take an alien ship and a guy like Hobbes to bring us back together."

A few minutes later, the guards switched off the overhead lights, and the tent went dark except for the camp light bleeding in through the canvas. Eleanor listened to the sounds that continued outside, the vehicles driving around, and even people talking as they walked. She couldn't figure what everyone was doing here. The security forces made sense. But what about everyone else? Were they scientists? UN staff? Something about this whole situation was fishy, even beyond the imprisonment and threats. Hobbes had a hidden agenda. She felt certain of that, but she could only guess what it might be.

Eleanor lay awake until she could hear Uncle Jack's snoring coming from his cot. Then she rolled onto her side, away from Julian.

"Mom?" she whispered. "Are you awake?"

Silence.

"Mom?"

Nothing.

Eleanor wasn't even sure what she wanted to say. Maybe she should apologize for what she'd done at dinner, even though her mom was the one who should be apologizing to her, and in a very big way. Eleanor thought about reaching over and waking her up, but worried that would make too much noise and rouse the others. After a few moments of indecision had passed, she gave up trying to figure out what she wanted and rolled onto her back to try to sleep.

Eleanor woke to the sound of the cage door opening. When she opened her eyes, she saw Hobbes walking in, flanked by two soldiers. The light coming in through the tent had the pale blue tinge of early morning. Hobbes clapped his hands twice.

"Wake up!"

Those who hadn't stirred at the sound of the cage door opened their eyes and sat up in bed.

"This isn't boot camp, Hobbes," Watkins said.

"We aren't running a resort, either." Hobbes looked at Eleanor. "You're coming with me."

Eleanor narrowed her eyes at him but said nothing.

Hobbes turned to Watkins. "You, too. The rest of you will stay here."

"No way." Uncle Jack heaved himself to his feet, holding his side and grunting. "You're not taking her without me."

"Or me," Eleanor's mom said.

"I appreciate your desire to protect her," Hobbes said. "Trust me, I do. But you're staying here." He turned toward the cage door. "As long as Eleanor here does as I ask, you've got nothing to worry about."

Eleanor looked at Uncle Jack and her mom and nodded to them both, trying to reassure them. "I'll be back," she said, before following Hobbes outside the cell.

Watkins came behind her, and after closing the door and relocking the cage, Hobbes led them from the tent. Outside, Eleanor could see it would be another overcast day, and it was later in the morning than she thought. As she and Watkins walked beside Hobbes, the two guards a few steps behind them, she noticed the continued activity around the camp.

"Who are all these people?" she asked.

"UN peacekeepers," he said.

"Not the soldiers," she said. "Everyone else."

Hobbes glanced to either side. "Support personnel."

"What kind of support?" Watkins asked.

"The usual." Hobbes waved his hand casually. "You'll find out soon enough."

Eleanor didn't know what that meant, but she did know Hobbes wasn't going to say anything more about it, so she let it go. They crossed the camp and came to a tent at the center of a flurry of activity. A few soldiers stood guard, but a much greater number of so-called support personnel came and went, or stood in conversation. As Hobbes approached, they all fell silent and stared at Eleanor and Watkins.

"I think our reputations precede us," Watkins said.

"I wonder what they've heard," Eleanor said. "Are they staring at global terrorists, or are they staring at freaks who can talk to aliens?"

"Perhaps both," Watkins said.

"That's enough talking." Hobbes pulled the tent flap aside and nodded them in.

This time, Eleanor found a setup very similar to the G.E.T. encampment in Cairo. Large screens displayed satellite images and new broadcasts, while UN staff manned numerous computer terminals arranged in rows. Eleanor searched them for any images of the alien ship, but Hobbes rushed them through too quickly toward a temporary wall that ran down one side of the tent. It had several doors, marking ceiling-less rooms, and one of them bore a sign with Hobbes's name.

"My office," he said, unlocking the door. "Enter."

This wasn't where Eleanor had expected him to take them. Inside, the room looked exceedingly normal. A generic veneered wooden desk, with two slim armchairs in front of it. The desk bore a framed picture, but it faced away from Eleanor. The office even smelled of freshly brewed coffee, a familiar aroma Eleanor realized she hadn't smelled in a very long time, and she spotted the coffeemaker on a small table against the temporary wall.

"Please," Hobbes said, closing the office door behind them. "Have a seat. Would you like some coffee? It's crap, but it's coffee."

"I'll pass," Watkins said, taking one of the armchairs.

Eleanor took the other, working to restrain her anger. "You can try as hard as you want, Hobbes, but you will never be the good cop."

"No?" Hobbes poured his coffee into a mug so stained inside that Eleanor wondered if it had ever been washed. "And why is that?"

"You threatened to kill my uncle."

Hobbes replaced the coffeepot. "Not directly."

"Not directly?" Eleanor said. "That still sounds pretty bad cop to me."

Hobbes put the mug down on the desk and sat down in his chair. "There are a number of people who would disagree with you. They sent me here to save lives."

"And you decide to start by threatening my uncle's?"

Hobbes sighed. "Believe it or not, I don't feel any need to convince you. So fine, I'm a bad cop, and this is a bad cup of coffee." He took a sip. "There are more important things to discuss."

"Such as?" Watkins said.

"The ship, obviously. You've been in contact with it, so that makes you two the earth's foremost alien experts."

"I wouldn't say that." Watkins crossed one leg over the other and leaned back in his chair as if he were sitting in his living room back home. "We haven't even seen the ship."

"It's . . . something else," Hobbes said. "But seeing it doesn't tell us anything about it. In fact, I'm not even sure we're really seeing it." He paused. "You know what I mean by that?"

Eleanor knew exactly what he meant.

Hobbes continued. "None of our equipment can give us any information on it. If you believe the data from our sensors, the thing isn't even there. But it is." He held out his hand as if the ship were on his desk. "It's right there."

"What's your point?" Eleanor assumed he was

trying to win them over to his side, sharing information with them, giving them the appearance of cooperation, but doing an obvious and clumsy job of it.

"I don't have a point," he said. "I have a question."

"What is your question, then?" Watkins asked.

Hobbes gave them both a long, pointed look. "Do you know if there are aliens inside that ship?"

Eleanor looked over at Watkins. He cocked his head to one side and then turned toward her. That question would be very important to someone like Hobbes, who knew nothing about the ship, other than where it came from. But Eleanor knew, intuitively, that the only being on that ship was the intelligence that controlled it. The look that passed between her and Watkins confirmed that he thought the same thing, even though the rest of the earth's inhabitants probably feared otherwise.

In that moment, Eleanor realized they could potentially take the upper hand, if they played things right.

"We don't know," Eleanor said. "We've only ever connected with the alien technology. Not with the aliens themselves."

"So there *could* be aliens on that ship," Hobbes said. "Is that what you're telling me?"

"Anything is possible," Watkins said.

Hobbes leaned back in his chair, rubbing his chin.

"You find a car parked on your lawn, you know some-one must have driven it there."

"Ah, now I see," Watkins said. "That's what all of this is for. Your support staff. You're preparing for a First Contact scenario."

Hobbes nodded. "Biologists. Linguists. Anthropolo-gists. You name it."

"But what are you hoping for?" Watkins asked. "These aliens did not come in peace. The Concentrators—they're like teeth. They came to kill the earth, to extract its blood. This is war."

"We know that," Hobbes said. "We don't expect a handshake."

"Then what do you expect?" Watkins asked.

Hobbes looked at the photo on his desk. "We have a number of contingencies in place."

"That's not an answer," Eleanor said.

"It's the only answer you're going to get." He took another sip of his coffee.

"Is that your daughter?" Eleanor pointed at the pic-ture.

Hobbes turned the photo around so she could see it. From within the frame, a teenage girl smiled out at her, sitting next to Hobbes on a park bench with her arm through his. The Hobbes in the photo looked at his daughter with the same loving expression as the

Hobbes in the office looking at her picture.

A moment later, he turned the frame back around. "Here is what will happen. In a few minutes, the three of us will leave for the site of the alien ship. You both will connect with it, convey to it that we mean it no harm, and get it to open its doors."

"How are we supposed to do that?" Watkins asked.

"That's up to you," Hobbes said. "But Eleanor here has managed to shut down four Concentrators, and you've managed to start a couple of them back up, not to mention controlling the World Tree. I believe you'll figure something out. Now, ask me."

"Ask you?" Eleanor said.

"Yes, ask me."

"Ask you what?" Watkins said.

"Ask me what happens if you don't do what I tell you to do." He took a sip of coffee, and over the rim of his mug, his eyes had gone cold and empty. "Ask me what happens to your mom and your uncle."

Eleanor's vision tunneled. This was what she had feared after talking with Finn. Hobbes had control of her the same way he had controlled her mother, by threatening the people she loved, and so long as she believed he meant to carry out that threat, he had her.

"What about me?" the old man asked. "What happens if I don't do what you tell me to do?"

Hobbes wagged a finger at him. "You had me up most of the night asking that same question. But I think I figured it out."

"Oh?" Watkins folded his arms.

"It was actually Eleanor who gave me the idea."

Watkins glanced at Eleanor, but she had no idea what Hobbes was talking about.

"What idea did Eleanor give you?" Watkins asked.

"She told me that you had joined your minds together somehow to stop the alien intelligence." He came around the desk and sat on its edge. "I've known you for years, Watkins. We never got really personal with each other, but I am sure of one thing about you."

"And what's that?" Watkins asked.

"You are a lonely old man."

That word. The way he said it. *Lonely.* It slowly settled over Eleanor what he meant, and how he would try to control Watkins, by using her. But she knew that would never work. Watkins didn't really care about her, and she expected him to laugh or to smirk at Hobbes.

But he didn't. He went quiet.

"Now you see," Hobbes said. "And I see you. No wife. No kids. All alone. But now there's Eleanor, the only person who has the same power you do, the same drive to use it—the only person who truly understands what you're going through, what you're trying to do. And my guess is, you don't even know what to make of it. But you know it means something to you. And you're not going to let me take that from you." Hobbes drained the rest of his coffee in one long gulp.

Eleanor had suddenly and inexplicably found herself being used as a pawn in the same way Uncle Jack had unknowingly been used, only this didn't make any sense. It didn't seem possible that this could work, not on Watkins.

"You wouldn't do anything to her," Watkins said. "You're not stupid. You know I can't get into the ship without her."

"I'm aware of that," Hobbes said. "So you'll just have to decide whether I'm bluffing or not. Ask yourself if that's a risk you're willing to take."

They were talking about Eleanor as if she wasn't there, as if she couldn't hear the threat Hobbes had just made against her. No way would Watkins surrender to Hobbes for her sake, which meant Hobbes might soon carry out his threat. Eleanor looked around the room, panic taking over, wondering if the door was locked.

"Well?" Hobbes asked.

"I'm not," Watkins said.

"You're not what?" Hobbes asked.

"I'm not willing to take the risk," Watkins said. "I'll do what you want."

Eleanor couldn't believe it. She didn't know what to think or feel about it.

"A wise choice," Hobbes said. "Now that's settled. And you both have a job to do."

— CHAPTER —
21

W E'RE NOT GOING ANYWHERE WITHOUT MY MOM AND Uncle Jack," Eleanor said, still reeling from what had just happened.

"You're not in a position to make demands." Hobbes walked toward the door.

"Yes, I am." Eleanor got to her feet. "If you want my help, I need to know you'll keep your end of the bargain. I need to know they're safe."

"I would also point out," Watkins said, "that the connection with the alien ship will require tremendous concentration. That may not be possible if Eleanor is distracted by worry for her family."

Hobbes reached the door and then turned around

to face them. "Not both of them," he said. "Pick one. Your mom or your uncle. The other stays here."

Eleanor shook her head. "They both come or—"

"One," Hobbes said. "Or none. I need my own assurances."

Eleanor knew he ultimately held the power, and if he wanted to he could keep both her mom and Uncle Jack at gunpoint. But she had managed to negotiate something out of him. And one was better than none.

"I want my mom," she said, a little surprised at the swiftness of her choice. But with his injury, Uncle Jack needed to rest, and his cot in the cell would probably be the best place for that.

Hobbes nodded. "I'll go get her." Then he opened the office door, and two armed soldiers marched in. "Take Eleanor and Watkins to the convoy. I'll meet you there."

"Yes, sir."

Eleanor looked at Watkins. He proceeded through the doorway with his hands clasped behind his back, a mild smile on his face, as if nothing had changed since he'd walked in. But something *had* changed, and Eleanor was confused by it.

The soldier nearest her gave her a little nudge, and she moved forward, following Watkins through the door, and on her way back through the tent, she tried again to catch a glimpse of anything useful on the computer monitors and screens.

"Keep moving," the soldier behind her said.

She turned to give him a scowl, and didn't change her pace at all. When they exited, the two guards directed them toward a large break in the tents where numerous vehicles waited, arranged in a double column. The forward trucks had large guns mounted on them, followed by several armored vans, with a few six-wheeled tank-like vehicles at the rear. The soldiers with Eleanor and Watkins loaded them into one of the vans by themselves, but left the doors open and stood guard.

"It seems we're finding our way to the alien ship," Watkins said. "One way or another."

"I'd rather the other way," Eleanor said.

She didn't know how to talk about what had just happened, or even if she should. Hobbes was probably right, and Watkins wouldn't even know how.

"I have a theory," Watkins said.

"About what?"

He flicked his eyes toward the guards and lowered his voice. "What's really going on here."

Eleanor leaned in close. "What?"

"I have heard rumors of a second version of the Preservation Protocol—a plan B, to be used in the event that our attempts to draw energy from the Concentrators failed."

"What did it say?"

"I was never involved with it, as the G.E.T.'s responsibility was only plan A. But the rumors—"

Hobbes appeared from behind the van, and Watkins leaned away from Eleanor. Then Eleanor's mom appeared, and Hobbes helped her climb into the same row as Eleanor and Watkins, a slightly confused and worried look on her face.

"There," he said. "As promised. And Jack will remain here."

Eleanor didn't need the reminder.

"We'll move out shortly," Hobbes said, and walked away, though the same two guards remained.

"Are you really going to do this?" her mom asked.

"I thought you wanted me to cooperate," Eleanor said.

"But why did you change your mind?"

"The same reason you turned us in."

Her mom showed a moment's confusion across her wrinkled brow, but then seemed to realize what Eleanor meant. "I'm sorry."

"He's safe now," Eleanor said. "But I'm sure he wasn't happy about being left behind just now."

"Not at all," her mom said. "I'm surprised you

didn't hear him shouting from here."

"He is fortunate to have two people care about him as much as you do," Watkins said. "That is what this is all about, isn't it?"

"Yes," Eleanor said.

The front doors opened, and Hobbes climbed into the front passenger seat, while another soldier got behind the wheel and turned the key. Eleanor looked outside and saw the rest of the vehicles filling up with additional soldiers and support staff. Hobbes spoke into a handheld radio.

"All clear back here. Let's move out."

The head of the column leaped forward, and row by row, each segment followed until Eleanor's van roared ahead. They moved through the encampment at high speed and drove through the perimeter gate without slowing, merging into single file as they streamed into the narrow English road.

"How far away is it?" Watkins asked.

"Five miles," Hobbes said. "You two ready to do your thing?"

"We're still not even sure what our thing is," Eleanor said. "We've never attempted anything like what you're asking. We've never tried to directly *communicate* with the intelligence."

"You'll have time to figure it out," Hobbes said.

"We have a secondary installation at the site. You three will stay there. Get the feel of things. We want to get this right."

"What if we can't?" Eleanor asked.

Hobbes shook his head. "Not an option."

"What do you mean?" Eleanor said. "That's not—"

"If I may," Watkins said. "Hobbes, you are accustomed to throwing yourself against a problem until it gives way. But brute force will not work here. We are doing a job you cannot do and don't understand, so you feel disadvantaged. But blindly throwing your weight around, making demands, isn't going to produce results. It will simply make this more difficult than it already is."

Hobbes craned his neck and looked back at Watkins, then Eleanor. "You'll figure something out, Watkins. You always do."

Eleanor stared at him until he turned back around.

They drove through some of the same countryside Eleanor had crossed on foot before heading a few miles into new territory. They had to be getting close to the site. Eleanor had worked to keep the ship's intelligence out of her head, but as they drew closer to it, she became aware of its shadow growing in the corners of her mind. She remembered it strangling her thoughts, choking the life out of her. Cold dread reached down her back at the thought of confronting it again, and if she allowed herself to think of the rogue planet beyond it, her dread became terror.

Hobbes pointed toward the horizon ahead of them. "The ship will come into view in a moment."

Eleanor watched for it, her stomach as tight as her fists as they followed the contours of the land, rising up and down, and then rounded a bend.

And then she saw it.

"Good Lord," Watkins whispered.

It was even larger than Eleanor had imagined it, the size of a small skyscraper, or perhaps even bigger than that. It was hard to tell. Her mind found it difficult to hold the black ship in one thought. Dozens, perhaps hundreds of spiny legs protruded from its central mass, all bent at impossible angles. Some of them had clawed deep into the ground. It reminded Eleanor of the pictures of invasive cancer cells she'd seen in biology class. Everything about it screamed into her eyes that it was wrong, and it should not be there. She felt the visceral need to run from it, to be as far away from it as she possibly could be, as if her prehistoric ancestors cried out in warning from somewhere deep inside her.

"You're shaking," Eleanor's mom said, putting her arm around her.

Eleanor looked down at her body, her hands. She hadn't realized she was shaking, but she couldn't stop.

"You get used to it," Hobbes said.

"You get used to that ship?" Watkins asked.

Hobbes seemed to be reconsidering. "Well, somewhat."

As they drove closer to it, the ship loomed larger, its legs stretching up and over them, bringing them into its shadow. It wasn't until they had reached the UN station near the ship that she even noticed the Stonehenge monument at its feet. Next to the alien spacecraft, the megaliths appeared small, the achievement of their prehistoric architects nothing more than that of children playing with blocks.

"The stones are an average of thirteen feet tall and weigh twenty-five tons," Hobbes said, following Eleanor's gaze.

She looked again, scaling up. "The ship is a dozen times the size of those stones."

"Sometimes it looks even taller," Hobbes said. "Come on, let's show you around."

Eleanor was the last to get out of the van, and she did so very slowly, without taking her eyes from the ship. Even more than the Concentrators, this alien presence filled her with disquiet, and not simply because of its size. Eleanor felt an aggression and contempt radiating from it that had nothing to do with the intelligence lurking inside. The ship itself seemed to challenge the worth of the human species simply by its being there.

The sight of it stole away what little confidence Eleanor had felt. They wouldn't be confronting the intelligence out in the open this time. They would be attacking its fortress.

"Come," Hobbes said. "Let me show you around."

The UN facility they had come from held a fraction of the tents that made up its larger counterpart here in the shadow of the alien ship. Those that Eleanor could see into seemed to be entirely filled with scientific equipment. Beyond the tents there were floodlights waiting for darkness to shine. There were also a dozen or more tanks, their gun barrels aimed up at the ship.

Eleanor's mom gestured toward them. "I thought you were trying not to provoke the aliens."

"We haven't blown it up yet, have we?" Hobbes said.

"Assuming you could," Watkins added.

Hobbes scoffed at that, and then said, "Your sleeping quarters are this way."

He walked off, and as Eleanor went to follow him, her mom touched her arm. "You've been very quiet."

Eleanor glanced up at the ship, and then quickly away. "I'm fine."

"I try not to look at it," her mom said. "If I stare for too long, it's like my mind gets stuck trying to figure it out. Is it organic? Inorganic? Is it insect? Aquatic? It defies categorization."

"It's . . . none of that."

"It reminds me of what philosophers have said about gazing into the abyss."

"Dr. Perry," Hobbes said. "Eleanor. This way."

Eleanor turned toward him where he waited with Watkins, and then the four of them continued their tour of the facility. Aside from the tanks, the soldiers had very little presence here. It seemed all the personnel belonged to some branch of science or government. When they reached their tent, Eleanor expected to find another cage, but there wasn't one. Just the cots and sleeping bags, but there were a lot of them. It seemed they would be sharing the space with others.

"Now that you've seen some of the operation," Hobbes said, "let's move closer to the ship. I'd like your assessment."

"Can it wait?" Eleanor's mom said. Eleanor could tell that her mother knew the alien ship was affecting her, working its way into her mind. "You should give her some time to adjust."

Eleanor wondered where that show of concern had been back in Cairo. She didn't need her mom to look out for her anymore, after everything Eleanor had done on her own.

"I don't have that time to give her," Hobbes said.

"What good will it do if she's overwhelmed?" her mom asked.

"It's okay," Eleanor said. "I'm ready."

"So am I," Watkins said. "Lead the way, Hobbes."

They left the sleeping quarters behind and walked away from the encampment, passed the ring of tanks, toward Stonehenge, which stood a few hundred meters away. As they walked, Eleanor kept her eyes on the ground and shored up her mental defenses, trying to keep her mind contained so she didn't alert the ship's intelligence.

They passed the first of the alien legs where it stabbed deep into the ground, thick as a lamppost. It reminded Eleanor of the Concentrator's trunk, and the closer they got to the ship, the more of them there were, creating a forest. Then they crossed the low remnant of a raised earthen ring that encircled the monument, before finally approaching the towering stones. Above Stonehenge, the ship had already swallowed them into its presence.

Hobbes pulled a handheld sensor out of one of his pockets. "The ambient temperature around the ship is always five degrees warmer than it is back in the camp."

"It's the earth's telluric energy." Watkins laid a hand on one of the megaliths. "The ship must be drawing it up through its legs, just as the Concentrators did."

Eleanor added, "I bet that's also how it plugged into the network of ley lines and took control." Somehow the ship's intelligence had traveled along those lines, or at least used them to communicate with the World Tree.

Eleanor turned her attention to Stonehenge. The earth here almost vibrated with current. The monument's prehistoric builders had placed it over a nexus of ley lines, which Eleanor could only assume must have been intentional. Perhaps these massive stones had somehow interacted with the ley lines, a kind of primitive energy control center, just as the ancient Egyptians had harnessed their own Concentrator's power.

"Impressive, isn't it?" Watkins said. "How they cut these stones, brought them here, and stood them up."

"Very impressive," Eleanor's mother said.

It was hard for Eleanor to get too excited about it with the ship bearing down on her.

"I'm going to check things out," she said.

Watkins stepped toward her. "I'll come with you."

"Be careful, sweetie," her mother said.

Eleanor turned toward her. "Maybe it would be better if you stayed here."

Her mother opened her mouth as if to say something, but then just nodded. It wasn't that Eleanor thought there would be any imminent danger. She simply found her mother's worry irritating, the wrong concern at the wrong time, and she didn't need to be told to be careful every two minutes. Eleanor turned to Hobbes. "It would be better if you stayed over here, too."

"Not a chance," he said, marching right past Eleanor and Watkins toward the ship.

Watkins shrugged and followed after him, and so did Eleanor after exchanging another glance with her mom. They exited Stonehenge on the far side, and approached a side of the ship devoid of legs, where there appeared to be a kind of portal near the ground. It reminded Eleanor of the mouth of an octopus in the middle of its tentacles.

Watkins rubbed his chin. "This appears as if it might be a hatch."

"That's what we assumed," Hobbes said. "But there doesn't seem to be any way to open it."

Eleanor studied its size and shape: an oval three

times as tall as Hobbes. She wondered if that's how large the beings who had built the ship were. Next to the hatch, she spotted a console panel similar to those the Concentrators each had. That would be a potential point of connection with the ship's intelligence, when they felt ready to attempt it. But before they did anything, she wanted to have a thorough look at it.

"I'm going to walk around," she said, leaving the hatch behind.

Watkins and Hobbes fell in beside her, and they traveled a wide path around the ship, mapping the dozens of legs digging into the ground, trying to gain a better understanding of the ship's elusive geometry. The trip around it took quite some time, and its legs appeared to have pulled its belly tight against the ground, as if a precaution against removal. When they reached the hatch where they had started, Eleanor turned and peered into the megaliths of Stonehenge, and saw her mother sitting on one of the fallen stones.

"What do you think?" Hobbes asked.

"This is quite unlike the Concentrators," Watkins said. "It has a different character. A different purpose."

"What would you guess its purpose to be?" Hobbes asked.

"I don't think we can even imagine what its purpose is," Eleanor said. "I think you would have to have the mind of an alien to really understand it."

Hobbes folded his arms. "Can you connect with it?"

Eleanor looked at the console beside the hatch. The hardware was there. The question was whether she and Watkins would be strong enough. But even if they were, she wasn't sure yet whether she wanted to just open it up for Hobbes. She had to figure out if she could destroy the intelligence first.

"I think we should wait until we're rested," Watkins said. "The process is extremely taxing, and we may only get one chance at it."

Hobbes didn't like that answer, and his heavy scowl showed it. "Tomorrow morning, then. This is your only chance."

━ CHAPTER ━
22

HOBBES GAVE ELEANOR AND WATKINS NO OPPORTUNITY to confer privately after that. He stayed by their side for the rest of that afternoon and evening as they did some more exploring of Stonehenge and ate another meal of field rations, and then Eleanor, her mom, and Watkins went to bed in a tent full of strangers. But the strangers didn't bother Eleanor.

It was the alien ship that kept her awake.

Every time she closed her eyes, she saw it, and even when her eyes were open, its presence never left her mind, nothing between her and it but a thin stretch of canvas. She could almost sense something reaching for her, crawling along the currents in the ground beneath her cot. If she remained alert, she would be able to fight it off. If she fell asleep, she would be vulnerable.

But she could not stay awake forever.

Eleanor stood at the base of what appeared to be a mountain, but it wasn't made of rock and earth. Endless nested ducts and pipes seemed to twist and writhe across its steep and angular facets liked exposed muscle. It rose to the height of a true mountain—a black, pyramidal massif that dominated the horizon, and something called to Eleanor from its summit, where she saw a distant green light. She would have to climb to find out what waited for her up there, but as she stepped toward it, she heard a noise behind her, a kind of metallic whine.

She glanced back. Then she screamed.

The thing coming toward her was a monstrous creature of spindly legs and snapping jaws, but it moved with mechanical intention, not fully alive, and at the end of its arms it had four circular saws that preceded it at different angles. Eleanor knew intuitively the purpose of those blades. To the beings who had created this sentry, dismemberment was the ultimate violence, to be separated from the being of which you were only a part.

She turned and ran, but the machine clicked and

clattered after her with surprising speed and agility. She knew somehow her only chance of escape would be to reach the summit of the mountain, so she raced up the side, scrambling and slipping and nearly falling more than once.

Once she had achieved a modest height, the sentry gave up its chase and returned to its post at the mountain's base. Eleanor allowed herself a few moments of rest, looking out over a shadow landscape thick with spires and spines as far as she could see, ash-swept and utterly empty except for automated, perpetual machines. A world-city constructed outside Eleanor's understanding, made dark and impenetrable by her own mind as she simply gave up trying to comprehend it.

Swarms of alien ships flew through the air, and storms of static crackled across the surface, striking the ground with lightning and filling the air with the smell of ozone as the planet moved through space, the stars overhead unrecognizable from those where the world had been born. The earth was out there, a distant, pale blue dot, and Eleanor realized she stood upon the rogue planet, the only truly living thing on that entire world, separated from her home by a vast expanse of cold space.

But she wasn't alone.

The mountain's summit still called to her, wordless but forceful and absolutely clear. The silent observer she had sensed back in the Himalayas. Something up there needed her help.

When Eleanor awoke, she felt as though something had just whispered in her ear, near her head, its fleeting presence retreating before she could rouse herself to grab hold of it. She sat up, the tent dark, letting her know it was still the middle of the night. She listened. All was quiet. Then she lay back down, thinking about what she had just dreamed.

She felt as if she had been shown something.

By something.

But it hadn't come from the ship's intelligence, which she would have recognized instantly. This new presence must have been what she'd felt before she drifted off to sleep. The silent observer. It had reached her through the network of ley lines. It had shown her something it wanted her to see. It had called to her from the summit of that mountain. It wanted her to come to it. It needed her, and she no longer felt quite so alone.

She immediately brushed that thought aside. It seemed too ridiculous. An impossibility. It was a dream, after all. But hadn't this all been impossible, like a dream? The question kept her awake, her mind filled with the image of the black mechanical mountain, its distant flicker of green light.

The only other time she had experienced anything like this was when she'd had a vision at the base of the first Concentrator she found, in the Arctic beneath the ice. That had felt real, too, and she now understood better where it had come from. Her sleeping mind must have inadvertently connected with the intelligence in the Concentrator, and she'd been given a glimpse of its workings and where it had come from.

But if that had been real, was this?

She'd been sleeping practically on top of the most connected place on the planet, where all its energy coalesced, and the alien ship was plugged directly into it. If something not of this world was trying to reach her, this would be the place to do it. But why would something from the rogue planet try to reach her at all? And why would it need her help?

This presence hadn't felt like any of the alien intelligences she had encountered. It held no hostility toward her, and she felt certain its purpose wasn't to harm. Maybe it was a peaceful part of the rogue world. Maybe it was a prisoner of the rogue planet, and it needed her to break it free. Whatever it was, Eleanor believed it possible that the presence could help her, just as she could help it. Maybe it could even offer her a way to end the Freeze.

A light bobbed outside, coming quickly toward the tent, and then someone walked in shining a flashlight. The bright beam flashed over Eleanor's face, blinding her for a moment.

"Turn that light out," someone muttered from the other side of the tent.

"I need Hobbes," the woman with the flashlight said.

Eleanor heard Hobbes mutter something she couldn't understand, and then he asked, "Why?"

"It's the ship," the woman said. "We've got activity."

A second passed, and then Hobbes was on his feet. "I need Jeffries and Ntaba, now." Then he turned to Eleanor and Watkins. "I guess you're up to bat."

Eleanor knew it wasn't a coincidence that the alien ship had become active after her dream, but she wasn't going to say anything to anyone yet. She climbed out of bed, and her mother stood up beside her, her mouth open as if she was about to say something. But then she didn't, and Eleanor knew she'd been about to tell her to be careful and had caught herself, but now she didn't know what to say.

"Don't worry," Eleanor said. "I will be."

Her mom smiled.

"Shall we?" Watkins said, moving stiffly toward the exit.

Eleanor nodded and followed him, wondering what kind of dreams he might have had.

Outside, Eleanor looked up at the ship. Spotlights did their best to illuminate its surface, but with the spacecraft's legs and angles, it only appeared to be covered in more chaotic and shifting shadows. But lights had also come on within the ship. They glowed in clusters that gave the impression of spider eyes.

"You two." Hobbes actually snapped his fingers at Eleanor and Watkins. "Stay with me."

He marched toward the tents where all the scientific equipment could be found, and as Eleanor and Watkins followed after him, her mom close behind, she asked the old man whether he'd just had an unusual dream.

"Not that I can recall," he said. "Why?"

"I'm not sure yet," Eleanor said.

As they neared the first tent, a scientist approached Hobbes with a stack of readouts that didn't appear to have been organized yet.

"Status?" Hobbes said.

The scientist, a middle-aged Asian man, cleared his throat. "Thirteen minutes ago, we detected a surge on the infrared monitors."

"The ship is heating up?" Watkins asked.

"Parts of it are," the scientist said. "Then its lights came on, and our sensors detected subaudible vibrations from inside. Things are moving."

"What kind of things?" Eleanor asked.

"Unclassifiable," he said. "It also appears some of the legs may have shifted, but we'll have to cross-check with previous imaging to confirm. There's just so many of them."

Hobbes nodded. "Let me know what you find out."

The scientist returned to his work, and Hobbes pulled Eleanor and Watkins aside. Eleanor's mom stood behind her, leaning forward to listen in.

"Any idea what's going on here?" Hobbes asked.

"None," Watkins said.

"It looks like something woke it up." And Eleanor believed she knew exactly what it was, which meant she had no more doubt whether what she had experienced had been a dream. There was a mountain up there on the rogue planet. She was sure of it.

"Do you have any idea what it's doing?" Hobbes asked. "What it's going to do?"

Neither Eleanor nor Watkins had an answer to give him.

"But this sudden activity does appear neutral thus far," Watkins said. "Neither hostile nor defensive."

"Can you be sure of that?" Hobbes asked.

"Of course not."

Hobbes turned to face the ship, staring up at it with his arms folded, chewing on a thumbnail. Eleanor wondered what options he might be considering, as she considered hers. The feeling had only grown more intense that something up there needed her help. But if she were to even entertain the idea of answering the call of the black mountain, there would be only one way to reach it, and in that moment, Hobbes had a bunch of tanks pointed at it.

"I think we can get inside it," she said. "And I think we should try."

Watkins looked at her in surprise.

"Why do you say that?" Hobbes asked.

"Right now, it could be getting a weapon ready, or it could be firing up its engines to return to the rogue planet—and who knows what'll happen then." She pointed up at the ship. "The only way to know is to go inside and find out what it's doing."

Hobbes regarded Eleanor askance for a few moments. "When?"

"Now," Eleanor said. "We can try to get in now, while there's time, and if it doesn't work, you have . . . other options." She nodded toward the tanks.

"What do you think, Watkins?" Hobbes asked.

"I—" Watkins looked at Eleanor, and Eleanor gave him a nod. "I will defer to Eleanor," he said.

"Then let's do this." Hobbes set off toward the ship, and Eleanor followed him. As they walked, Watkins leaned in close to Eleanor, and she knew he was about to ask her what she was doing. Before he could, she whispered, "Just trust me," and that seemed to appease him for the moment.

Stonehenge had a haunted quality about it at night, the standing stones like gray ghosts as they walked among them to the ship's hatch. Eleanor stood before it, and tried to mentally prepare for the task at hand by clearing her mind, focusing on taking deep breaths.

"Linguistics, report to the ship," Hobbes ordered into his handheld radio. "Tactical, set up a perimeter, full contingency. We don't know what might come through the door once we get it open."

"That won't be necessary," Eleanor said.

"What makes you say that?" Hobbes asked.

"The ship is empty."

"How do you know?"

"I just have a feeling."

Hobbes spoke into his radio again. "Tactical, bring around five Scout tanks. I don't want to take any chances. Hobbes, out." He put the radio away and said to Eleanor, "I trust my own paranoia over your feelings."

Eleanor resisted rolling her eyes at him and returned her attention to the ship. Her mom stood on her left side, and Watkins stood on the right. None of them spoke, and then the linguistics team and soldiers began to arrive, and Hobbes stepped away to give them orders.

"What is this?" Watkins asked, quickly and quietly.

"We're boarding the ship."

"And what is your plan for the intelligence?"

"We kill it," Eleanor said.

"What about Hobbes?" Watkins said. "His fear of provocation?"

"It won't matter," Eleanor said. She decided not to tell them about her plan because she was still forming it, and because she couldn't risk what might happen if they objected, and Hobbes overheard.

"I think it might matter to Hobbes," Watkins said. "He was—"

"I know what I'm doing," Eleanor said just as Hobbes returned.

"We should be set up in ten minutes," he said. "Then you can open the ship."

Eleanor heard the sound of engines, and she saw

the tanks pulling up, their guns now aimed disconcertingly at the ship's hatch, right where she was standing. Nearer to them, the linguists had set up a temporary workstation with several computers for recording and analysis. None of their efforts would be necessary, but she watched and waited until Hobbes was satisfied.

"We're ready," he said. Then he took a place next to Eleanor, and she noted a change in his body language and posture. He seemed somewhat distracted, checking and adjusting his uniform, and he kept patting one of his pockets. Eleanor wondered what he was hiding.

She leaned toward Watkins. "Are you ready?"

"I believe I am," he said. "We approach this as we did before?"

"Yes."

Together, they stepped up to the control panel beside the hatch. Its contours looked familiar, and it appeared to be made of the same metal as the Concentrators. Then they raised their hands, and with a nod to each other, they laid their palms against the console.

It felt as if the ship's intelligence had been waiting for them. It lashed out almost as soon as she attempted to enter its space, raking her mind with claws and fangs. She recoiled from it, back into her bedroom, until she found her bearings and pushed back.

"Watkins, are you here?"

"I am where you last found me."

Eleanor worked to summon the memories that had allowed her to join her strength with his before, to feel the isolation and pain that they shared. She left the safety of her bedroom and found the scared and lonely boy hiding in the same janitor's closet. She brought him out, and together with him felt even stronger than she had the last time.

They faced the ship's intelligence, and they attacked.

Right away, this battle felt different from the others. The alien mind had a certain arrogance that those in the Concentrators had lacked. They had felt more desperate, weakened by thousands of years in exile on earth. This one had an undeniable will and single-mindedness.

"This one is a fighter," Watkins said.

A fighter. Maybe that was it. The previous intelligences had been created to inhabit and run the Concentrators. This one had been sent down to bring the system back under control. Like an enforcer, it was built to fight. But what would a fighter do without an opponent?

"Wait," she said. "Let's try easing up for a second."

"Easing up?

"Just try it."

So they did, and they found that as they relaxed their assault, their opponent relaxed its defenses.

"It's like a finger trap," Eleanor said. "The harder we fight, the harder it fights."

"Then we must keep it thinking we aren't here to fight."

"Let's just sit still and see what happens."

They went quiet and idled in that void space within the ship's machinery. It was the first time Eleanor had ever been able to really reflect on the experience of being inside, and she found it like an extreme form of daydreaming, or even reading a book. Her body was in one place, but her mind was somewhere else.

The intelligence waited in front of them, poised, ready to pounce. Eleanor sensed its nature, its existence one of caged dormancy until called upon to fight.

"We need to sneak up on it," Eleanor said.

"How?"

"We move slowly. Patiently. It's basically a guard dog. If it gets used to us, we might be able to get past it."

"I doubt Hobbes will be very patient."

"He doesn't have a choice now. All he can do is watch and wait."

So minutes passed in the void. Perhaps even hours. Eleanor lost the sense of time, focusing all her attention on the enforcer. Gradually, its posture changed, like a mass of shadow softening around the edges. She sensed it relaxing, allowing them to creep closer, and closer, and closer, until they were almost on top of it.

They waited a bit longer, and then they fell at once upon it, crushing it with the weight of their combined minds. The surprised enforcer had no time to marshal a defense, though it tried, but they were able to tame it, pinning it down until it submitted to them. Eleanor felt it go slack beneath them, and when they released it, the enforcer retreated deep into the void, perhaps finding a distant recess in the ship's machinery to hide.

"That's it," Eleanor said. Now they could reach into the unguarded space with their minds, and it was like the entire ship flowed in, the controls at their disposal.

She could feel Watkins's satisfaction, which matched her own. "The ship is ours."

— CHAPTER —
23

ELEANOR SEPARATED HERSELF FROM WATKINS AND OPENED her eyes, but she left her palm against the console. Watkins stood beside her, and when she looked behind her, she saw her mother and Hobbes standing by. Having driven off the ship's enforcer, she took control of the hatch and opened it with a thought.

The oval span split down the middle, where there hadn't been a seam, and became a spreading chasm of darkness. Eleanor stepped in front of it, feeling a rush of cold, sterile air pour over her, while all the people behind her stirred, and some of them gasped.

"They did it," Hobbes said.

A moment later, he was standing beside Eleanor,

staring into the opening, fidgeting—as if he expected an alien to emerge from it at any moment and he already had a speech prepared.

"The ship is empty," Eleanor said.

He barely glanced at her, and scowled as if she were distracting him, patting whatever he had in his pocket with one hand, and his holstered sidearm with the other.

Watkins joined them, followed by Eleanor's mom, while the linguists and soldiers hung back. Several moments went by, and no alien appeared. Hobbes's expression turned to one of puzzlement, then to frustration, and Eleanor sensed that if she did not act soon, she would lose her chance.

"I'll need you, Watkins," she said. Then she walked straight toward the opening.

"Eleanor?" her mom said. "Sweetie, what are you doing?"

Eleanor reached the border of shadow and crossed it without hesitation, entering the ship.

"Eleanor!" her mom shouted.

Then Eleanor heard Hobbes swear and start shouting into his radio.

Eleanor kept moving. With each step, her eyes adjusted to the relative darkness, revealing more of the ship. She walked down a corridor as wide and tall as the hatch, but her footsteps didn't echo, as if the space simply swallowed all sound. The surface of the floor and the walls, while solid to the touch, appeared viscous, like a flowing river of crude oil lit from within by a pale, ambient glow. The air smelled of nothing.

"Eleanor?" Watkins said behind her, sounding almost frightened.

She turned around and saw his approaching silhouette against the light from outside.

"I'm here," she said.

"What—what are you doing?"

"I'm taking the ship up to the rogue world."

He said nothing.

Beyond Watkins, she could see that her mom and Hobbes had entered through the hatch as well. Eleanor resumed her journey inward. Her connection with the console outside had given her an understanding of the ship's layout, and she knew where to find the pilot's cockpit.

"Eleanor!" Hobbes said. "Don't take one more step!"

"Sweetie, please!" her mom said. "Come back!"

Eleanor scurried ahead. If she moved quickly, soon there wouldn't be anything they could do to stop her. Numerous chambers opened off the main corridor, and the passage forked several times into side channels, but eventually Eleanor reached a ramp leading up to the ship's cockpit. As she climbed up and stepped inside it, she thought of Luke, and wished he were there to appreciate what she was seeing.

A tall, wraparound window offered views of Stonehenge and the surrounding countryside from high above, as well as the rest of the ship and its myriad jointed legs reaching out and down into the ground.

The pilot's chair, if it could be called a chair, had clearly not been made with human dimensions or shape in mind. It looked like something that had been brought up from the bottom of the ocean, sculpted by the sand and the endless currents, a sprawling and graceful repository for a living thing Eleanor couldn't imagine. A central console rose up on a pedestal before it, and Eleanor crossed the room to stand in front of it. Aside from these central features, the cockpit had no other features, the walls like those in the rest of the ship.

A blade of spotlight sliced across the window. No doubt the UN soldiers knew Eleanor had gone into the ship. No doubt they still had their tanks and guns pointed at it. At her. But they wouldn't shoot if Hobbes was on board. Eleanor doubted the inferior technology of their guns could do much damage anyway.

She looked down at the console, and laid both her palms against it.

The ship came alive at her touch, but not in the way of the Concentrators she had dealt with. This was simply a responsive tool, not an intelligence, and it waited for her to accept what it offered. Eleanor took a breath, and let the ship into her mind.

The sudden rush of information staggered her, and she gasped, nearly breaking away from the console. But after a moment, her mind began to adjust to it, and when she looked up, the blank walls and window of the cockpit had been replaced and overlayed with bright, glowing imagery she couldn't understand. There were charts and maps of stars, readouts from different parts of the ship, messages in a language as indecipherable as the architecture of the Concentrators.

"Eleanor!" she heard Hobbes shout. He was getting closer, and would find his way in here any moment. "I don't know what you think you're doing!"

Eleanor knew exactly what she was doing. She reached her mind into the ship, as she had done with the Concentrators. She mentally returned down the corridor through which she'd come, and she found the main hatch. Watkins, her mom, and Hobbes were on board—the ship could sense their movements—and Eleanor hoped that at least her mom and Watkins would forgive her.

She shut the main hatch, sealing them all in.

Then she brought her mind back up to the cockpit.

"Eleanor!" Hobbes shouted.

He was very close now, marching up the ramp toward her, and she looked over her shoulder just as his head snarled into view.

"Kid, you are entering a world of hurt," he said.

Eleanor reached with her mind toward the cockpit door.

"This is—"

She closed the door just as Hobbes reached it, the last look on his face one of fearful fury.

Eleanor smiled to herself. No one would bother her now. No one would stop her from doing what she needed to do. That was all she had wanted from the beginning.

Eleanor turned her attention back to the ship's main controls, and the elegant, prismatic displays that danced in front of her. She still couldn't make sense of them, but hoped she would be able to connect with the ship without them. She had to trust that the DNA she carried would make her compatible enough to fly it. Into space.

Into space.

If Eleanor's hands had not been pressed up against the console, she knew they would have been shaking.

Now that she had sealed herself into the cockpit, she could hear her own heartbeat thumping through the silence.

"I can do this," she said aloud.

But she didn't know how. Even if she could figure out how to get this ship into the air, how would she know where to go? From the surface of the earth, whole planets looked like specks. Space was big. So big the word became meaningless. How in all that vastness would she find the rogue world and the black mountain that had called to her for—?

She stopped.

A call.

That was the answer. The ship had to have some way to communicate. Perhaps Eleanor could use it to contact the rogue world. The black mountain. Something there had reached out to her. Why couldn't she reach back?

She went back into the ship's systems, proceeding by feel with her mind, exploring its different functions, letting the ship guide her when it could. But stuff wasn't exactly labeled in stencil, like GIANT ALIEN PROPULSION THING, or THERMAL EXHAUST PORT. Eleanor didn't have the ship's vocabulary, and the ship didn't have hers. But it *had* connected with her mind to a certain degree. What if it could sense what she wanted?

Eleanor closed her eyes and imagined the black mountain as she had seen it in her dream. She recalled its shape, its texture, its height as it rose above the world-city. She imagined the green light at its summit, and the call for help that had come to her. She tried to send back a message of her own, as simple a pure thought as she could form, one rooted in the only thing she really knew.

I'm here.

She pushed this thought with her mind toward that green light in her memory, and suddenly a new display glimmered before her with scrolling, oscillating waves of color. A moment after that, she felt a familiar presence approaching her, and if a mind could have a voice, this voice sounded like the one she had heard in her dream.

I'm here, she thought again.

The black mountain responded immediately. She felt it move through the ship, and then the ship moved into action. Deep within its core, the giant alien propulsion thing surged with power, sending minor shock waves through the floors and walls. Out the window, Eleanor saw the ship's legs extracting themselves from the ground, sending dirt and debris flying. The UN soldiers and staff scurried to safety as the legs bent up and folded inward, like a spider's when tucked away deep in its funneled lair. The ship was preparing to fly.

Eleanor didn't know exactly where they were going, or how they would return. She thought of her uncle Jack, and it broke her heart to be leaving him behind again.

"Good-bye," she whispered to him, hoping that somehow he could hear it the way she had heard him when she was lost underground.

A deep and resonant drone rose up from beneath Eleanor's feet, thrumming the bones of the ship, and the vessel up into the air. Eleanor maintained hand contact with the console, even though she wasn't exactly in control of the ship anymore, and watched out the window as they ascended. The fields and pastures below grew smaller and became a kind of geometric abstract painting. The ship soon reached the height at which *Consuelo* had flown them around the world— tough, reliable *Consuelo*—and then rose even higher.

The horizon began to bend, as if a strongman had taken one end in each hand, and Eleanor watched the sun rise against the curvature of the earth, spreading light over a globe of white, brown, and blue, gauzed in the thin haze of its atmosphere.

How many people in the history of the world had seen their home this way? Before the Freeze, Eleanor had heard that kids dreamed of growing up to become astronauts. There were no astronauts anymore, and that wish had never been Eleanor's. Yet here she was, in space.

Over time, the earth grew smaller, and soon, the entire world fit within the frame of the ship's window, and Eleanor could see the white of the glaciers covering half its surface as though someone simply taken an eraser to the image.

Suddenly, the ship spun, sweeping the earth from Eleanor's window, pointing her in a new direction. The droning of the engine then fell to a lower note, and the ship launched itself forward, though it was hard to tell how much faster it was traveling now without something to give her reference. The stars seemed not to move at all, and Eleanor couldn't see the earth's moon, but she scanned the section of space ahead for signs of the rogue world.

Minutes passed. She heard a pounding on the door outside, but eventually, her mom or Hobbes or whoever it was gave up, and Eleanor did her best not to think about them.

Hours passed.

Eleanor became tired, and wished the seat behind her had been designed with human anatomy in mind, so that she could sit down. As it was, she couldn't find a comfortable position anywhere on it to rest.

And still the ship flew on. Into nothing. Nothing changing.

Eleanor slowly realized that the pictures of the solar system from her science classes were a lie. They got the scale completely wrong. They weren't like marbles rolling around out here. She would have been able to see marbles. They were more like motes of dust, barely visible from one to the next, with emptiness between them.

Over time, that emptiness settled a nameless dread over Eleanor's mind. A feeling of smallness and insignificance. And powerlessness. Even meaninglessness. She reached a point where she couldn't look into it anymore, and she took her eyes from the window, trying not to think about how far she was from home.

Her exhaustion increased.

All she wanted to do was lie down and shut out the void.

She even thought about removing her hands from the console, and just as she had resolved to do so, an impression intruded on her mind. The black mountain conveyed to her a feeling of urgency.

Close.

Eleanor looked out into the stars and saw nothing.

Close.

She scanned the unchanging stars. Waiting. Watching.

Until she thought she saw something. Or the absence of something, an absence that seemed to be growing. She kept her eyes on it, and soon that absence had spread, becoming a round, black pit. A hole in space.

That was the rogue world.

Lightless. Cold. All alone on its hunt, and seemingly unaware of her.

The dark planet grew in size just as the earth had shrunk, until its horizon leveled, and the blackness of its surface resolved into hideous shapes and shadows. The ship descended, flying over and through labyrinthine canyons of twisted, angular towers that appeared to have been melted, dripped, and shattered into shape. This was the world-city from her dream.

She saw no light down there, except for what reached the rogue world from her own sun, looking dimmer and weaker than it should. The alien planet seemed completely lifeless, and while she knew that to be strictly accurate, she hadn't forgotten the deadly machine that had chased her, and she shared the sky with distant swarms of ships just like the one she was piloting.

Close.

Eleanor searched the horizon for the black mountain, and soon found it, a pyramid looming over the city at its feet, its pale green light a single spark in a plain of ashes. They sailed toward it, and Eleanor felt something new from the entity that had reached out to her. A feeling Eleanor knew well, and worked hard to keep.

Hope.

She did not understand this being. It felt entirely different from the alien intelligences she had encountered. But she trusted that her questions would be answered when she reached the summit.

The ship sailed closer, the black mountain swelling in size. Eleanor wondered whether it would set them down at the base, or fly them to the summit. Of the two, she definitely—

There was an explosion, and the ship suddenly jolted and heaved, pitching sideways, throwing Eleanor from the console. She stumbled down along the angled floor, slamming hard into a wall of the cockpit. All the lights and displays had gone out as soon as her hands had lost contact with the ship, and the connection with the black mountain was now severed.

Through the window, she saw one of the other ships flying alongside her, its legs flared, pointing like daggers at Eleanor's vessel.

They were under attack.

Eleanor thought of her mom and Watkins, praying they were okay on the other side of the door, and then labored to her feet. She had to get back up to the console and regain control.

She scrambled and climbed up the floor until she was able to grab the base of the console, hook her elbow around it, and then slowly pull herself to her feet. As soon as she was in position, she smacked both her palms against the console, desperate to talk to the ship.

The connection failed. And failed again.

She had to concentrate, somehow, while the ship barreled ahead halfway on its side. She spared a moment for deep breath, and another to close her eyes, and then she tried again. This time, it worked, and she welcomed the flood of the ship into her mind. The lights and displays came back up across her vision, many of them flashing urgently, some having simply gone dark.

The black mountain was still there, too, in the ship and on the horizon.

Close.

"Close?" Eleanor shouted aloud. "How is that supposed to be helpful?"

She tried to reach with her mind for the ship's navigation, but it was either damaged or beyond her ability to control, because she couldn't do anything to change their trajectory. She was able to right the ship by shifting her weight and stance within her mind, and then she dug in her heels to slow their descent as much as she could. Even so, it didn't matter.

They were going down.

─ CHAPTER ─
24

ELEANOR COULDN'T MOVE. TERRIFIED OF WHAT SHE MIGHT see, she opened her eyes and looked down at her body. But her body wasn't there. Or it was, but it was encased in some kind of rigid foam. Where had *that* come from?

She was lying on her side against the cockpit's forward bulkhead, beneath the window. The impact of the crash must have thrown her there, and whatever this foam stuff was, it seemed to have cushioned her, probably saving her life.

Had it come from the ship? Some kind of alien airbag?

And how was she supposed to get out of it?

She tried to wiggle, and couldn't, so she put everything she had into bending at the waist, hoping to just crack the stuff open, but even then she couldn't escape it.

"Survive the crash," she said. "Then death by Styrofoam."

Something made a crumbling noise, like sand. She looked down and saw that some of the foam had started deteriorating. Just crumbling away and disintegrating. She tried to move again, and this time she could. The foam fractured and broke and turned to dust as she fought her way out of it, and by the time she was on her feet, there was only a trace of it left on the floor.

"So I guess that actually works pretty well," she said, patting the console. "Sorry for doubting you."

Through the window, she could see the black mountain in the distance, perhaps a few miles away. It was hard to judge the distance here. The architecture of the world-city that surrounded her shifted and dodged in her vision the same as everything else the aliens had built, and she wasn't looking forward to crossing any distance of it.

But first she needed to turn her attention to the cockpit door, which was sealed shut. When she laid her palms on the console to open it, she feared there would be no response. But as she connected with the ship, it reached back. Almost all its systems had gone dark, but there was basic power to central areas of the ship. She almost felt like she had to be careful in the wreckage with her mind as she reached to find the cockpit door, and she worried that it might not open. But it did.

Eleanor pulled her hands away from the console and turned around.

Her mother stood in the doorway, and of all the looks Eleanor had ever seen on her mom's face after all the stupid things Eleanor had ever done, she had never seen a look like this. Eyes open wide, mouth open wide, forehead twisted up. At first, Eleanor thought it was simply disbelief, but almost immediately worried it was anger, and her mom was so furious she just couldn't say anything.

Behind her, Hobbes made his feelings clear. "I'm glad to know you're not hurt, kid. Because I want to see to that personally."

"What are you going to do, Hobbes?" Watkins stepped out from behind the soldier. "She's a child. And we've just crashed on an unfamiliar planet in the depths of space. I think we have other things to worry about."

Eleanor's mom finally blinked. "Eleanor, how did you—"

"Mom, I had to. There was no other way."

"No . . . other way?"

"We're not going to have this conversation here," Hobbes said. "Eleanor is going to open that hatch, and we're going to exit this ship so that my team can get to work." He pointed at Eleanor. "Then we'll deal with *you*."

His statement puzzled Eleanor. "Your team?"

"That's right, my team." Hobbes shook his head. "Haven't you been paying attention? What do you think this is, some kind of—"

"Hobbes," Watkins said, wide eyes now focused past Eleanor, over her shoulder.

"Don't interrupt me, Watkins—"

"Look outside."

Hobbes glanced. Then he stared, and apparently forgot what he had been about to say.

Eleanor looked to see what had drawn their attention. Through the cockpit window she saw the world-city and the black mountain, just as they had been several moments ago. But then it occurred to her. The ship had no other windows than this one. With the cockpit door shut, she had been the only one who knew what was happening.

Eleanor realized then that her mom had been surprised, not angry, and it had simply taken longer for

340

Watkins and Hobbes to notice the view.

"Where—" Hobbes stepped up closer to the window, looking out. "Tell me this is a television screen."

"It's not," Eleanor said. "We're here."

"Where?" Hobbes asked.

"The rogue world," Watkins said, a grin spreading. "You clever girl."

"I can't believe this," Eleanor's mom said. "How—?"

"I connected with the ship," Eleanor said. "But before that, something up there contacted me." She pointed out the window, toward the summit of the black mountain. "It wasn't like the Concentrators or anything else. It needed help."

"Excuse me, help?" Hobbes pressed his thumb and index finger against his squinted eyes. "You're telling me you hijacked this ship and flew it into outer space because an extraterrestrial entity asked you for help?"

Eleanor thought for a moment. "Yes, that's what I'm telling you."

Watkins chuckled, and that drew the attention of Eleanor's mom.

"You think this is funny?"

"I find it amusing, yes. And absurd. And impossible. And yet, here we are." Watkins held up his hands.

Eleanor's mom shook her head, and then took Eleanor firmly by the shoulders. "Sweetie, I . . . I don't even know where to begin."

"Then let me," Eleanor said. "Last night, I saw the rogue world in a dream. I saw this city. I saw that mountain. Something up there needs me to do something. I don't know what, and I don't know how or why, but I know it has something to do with the Freeze. I . . . I was out of ideas. And I know that whatever is up there can help us. When I connected with the ship, whatever is up there took control and brought us here."

"How far did we travel?" Hobbes asked.

"A long way," Eleanor said. "The sun looks smaller from here. That's all I know."

"I might be able to estimate our position if I can get a look at the sky outside," Watkins said.

"Outside?" Eleanor's mom put her hands on her hips. "You're not suggesting we go out there."

"We have to," Eleanor said. "I have to get to the top of that mountain."

"Eleanor, listen to me," her mom said. "This is an alien world. We have no idea what dangers there are."

"I have *some* idea," Eleanor said, but decided that saying anything more about it wouldn't help the situation. "Besides. This ship is damaged. We won't be able to fly it home."

"It felt like a crash." Watkins glanced back down the corridor. "And apparently it was. The ship deployed some kind of protective casing around us."

"And now we need to move," Eleanor said. "We crashed because another ship attacked us."

"Attacked one of their own?" Hobbes said.

Eleanor nodded.

"So what are we dealing with?" Hobbes turned to Watkins. "Civil war? An insurgency?"

"You won't have any of your questions answered until we climb that mountain." Eleanor moved toward the cockpit door, but her mom stepped in front of her, preventing her from leaving.

"Sweetie, we don't even know what kind of atmosphere this planet has."

That wasn't something Eleanor had considered. In her dream, she'd stood outside, breathing just fine, but that didn't mean she could breathe on the actual planet.

"The ship's atmosphere is apparently compatible with our biochemistry." Watkins inhaled deeply through his nose. "So either the aliens who built it shared our environmental needs, or the ship was prepared for humans."

"We should just go see," Eleanor said. "I'll open the hatch, and Hobbes can use his sensor thing. I can close the hatch if I need to. Then we'll know."

The three adults looked back and forth among

themselves. They left the cockpit and found their way back down the ramp, through the corridor, to the ship's main hatch. This doorway had its own control console, and after placing her palm on it, Eleanor easily opened the door.

Hobbes stood in the rushing exchange of air with his handheld sensor, staring at the little display screen. "Seventy-eight percent nitrogen. Twenty-one percent oxygen. Other gases." He looked up from the device. "It's like earth."

"Remarkable," Watkins said. "I wouldn't have thought a rogue planet could sustain an atmosphere."

"At least we can go now," Eleanor said, growing more anxious. "Right?"

"Right." Hobbes stepped forward. "But we know there are hostiles out there. One of them brought down this ship."

"What are you saying?" Eleanor's mom asked.

Hobbes pulled his sidearm from its holster. "It means I lead the way."

In this situation, his bravado didn't bother Eleanor. He was a soldier, and the only one with a weapon. Hopefully it wouldn't be needed, but if it would, she was happy to let him go first.

Hobbes exited through the main hatch first and scanned their surroundings before motioning for the other three to follow him out. The air, though breathable, was as cold as it had been in the Himalayas. Eleanor shivered a little and followed Hobbes down a ravine-like street toward the black mountain, leaving the ship behind.

Alien structures leered to either side, their walls like melting wax, scratching and clawing at the never-ending night above them with black talons. Nothing within the buildings gave off any light, and what little sunlight reached them got mired in their vermicular surfaces. As Hobbes marched Eleanor and the others forward, sweeping the city with his gaze, they kicked up a layer of dust so deep and fine it almost looked like they were walking through knee-high fog.

"This place is a ghost town," Hobbes said.

"A ghost *world*," Watkins added.

"What do you think happened to them?" Eleanor's mom whispered.

"I don't know," Eleanor said. "But I think it happened a really long time ago."

Nevertheless, they crept along the streets, sometimes in the shadow of the world-city, sometimes in the weak light of the sun, as if they might disturb something that shouldn't be. On earth, Eleanor might have known how far they walked, and how far they had yet to go. But here, with the world shifting before

345

her eyes and in her mind, Eleanor could only keep moving, and hope they reached their destination soon.

Not far from them, a static storm raged, lighting half the sky with searing flashes. Watkins speculated that the churning clouds were made of dust. Hobbes worried it was moving in their direction, posing a danger, so he told them all to walk faster, and a short while later they turned a corner and saw the base of the mountain up ahead. The dark peak filled its corner of the sky.

"I don't suppose there's an alien elevator some-where nearby," Watkins said.

"I think we have to climb it," Eleanor said.

The old man sighed and nodded. "I'll do my best."

Eleanor looked up at the green light, the beacon on which she had staked the world. That glowing point and this mountain represented the end of her journey. She had done everything she could, and traveled as far as she could, and if this failed, there was literally nowhere else to go, and nothing else to do.

Something whined in the distance, and Eleanor recognized the sound without having to turn around.

"We need to run," she said.

Behind them, a few streets away, one of the terrible machines crawled around a corner and hurtled toward them, legs clicking, circular blades outstretched.

"Everyone behind me!" Hobbes shouted. "Eleanor, do you know what this is?"

"I saw one in my dream!"

"Hostile?"

"It's a sentry."

"What's it guarding?" Watkins asked. "There's nothing here."

"You want to stay and ask it or get out of here?" Hobbes said. "You all make a run for it. I'll bring up the rear and hold it off if I can. Now go!"

Eleanor hesitated a moment, and then turned toward the black mountain. She, her mom, and Watkins broke into a sprint, and a few paces on they heard the first gunshot, a crack that seemed to echo off every uneven surface on every building nearby, growing louder and more piercing.

Eleanor looked back as Hobbes fired another shot, and another in a controlled retreat before the machine. She couldn't tell if his bullets had done any real damage to it, but the monstrosity had slowed down.

"Come on!" she shouted to him. "Hurry!"

Then she, her mom, and Watkins started up the mountain, grasping at the mass of serpentine pipes and conduit, pulling themselves up with their hands

347

as much as their legs and feet.

Another gunshot rang out. Then three more in rapid succession.

Eleanor glanced down to see Hobbes take a running leap up the side of the mountain, the machine behind him moving considerably slower than it had been, two of its appendages dragging uselessly along the ground.

"I'm with you!" Hobbes shouted. "Keep going!"

Eleanor didn't know how closely the machine could follow with the damage it had sustained, but she continued climbing. Her mom kept pace with her, and sometimes led the way, but Watkins always trailed behind, his jaw set with pain and determination. Some distance on, Hobbes caught up with them.

"That thing is still following us," he said. "And two more just reached the base."

Eleanor looked back down the slope at the scuttling machines. "In my dream it gave up."

"These aren't," Hobbes said. "And I don't want to keep wasting bullets on them in case we need them later, so let's keep moving."

They climbed. And climbed. The mountain had folds, gaps in the pipes that snagged their toes, places where it leveled off, and spots where it was so steep they had a difficult time ascending.

"Do you remember the Great Pyramid, Eleanor?" Watkins said. "We've climbed something a bit like this before."

"I don't know that it's quite the same thing," Eleanor said. "And I think we're already much higher than that."

From her vantage point, she could see the world-city's unbroken expanse for miles and miles, a thick bramble of alien thorns stretching to the horizon in every direction. When she looked up, she saw the green light glowing brighter. Clearer. Closer.

Close.

— CHAPTER —
25

THEY WERE ALMOST THERE. BUT SO WERE THE SENTRIES, which had steadily gained ground on them in their relentless pursuit. Eleanor's mom looked exhausted, her movements sluggish, her eyes dark. Eleanor felt the same way. Her muscles had gone from burning to simply quitting without warning. Watkins bore a constant grimace, and Hobbes, the only one of them who didn't seem tired, now helped the old man with every foot he climbed.

But they were almost there.

The green light had vanished from view. At first Eleanor worried it had gone out, but she realized the top of the pyramid was flat, and the light had simply dropped behind that high horizon.

"Almost there," Eleanor's mom said, but it sounded like she may have been talking to herself.

"There better be some kind of shelter up there," Hobbes said. "Those things are right on top of us."

With her hands against the metal pipes, Eleanor could feel the vibrations caused by the sentries' rigid legs, and wondered if Hobbes would have to waste a few more bullets before they reached the top. The static storm had rolled closer, too, violent gray, and Eleanor felt the wind that drove the surge of dust toward them. If lightning struck the mountain while they were climbing it . . .

"Almost there," Eleanor said, talking to herself.

They had a hundred feet to go. Then eighty. Then fifty.

Eleanor put her head down, staring deep into the warren of pipes. Climb. Climb. Climb.

Close.

The voice was still with her, stronger as she'd drawn closer to the summit.

Climb.

Eleanor reached her hand up to grab onto the next pipe, and felt air. She looked up into the green light, and she was there. She had made it. Her mom heaved up next to her, as if tossed ashore by a storm, and they helped each other to their feet, surveying the top of the mountain.

The light shone from the top of a building shaped like a giant, thorny seashell, a calcified vortex spiraling upward. From this height, Eleanor saw even more of the empty world-city below, and though much of it looked the same as what she had already seen, there were indistinct features on the horizon. Perhaps mountains, perhaps skyscrapers, they filled Eleanor with dread.

Hobbes climbed up next, and then pulled Watkins up after him. The old man looked pale, his eyes absent, and he staggered forward.

"Easy there," Hobbes said, catching him before he fell.

The sentries would be there any moment. "Let's hurry," Eleanor said.

So they rushed and stumbled toward the shell. Eleanor saw no door, no opening. Behind her, she heard the clatter and clang of sentry feet.

"They're up here!" Hobbes shouted. "Take him!" He handed Watkins off to Eleanor's mom and pulled out his gun, aiming it at the machines with their saws. "What's the plan now?"

Eleanor didn't know. They scrambled up to the shell, and she scanned its rough surface, frantic for a console or control panel.

"Sweetie?" her mom said.

But Eleanor didn't know what to do.

Hobbes fired a shot. The bullet struck what might have been one of the sentry's eyes with a spark and ricocheted. "I don't know what part of this thing to hit!"

Eleanor looked up at the green light. It shone with a glow that almost had substance. Light she could touch. "I'm here!" she shouted. "What do you want?"

Close.

The voice felt as if it were right next to her ear, tingling her neck. She closed her eyes and reached out to the entity.

I am here.

The shell loosened its coils, opening, and the same green glow burst from within, like light through fingers. Then a blinding doorway appeared, a spreading fissure in the shell's grain.

"Inside!" Eleanor shouted.

Her mom went first, carrying Watkins with her, and they vanished into the light.

"Hobbes!"

"You first, kid!" he said, and fired another shot.

The sentries were almost there, nearly climbing overtop of one another to reach them. Eleanor passed through the portal, blinded, and a moment later she felt Hobbes come through and bump into her.

The fissure started to close, and Eleanor heard the painful shriek of metal grinding against stone. But the sentries were too late, and though she could still faintly hear the muffled sounds of their assault, the door was shut. The light faded as if settling at Eleanor's feet, and she looked around.

They stood within the hollow shell, perched on a narrow ledge, and Eleanor realized the part of the structure they had seen from the outside was only the tip of it. Its spiral descended into the heart of the black mountain. Here at the top of it, they faced a pit perhaps twenty feet across that opened wider and wider the deeper it went, their ledge little more than a thread following it downward. The cumulative haze of the green light obscured exactly how far it might be to the bottom, and Eleanor felt the height pulling on her stomach with vertigo.

Hobbes peered down into the chasm. "I'm guessing we go that way."

A subtle, hollow wind blew through the space. Eleanor still felt the entity as if it were beside her, rising up out of the shell. "Yes."

Eleanor's mom was still panting. "I don't know if Watkins—"

"I'll be fine, Dr. Perry," the old man said. "You can leave me here."

"No," Eleanor said. "We're sticking together."

"Besides." Hobbes holstered his gun. "We might need you."

"I can't imagine I'll be any help anymore."

"Never thought I'd hear you say something like that, old man." Hobbes took Watkins's arm from around the shoulder of Eleanor's mom and placed it over his own. "Even if it's true, I never leave anyone behind."

Eleanor smiled and nodded at Watkins. Then she turned and took the first step down the spiral, trying to keep her eyes from the glowing pit, focusing on the path. The other followed her, and they slowly swung their way around and around, deeper into the mountain's interior. To her it felt like they traveled in the eye of some kind of vortex. She felt whorls of energy, not unlike the ley lines on earth, rushing up and down the structure.

"What is this thing?" Hobbes asked, with a little bit of a grunt.

"I think it might be like a radio tower or something," she said. "Sending and receiving." Maybe that was how the entity had called to her, and then brought the ship home.

"Then why are those sentries attacking it?" her mom asked.

That confused Eleanor, too.

"If it's a radio tower," Hobbes said, "that means someone is broadcasting."

"In a way," Eleanor said. She glanced back at him and noticed him patting his pocket again, as if checking to make sure something was still there.

He still had a secret. His own agenda. Eleanor had brought him here without knowing what he really intended to do, and she would be responsible for whatever he did.

She stopped walking and turned to face him. "What is that?"

"What is what?" Hobbes asked

"What is in your pocket?" Eleanor pointed.

Her mom looked, and Hobbes frowned at Eleanor. "Nothing."

"It's not nothing," Eleanor said. "I've seen you obsessing about it. What is it?"

Hobbes looked back and forth between Eleanor and her mother, still supporting Watkins, who clung to his large frame. "It's classified."

"Classified?" Eleanor's mom said. "As if you're still on some kind of mission for the Security Council?"

"I am," Hobbes said. "I still have orders."

"What kind of orders?" Eleanor asked, incredulous that after every impossible thing that had happened, he still even thought about his orders.

"Yes, what kind of orders?" her mom echoed.

"It's classified."

"It might be classified on earth," Eleanor said, "but we're not on earth, and you need to tell us what's going on."

"I don't need to tell you anything," Hobbes said. "I don't care if we're on a moon made of cheese, you—"

"Eleanor, catch." Watkins lobbed something into the air toward her.

Eleanor reached up and snatched it, almost by reflex, as Hobbes felt his now-empty pocket, his eyes widening with anger and surprise.

"That was a mistake," he said, shoving Watkins away from him.

The old man stumbled, but Eleanor's mom stepped forward and caught him before he slipped, saving him from a fall into the chasm. Hobbes reached for his gun, and Eleanor flinched, but a second later she saw that the gun was missing from its holster.

Watkins had it aimed at Hobbes. "I do know how to use this," he said. "You taught me."

"I remember. That's on me, I guess."

"What was he hiding?" Watkins asked Eleanor,

without taking his eyes or the gun off Hobbes.

Eleanor looked at what she held in her hands. It seemed like some kind of portable drive, but it had a series of buttons used for controlling digital media, and a convex lens. "I think it's some kind of player. Or a projector."

"You press that button," Hobbes said, "you won't be able to put the genie back in the bottle. Hand it over, and I'll pretend like this whole thing never happened."

Eleanor pressed the power button, and the lens lit up, projecting a holographic image of the UN seal into the air, a map of the globe supported by olive branches. She hit the play button, and the projection changed to a menu listing the languages of earth. She scrolled to English.

The projection changed again, this time to the image of the president of the UN, a woman from the Union of the Congo Republics, but Eleanor couldn't remember her name.

"Greetings," she said. "On behalf of the human race, I welcome you to our world. . . ."

"What is this?" Eleanor's mom asked.

Hobbes ignored her.

"We regret that our first meeting is taking place under these circumstances. It was not our intention to engage in hostilities with you, and it is with the hope of peace that I speak to you now. I understand our world has resources you desire. I am confident that we can come to an agreement over those resources, in exchange for your forbearance."

"An agreement?" Eleanor said. This image was meant to open negotiations for a treaty of some kind. That's why Hobbes had brought it. He had expected and hoped to deliver it to the aliens who had built the Concentrators.

"We would like to meet with you to discuss our proposal," the UN president said. "Furthermore, we would like to resolve this matter before tensions escalate any further. Until then, I wish you peace and prosperity."

Her image remained for a few seconds more, smiling, and then it vanished.

Eleanor held up the device in her fist, facing Hobbes. "What is the proposal?"

Hobbes looked right over her head, sneering.

"It's the second Preservation Protocol," Watkins said. "The contingency plan. It has to be."

Hobbes lost his sneer, and shook his head.

"What is in the second plan?" Eleanor's mom asked.

Hobbes was silent.

"Look around you," Watkins said. "Do you see where you are? I'm not talking about jurisdiction here.

I'm talking about the fact that I could shoot you and no one would ever know. And I am perfectly willing to shoot you, Hobbes. Are you perfectly willing to die here on this desolate rock?"

Eleanor believed Watkins meant it. She had already watched someone die from a gunshot that Watkins had indirectly fired, and she did not want to again.

"Please, Hobbes," Eleanor said. "What would you even be dying for?"

"The world," Hobbes said.

"No," Eleanor said. "Not for the world. You'd be dying for the people who think they control the world. Who think they can pick and choose who lives and who dies . . . Wait. That's it."

"What's it?" her mom asked.

"The second Preservation Protocol. They let the aliens take most of the energy, without putting up a fight, and in return the aliens leave enough energy for certain members of the human race to live."

"It couldn't be," her mom whispered. "Hobbes, please tell me—"

But the subtle smirk on Hobbes's face confirmed it, whether he meant it to or not.

"It's not any different from what you were going to do," Eleanor said to her mom.

"It's entirely different!" her mom shouted.

The situation had somehow, suddenly, become about her mom's decision to support Watkins, the whole reason Eleanor had left her mother behind. "How, Mom?" Eleanor asked. "How is it different?"

"You can't negotiate with nature! All you can do is adapt to it, and those who can't adapt will die. The universe is hostile. It drives evolution forward so it can feed on the remains. You can't plead for mercy from an ice age." Then she turned to Hobbes. "And you shouldn't plead with terrorists."

Hobbes shrugged. "Sometimes the only way to survive a mugging is to give the mugger what they want."

"But you're not doing this for you," Eleanor said. "You're doing this for your daughter. The UN promised you Mariah would live, didn't they?"

Hobbes scratched at one of his eyebrows and looked away.

"I'm sorry, Hobbes," Eleanor said. "You might think you're doing the right thing, but you're not." She looked down at the device in her hand. "It doesn't matter anyway. There's no one here to negotiate with." Then she tossed the player into the chasm.

"No!" Hobbes shouted, lunging toward her.

Watkins moved to intercept him, but Hobbes was

quicker, and he seized Watkins by the throat with one hand, and with the other he grabbed Watkins's wrist, pushing the gun aside.

"Let him go!" Eleanor shouted.

"You pointed my own gun at me, old man," Hobbes growled.

Watkins choked and gagged.

"Let him go!" Eleanor snatched and clawed at Hobbes's arm, trying to pull his fingers away from Watkins's throat.

But Watkins struggled to fight back, too, and he suddenly threw his body against Hobbes, setting the soldier off balance, and in the next moment Eleanor felt them slip past her hands, and they both went over the edge.

⤙ CHAPTER ⤚
26

N o!" Eleanor screamed. Then she turned and ran down the spiral pathway.

"Eleanor, wait!"

But Eleanor couldn't wait, and she wouldn't slow down, so she stayed as far away from the edge as she could, and she raced around and around and around, deeper and deeper and deeper, until at last she reached the bottom of the chasm, stepping into a round, open space without any doors, or windows. The green light she had seen from above filled it to a height of three or four feet, as water fills a well, flowing and drifting, splashing up against the sides, lapping at the path.

Watkins and Hobbes hung suspended in the air a

foot from the ground, as if held up by the light. They didn't appear harmed, and Eleanor realized she hadn't heard anything after they had fallen, which made her think that the light had somehow caught them before they'd hit the ground.

She waded into the light toward them to get a closer look. Their eyes were closed, and they didn't move, or speak.

"Eleanor," her mother whispered.

She turned.

Her mother stood on the pathway, apparently afraid to come all the way down to the bottom.

"It's okay." Eleanor motioned her forward. "Come on."

"No," she said, shaking her head, and then she pointed at Eleanor's chest.

Eleanor looked down. The light had begun to stick to her, and even climb up her clothing. She didn't feel anything. It didn't seem harmful. But she found it disconcerting to think about, and tried to brush it off, sending away little whiffs of glowing green.

Here.

Eleanor felt the entity more strongly than she ever had. Its voice had its hands on her shoulders, huge hands like Uncle Jack's, that made her feel small.

"I am here," she whispered.

Something stirred in the mist-light at the center of the room, and then a control console emerged from the floor, rising up dripping green glow in runnels. It was several times the size of the console aboard the ship, and when Eleanor stepped up to it, she felt very small.

But she lifted her hands to lay them down.

"Stop!" her mom said.

Eleanor didn't want to have this argument again. It only hurt and made her angry. How many times had they fought about it? How many times had her mom made her feel like there was something wrong with her?

"This is what I came here to do," she said, keeping her voice even. "And I'm going to do it."

"Sweetie—"

"This is exactly why I left you in Egypt," Eleanor said, sounding less even.

That brought her mom the rest of the way down the path, easing slowly into the green light as it swirled around her. "I know it is."

"This is me." Eleanor pointed at the alien console. "This thing, right here? All of this? This is who I am. This is—"

"Don't say that." Eleanor's mom waved her hands before her, crossing them like a shield. "Please don't say that."

"Why, Mom?" Eleanor raised her voice. "Why shouldn't I say it? It's the truth, isn't it?"

Her mom just shook her head.

"I don't care if it makes you uncomfortable." Eleanor jabbed her own chest with her bunched fingers. "You don't want it to be me, but it is. It's in my DNA, and I can't help it. Neither can Uncle Jack. It could just as easily be you, you know."

"I know that."

"Then why are you doing this?"

Her mom opened her mouth, but no words came.

"I can tell you why. It's really pretty simple." Eleanor paused. "You don't like who I am."

"Eleanor—"

"Do you know how it feels to know my mom wants me to be someone else?" Eleanor heard the pain in her own voice, and she let that question hang between them for a moment. "You know something else, Mom? This started a long time ago. Way before the aliens. Whenever I got bad grades, or got in trouble at school, or did something you thought was too risky or dangerous, I could see it in your eyes. You're disappointed in who I am."

Her mom closed her eyes and bowed her head, covering her mouth with one of her hands. "No, sweetie. No."

"What do you mean, no?"

Her mom looked up, and there were tears in her eyes. "I love you, Eleanor. And I am proud of you. You're the bravest, kindest person I know. I am hard on you, that's true, but that's only because I worry about you. I watch you being reckless, and it scares me to death. I'm not even talking about aliens here. I mean, it wasn't that long ago you tried to sled down a building."

The memory of that day, back in Phoenix with Jenna and Claire, felt like a different life from the one Eleanor had now.

"But you're right." Her mom nodded. "If I'm being honest, in the beginning of all this, I didn't want you to be this way." She gestured around them, the green light reflected in her eyes. "Who would want this for their child? But I never meant for you to think I don't love you. I do love you, and I should never have let my fear get in the way of you knowing that."

Eleanor wanted to believe her, but she kept the flood of emotions rising up contained. She had to have a clear mind for what stood in front of her.

"Listen to me," her mother said. "I don't always

367

understand you or why you do the things you do. Honestly, that may never change, and that's okay. You frustrate me and you scare me, but you amaze me, too, and in this moment, I wouldn't change a thing about you."

That was all Eleanor had ever wanted to hear.

"You be you." Her mom glanced at the console. "Do what only you can do."

Eleanor nodded. "I love you."

"I love you, too."

Eleanor laid her palms down on the console, closed her eyes, and projected her mind.

The entity waited for her, larger and stronger than anything she had ever felt, floating in an ocean of green light in which Eleanor thought she could drown. This wasn't a prisoner of the rogue world, or simply a part of it. This wasn't an intelligence installed in a piece of alien technology for a single, limited purpose. This was a *being*. This was like something out of a myth, the kraken or the leviathan, a mind vaster than Eleanor could comprehend or contain. This was the consciousness of the rogue world itself, and Eleanor knew that she and Watkins were no match for it. She couldn't imagine how many minds it would take, all joined together, to stop the entity before her.

"What do you want?" Eleanor asked, her voice

sounding very small, and very weak.

Here.

"I'm here," she said. "Why did you call me?"

Here.

"I am here," she repeated.

The entity said nothing, but then it moved, and when it moved, it was as if the entire ocean of green light moved, the entire planet tilting on its axis. She sensed its impatience. It wanted her to do something, but she had no idea what that might be.

"I don't understand," she said.

Here.

"Here, what? What does that mean?"

Be. Here.

How could she be more here than she already was? She had broken into an alien ship, crossed who knows how many hundreds of thousands of miles of open space, climbed up a mountain on another planet, and then descended down into that mountain. There wasn't anywhere left to go. To be more here, she would have to be the entity—

Be the entity.

Did it want Eleanor to join with it? To become one with it the same way she had with Watkins? Because that was impossible. To do that she needed something she could latch onto, a shared emotion, an

369

understanding, and she had none of that with this being. It had come from a different solar system, a different planet, created by a different species Eleanor still couldn't really imagine. What could she possibly find in it to share?

Be here.

"I am."

Be here.

"I am!"

Be here.

"I'm trying! But you need to stop killing the earth!"

Be. Here.

This entity was desperate. She tried to reach out to it, but it was too alien, and the rogue world had done too much damage. She hated it for the Freeze, for killing people and driving people from their homes. She hated it for all the suffering it had caused. It didn't matter to her that it was lonely, it—

Lonely.

Could that be it?

She had no idea how long the rogue world had been traveling through space. Millions of years? Longer? She had no idea how long the planet had been dead and empty. How long ago its builders had abandoned it. But she knew this entity had been alone since then, and Eleanor couldn't fathom that kind of isolation.

Her brief space journey here had almost been too much for her, the emptiness of it, and the vast distances between points of light and living things.

It hadn't always been that way. In school she'd learned about the big bang, back when all the matter in the universe, all the planets and stars, every atom, was all part of a ball so hot and dense the laws of physics couldn't even really explain it. The singularity, they called it. That ball had exploded, creating the universe and all that incomprehensible distance Eleanor had experienced, but before that moment everything was together and part of something. The atoms in Eleanor's body, and the atoms in the rogue world, had been a part of the same thing.

And maybe that was it.

Maybe that was the only thing Eleanor really shared with this being. If she looked back far enough, she had that in common with everything she could see and touch, and everything she had never seen and would never touch. All the beautiful and infinite variations of matter the universe had ever expressed all came back to the same beginning.

Eleanor looked at the entity once more in its ocean of green light, and she reached out to it. She reached for the matter that gave rise to its consciousness, the atoms that were the same as the atoms that made up her heart and her mind. She reached for the singularity within the entity that had given rise to it and to her, and she found it. With that key in her hand, her mind joined with the entity, and it opened the universe before her.

When Eleanor's mind returned, her mother stood beside her.

"Sweetie?"

Eleanor smiled. "Yes," she said. Her mind had been so far away, and so inhuman, that she needed to hear her mom say that to help her come back to who she was.

Everything she had just seen, through eons of wonders, and light-years of roaming, faded quickly. Without the entity's mind joined with hers, helping her comprehend it, all that it had shown her simply fell away, unable to fit. But she retained what she needed.

"We can save the earth," she whispered. But there were things that needed to be taken care of first. She looked over at Watkins and Hobbes, still resting in their cushions of buoyant green light, and changed the position of her hands on the console.

"What are you doing?" her mom asked.

"I'm sending Hobbes back."

"Back?"

"To earth."

Eleanor picked Peru. The Concentrator there hadn't been buried in an avalanche, and it would be safer than Egypt with the riots going on. She reached into the planet's reserves of energy and then activated the link.

The green light around Hobbes became active, swirling and flowing around him, coating him entirely in its glow, and when it had reached its brightest point, it simply vanished, taking Hobbes with it.

Eleanor's mom gasped. "What did you—is he . . . ?"

"He's fine," Eleanor said. "I teleported him."

"Teleported him?"

"Well, teleported his energy. The Concentrator will receive it and turn it back into him."

Her mom stared, openmouthed, and then simply laughed. "Watkins was right, you know. What else can you do?" But then she stopped. "Wait. Does that mean we could have teleported here?"

"No," Eleanor said. "The Concentrators send in only one direction, from here to there. The Builders didn't ever want a species that stumbled upon the Concentrators to accidentally travel from there to here."

"Builders?"

Eleanor looked around, trying to remember what the entity had shown her, but it felt like a dream she could barely recall having, let alone remember the substance of it. "All I can say is that their curiosity drove them to reshape their planet so they could ride it through the cosmos. But they weren't the last ones to inhabit it. After the Builders, other races found it, and corrupted it." She shivered and looked back at the console. "Now, Watkins."

This time, instead of teleporting him, she gently raised him up, cradled the entire way by the viscous light, and woke him.

When he first opened his eyes, he stumbled a moment before finding his footing. "I . . ." He blinked and rubbed his head vigorously. "I fell. Did I fall—?" He looked around, at the green light, at Eleanor and her mom. "Something—I think something caught me. It was . . . Where is Hobbes?"

"I sent him back to earth," Eleanor said.

"Well. That's good." Watkins cocked his head. "How exactly did you do that?"

"Matter-energy transfer," Eleanor said.

"Which you know all about, somehow?"

"I do now. I connected with the entity that controls this whole planet. I know why it called me."

"Why did it call you?" Eleanor's mom asked.

"That's a long story," Eleanor said. "A really, really long story. Millions and millions of years long. But

basically, the last aliens who lived on this planet disappeared. The entity can't even remember why or how.
But after they were gone, the planet's system went on
autopilot."

"Which means what?" Watkins asked.

"It kept itself alive by doing what it has always
done. What it was built to do. It found planets, it tapped
all their energy to survive, and then it moved on. It's
been doing that for millions of years, and in that time,
stuff has started to break down. Degradation errors
are creeping up in the artificial intelligences. They're
all turning wild, and the planet entity can't control
them anymore. That's why the ships and the sentries
attacked us."

"But why did it call you?" Eleanor's mom said.

Eleanor did not know how to tell her about the
next part. Eleanor was trying very hard not to think
about it at all. "It's tired and run-down. But it can't
stop, because of its programming. It has to meet its
minimum energy requirements, at all costs. Unless
certain conditions are met."

"What conditions?" Watkins asked.

"Someone has to take on pilot duties."

"Which you did?" he asked.

"It needed me to be here, in its place."

"I see," Watkins said.

"For how long?" her mom asked.

Eleanor took a deep breath in and then sighed it out. "If I leave, the entity has to take over again, and then it's back to draining the earth."

"Are you saying you can't leave?" Watkins asked.

Eleanor tried to smile and laugh, but it came out sounding like a sob, and then she had tears in her eyes. She didn't want to do this. But it was the only way. She had the ability to save the earth. She could save everyone, and not just the chosen few. She could keep the promise she'd made to Amaru as he died, and save his son. She could save Mariah, and Badri, and Nathifa, and Felipe, and Uncle Jack, and Luke, and Finn, and everyone she had ever cared about. She could save them all. Wasn't that worth it?

"Sweetie," her mom said. "This is ridiculous. Come away from there."

Eleanor stayed at the console. "We made a plan. The entity and me. I'm going to—"

"You're going to what?" her mom asked.

"I . . ." Eleanor didn't want to say it out loud. Keeping it in helped her control her fear. But her mom wasn't going to let up, and the plan wouldn't work without her. "I'm going to steer the planet into the sun."

Her mom looked at her a moment, then at Watkins,

then back to her. "You're not serious."

"I am serious," Eleanor said. "This is the only way."

"Eleanor, listen to me." Her mom leaned over, bringing their faces very close together. "You always said that you weren't going to let people die while the G.E.T. picked who got to live, right?"

"Right," Eleanor said.

"That includes you. You're not going to die. This is ridiculous—"

"Mom, if this planet isn't destroyed, it will just keep going. It will kill the earth, and then it will kill the next planet, and the next. We don't have any weapons on earth that can destroy it. Our sun is the only thing that can. Once the rogue world is gone, the earth will go back to its normal orbit, and the Freeze will be over."

"This isn't happening," her mom said. "Because you can't possibly be suggesting that I just leave you here. Because that would be insane. That would—"

"I'll stay," Watkins said.

Eleanor looked hard at him, wondering if he'd struck his head in the fall after all. "No, you won't."

"Of course I will," he said. "It makes the most logical sense. First, I'm the oldest by far, with fewer years ahead of me than I would probably hope for. Second,

377

like you, I have the needed ability to connect with the console and control the planet. Third, I have personal reasons."

"What personal reasons?" Eleanor asked.

"They are known as personal reasons for a reason."

"If you're trying to take my place," Eleanor said, "you're going to have to explain."

Watkins clasped his hands behind his back. "All right, then. I feel I owe it to the earth. Until quite recently, I was in charge of the G.E.T., and I made some grave mistakes, for which people have paid, some with their lives. You are aware of this. I want to honor them, and perhaps make up for what I did. Perhaps history will then judge me kindly." He paused. "And finally, I want to save you, Eleanor."

He spoke with his same, odd, pragmatism, a quality of his with which she had become familiar, and she realized she had grown fond of it.

"I hope you will trust me to do this," he said. "This is how I am choosing to confront the absurdity of our situation. A frontal assault. I hope you will remember me."

"Watkins." Eleanor's mom shook her head. "I don't know what to say."

"Of course you don't," he said. "Truthfully, neither do I."

"Thank you," her mother said. "I know I need to thank you. And I promise you, the world will know what you did."

Watkins nodded. Then he turned to Eleanor. "Do you trust me?"

Eleanor did not hesitate. "I do."

"Then show me how it's done."

— CHAPTER —
27

THEY CHOSE THE ARCTIC CONCENTRATOR, AVOIDING THE Himalayan and Egyptian locations for the same reasons Eleanor hadn't sent Hobbes to either one. But she didn't want to be anywhere near Hobbes, so they decided against Peru. That left the Arctic site, just outside Barrow, where Watkins said his team had already uncovered the Concentrator from its burial under the snow and ice. Where this whole adventure had begun.

"But we don't have the gear for temperatures that low," Eleanor's mom said.

"There will be a facility right near where you arrive," Watkins said, standing at the console. "You won't freeze as long as you get inside quickly. And let's not forget that the earth will soon be returning to its natural orbit, and warming up again."

"Plus," Eleanor said, "we can hide out in Barrow with Felipe if we need to until we can find Uncle Jack and Luke."

"I guess that's settled," her mom said.

They both stood in the midst of the green glow and watched as Watkins laid his hands on a different part of the console, just as Eleanor had shown him.

"Are you ready?" he asked.

"Ready."

"I have to admit," he said. "I'm curious what tele-portation would feel like."

"Wanna trade?" Eleanor asked, smiling even though she was already grieving.

"Not at all," Watkins said. "I may be the first and only human to fly into a star."

"That's true," Eleanor said.

He nodded, once. "Good-bye, both of you."

"Good-bye, Watkins."

The green light enveloped Eleanor, and within a few moments that light was all she could see, and then, in an instant, she saw white.

Snow and ice.

Eleanor stood at the base of the Concentrator, next to her mom, and a moment later, she could feel that it had gone permanently quiet. Watkins had shut it down from the rogue world, and now it was nothing more than a dead, leftover relic that scientists would undoubtedly study for years to come.

It was cold. Murderously cold. Eleanor was once convinced the cold would claim her eventually. That all it needed was time, waiting and watching for the chance to sink its teeth into her. But that was when Eleanor thought the cold might never end. Now she knew that it would end. Eleanor could be patient, too.

Not far away, they saw a new spherical Arctic habitat, and they jogged toward it, hoping to get indoors before they got frostbite. The Arctic Code of conduct for polar habitats mandated that they be let in.

"This reminds me of Amarok," Eleanor's mom said, her teeth chattering, clapping her hands together. "I wonder what happened to him and his people."

"I hope they made a new home for themselves," Eleanor said. "There's a place for them somewhere. I know there is. There's a place for all of us."

"You think so?" her mom asked.

"I do," Eleanor said. "We all belong."

MATTHEW J. KIRBY is the author of the acclaimed middle grade novels *The Clockwork Three, Icefall,* and *The Lost Kingdom,* as well as one book in the *New York Times* bestselling series Infinity Ring. He was born in Utah, but with a father in the military he has lived in many places, including Rhode Island, Maryland, California (twice), and Hawaii. As an undergraduate at Utah State University, he majored in history. He then went on to earn MS and EdS degrees in school psychology. Matthew currently lives in Utah. You can visit him online at www.matthewjkirby.com.